Le

She tried fanning herself with a napkin, which did absolutely no good. The corners of the festive room looked cool and shadowy, and she drifted toward one. She noticed that this Christmas tree was decorated differently from the one around which her family was congregating. The ornaments seemed to be tiny, wood folk carvings. She gravitated toward the tree for a closer look, and then, as if in a dream, she heard his voice.

"Leigh?"

She whirled around. The man was silhouetted against the fire, but because he stood so close, she saw his face distinctly. She would have known him anywhere.

Her breath caught in her throat. "Russ?" she whispered.

In that moment there was no one else around. No family, no holiday travelers—just the two of them, their faces illumined by the twinkling white lights on the huge Christmas tree....

ABOUT THE AUTHOR

Pamela Browning will celebrate the Christmas season with her husband and college-age son and daughter, as well as assorted family and friends. She believes wholeheartedly that the holidays are the perfect time for renewing old friendships, which she figures gives her the perfect excuse to spend more time on the phone than in the kitchen this December. Pamela and her family live in South Carolina.

Books by Pamela Browning

HARLEQUIN AMERICAN ROMANCE

237-SIMPLE GIFTS*
241-FLY AWAY*
245-HARVEST HOME*
287-FEATHERS IN THE WIND
297-UNTIL SPRING
354-HUMBLE PIE
384-A MAN WORTH LOVING

*The Heartland Series

PAMELA BROWNING

FOR AULD LANG SYNE

Harlequin Books

TORONTO • NEW YORK • LONDON
AMSTERDAM • PARIS • SYDNEY • HAMBURG
STOCKHOLM • ATHENS • TOKYO • MILAN

This book is dedicated to
the Palm Beach High School Class of 1960—
for auld lang syne

Published December 1991

ISBN 0-373-16420-3

FOR AULD LANG SYNE

Printed in U.S.A.

Chapter One

It was already late afternoon, the pale, wintry sunlight filtering through the almost-bare hickory branches outside the studio window. Leigh Cathcart stood back from the easel and studied the pansies she was painting on the canvas in front of her. Perhaps it was only the waning of the sun that made the brush strokes on her canvas seem lifeless, she thought, but by the time she decided to add the slightest touch of cadmium yellow to the mixture of oils on her palette, she heard the slam of the mailbox lid outside. *A good excuse to take a break,* she thought, glancing at her watch.

With one last doubtful glance at the painting, she wiped her hands on a turpentine-soaked rag and ran lightly down the stairs. When she pressed her face against the cool glass of the sidelight beside the front door she saw that the mailbox was stuffed with envelopes.

A crisp breeze blew a skitter of dry leaves across the sidewalk as Leigh stepped onto the front stoop. The mail carrier was retreating down the brick walkway, and he turned and waved. Leigh waved back. He wasn't her regular carrier, he must be one of those temporaries hired for the holidays. Funny, but with his long white beard and roly-poly figure, the man could have been a stand-in for Santa Claus. The idea made her smile.

The mail yielded a couple of bills and the first Christmas cards of the season, easily identifiable by their pristine white or festive red envelopes. One yellowed envelope, frayed around the edges, stood out from the rest, and Leigh pulled it from the pile out of curiosity.

She was surprised to see that the envelope was addressed to Miss Leigh Richardson, which had been her maiden name. No one had called her by that name for more than twenty years.

As she puzzled over the sprawling handwriting a sudden freeze-frame of a memory tugged at her heart. In her mind's eye she saw the image of a tall, dark-haired boy whose broad shoulders swung distinctively when he walked.

Russ, she thought with a shock of recognition. *Russ Thornton.*

The envelope bore his return address—or at least it had been his return address when she knew him twenty-two years ago.

She walked numbly into the living room and sat on the edge of the wing chair in front of the window. The postmark on the envelope was dated August 18, 1969.

A not-so-good year, Leigh thought. It was the year that Russ left for Canada in order to avoid the draft, the year that he had skipped out on her without a word. On the other hand, it was also the year that her daughter, Wendy, had been conceived, which more than made up for the rest.

But where had this letter been all this time? And why had it been delivered now? With trembling fingers she slit the envelope, unfolded the paper within and began to read.

Dearest Leigh,
You took a piece of my heart with you when you drove away from our special place yesterday. Please forgive the things I said in anger; you know I love you.

I must leave for Canada, and I believe that in time you will come to understand why I'm going. But Leigh, I cannot live my whole life without you. There can never be anyone else for either of us.

Marry me, Leigh. Don't let me leave the country with this unsettled between us! Whatever the difficulties, we can work them out. Say yes, wonderful Leigh, and we'll be together always. Knowing that you are my fiancée will make our separation so much easier.

I don't think I could bear to part from you if your answer is no. If it's yes, meet me on Sunday as usual at our special place. If it's no, you need not come and I will know.

Please say yes. We belong together.

I love you with all my heart, now and for always.

Yours,
Russ

Russ. Russ Thornton. If she closed her eyes she could picture him—the crisp, wavy hair, almost black, that curved over the back of his collar; snapping dark eyes; a wide smile slightly off-center. *Russ.*

Leigh slumped back in the chair and stared out at the tree branches whipping in the wind. Russ had wanted her to marry him. She hadn't known.

All the pain of his desertion came back to her in a flash. Stricken, she buried her face in her hands; tears streamed between her fingers and rained into her lap. At first she wept softly, but before long she was wrenched by great, gulping sobs.

Russ would have married her.

She had believed for all these years that Russ hadn't really loved her. But she had been wrong. He had written this letter and proposed to her. He had loved her even after their quarrel and in spite of all the cruel things she had said to him. *He had wanted to marry her!*

When her sobs finally died, she brushed the tears away and willed her stomach to stop churning. Slowly she bent to retrieve the letter, and in the fading light she read it once more to reconfirm its contents. She had not mistaken the words.

If only she had known back in August of 1969 that he wanted to marry her! Instead she had thought that Russ wanted her out of his life, and she'd been too proud to contact him first. After all, he was the one who wanted to leave, and she hadn't approved of his evading the draft by running away to Canada. In her heart of hearts, she had been terrified that she'd never see him again if he went either to Canada or to Vietnam, but to her way of thinking in those long-ago days, it would have been better to fight than to be branded forever a coward. And so he had gone, and she had never heard from him again.

Until now.

Leigh roused herself. How long had she been sitting there? Outside she heard the neighborhood children dispersing to their homes, and lighted windows sprang to life up and down the winding street. In a daze, she moved through the half darkness like a sleepwalker and turned on a lamp so that it spilled a shaft of golden light into the hall.

Slowly she walked into the kitchen and removed her paint-spattered smock. She set the letter on the counter, ran water from the tap into a kettle and put it on the stove to boil for a cup of tea. She stopped and stared at the letter for a moment in disbelief. Yes, it was real. It hadn't gone away.

The phone rang, but the sound didn't register at first. She didn't pick it up until the sixth ring.

"Mom?" It was her twenty-one-year-old daughter, Wendy, calling from college. Wendy was a junior at Duke University in Durham, North Carolina, and she was going to be married on December 26. "Mom, I've got the latest bulletin from Wedding Central."

Leigh sank down on the wide window seat in the breakfast area, her eyes resting on the letter. "What's going on?" she asked. Wendy's late-afternoon phone calls had become standard since she'd set the date for her wedding, but this time Leigh had to force herself to pay attention.

"Today at the bridal shop I saw the most beautiful satin roses. They hold rice or confetti or birdseed for the guests to toss. I want them for my wedding, Mom, but they can't order the exact shade of red I want. Can you make them?"

Leigh stifled a sigh. "I don't know. I can't promise anything until I've seen one."

"I'll send you a sample. I'm sure you can figure it out. I want them to be made out of the same satin as my maid-of-honor's dress. Oh, Mom, these roses would be just the right touch. In the shop, they were arranged in a gilt basket with small sprays of baby's breath, and the guests pull the roses out just before they throw the rice or confetti or whatever, but I want to use birdseed in my roses for the birds that stay around for the winter."

Leigh pinched the bridge of her nose between her thumb and forefinger. She felt a headache coming on.

"Mom?"

"I've never made satin roses before," Leigh said.

"You're the artist in the family—you're the only one I know who could get them exactly the way I want them."

It's amazing what we do for our children, Leigh thought, distractedly twisting a strand of auburn hair around her fingers.

"Do you need one satin rose for each guest? Is that the idea?"

"Oh, maybe we'll need a few extra so the basket will look really full. We're only having fifty guests, after all. I want a *big* basket of satin roses right by the door of the Timberlake Room when Andrew and I leave on our honeymoon."

"I wonder if I'll have time to do all this," Leigh said.

"I'm not getting married until the day after Christmas! Today's only December 1, you know. Do you realize I'll be Mrs. Andrew Martin Craig in only twenty-six days?" Wendy sounded enthralled.

Leigh managed a smile. "Wendy, darling, I certainly do. You and Andrew did a wonderful job of convincing me that you couldn't wait until after graduation to be married. If only—"

"Now, Mom, don't start again. Anyway, if we'd waited we wouldn't be able to have a winter wedding at The Briarcliff, and you have to admit that the setting is perfect."

"Oh, I'll grant you that, although I must say that dealing with the staff of an inn on the top of a mountain in western North Carolina is rather difficult when working from my home base of Spartanburg, South Carolina."

"How do you think I feel, stuck way over here in Durham? Thank goodness for the telephone. Maybe we should set up a conference call between you in Spartanburg, me in Durham and the inn staff on top of Briarcliff Mountain."

"Maybe someone at The Briarcliff knows how to make satin roses," Leigh said, snatching at this ray of hope.

"They wouldn't do half as good a job as you will, I'm sure of it. Oh, I almost forgot. Do you think Andrew and I could have that little bookcase in my room? The one with the glass doors on the bottom? It will look great in our apartment."

"Sure, I'd be glad for you to have it. In fact, Dad and I bought that bookcase when we first got married."

"Did I mention yesterday that Andrew has a job lined up for this summer? He's going to work in the local library. With my waitress job at Murgatroyd's we should just be able to make ends meet. In fact, I'm thinking of working there through my whole senior year."

"And Andrew?"

"We don't know if his library job will extend past August. Don't worry, Mom. We'll manage."

"So you say. Things happen," Leigh said before she could stop herself. She wished suddenly and poignantly that David were here. He had always been able to make Wendy see his point of view, and she was sure that he'd have wanted Wendy and Andrew to postpone their marriage for another year and a half. But David was dead, killed over two years ago by a drunk driver. She missed him; to this day she often expected to round the corner into the den and see her husband sitting in his favorite chair reading the paper.

"Must I remind you that you and Dad were married early in your senior year? I was born right before school was out. And you graduated with a baby in tow. Andrew and I don't plan to have children for a long time, so I'm sure we'll both finish college. Don't worry, Mom. Trust me.'' Wendy's tone was light and cajoling, and she couldn't possibly know that for Leigh, her careless words packed an emotional wallop.

Trust me. The expression, tossed so matter-of-factly into the conversation, echoed inside Leigh's head. They had been two of Russ Thornton's favorite words. *Trust me, I'm going to Canada. Trust me, you won't get pregnant.*

''Oh, I've got to run,'' Wendy said in a burst of energy. ''I just realized that I'm meeting Andrew for dinner in ten minutes. 'Bye, Mom. Thanks for everything. Love you.''

''Love you, too,'' Leigh said faintly. She hung up, reached automatically for the ever-present Things to Do list in the pocket of her jeans and wrote down ''satin roses.'' She glanced at Russ's letter on the counter to make sure it was still there. Nope, it hadn't gone anyplace. She'd better stop thinking it wasn't real.

It was time to eat dinner, but she didn't feel like eating. All she wanted to do was read Russ's letter over and over again. She retrieved the letter, settled herself amid the bright cushions of the window seat with her cup of tea, and studied every word. She ran her fingers across the lines of script, touched the letters of his name.

Russ Thornton. Oh, how she had loved him.

The world had been so different in 1969. The Vietnam war had been raging full-force. Apollo 11 landed on the moon. A crowd of four-hundred-thousand people gathered at a farm in the Catskills for the Woodstock Music and Art Fair.

And Leigh Richardson and Russ Thornton had fallen in love.

She'd actually met him the summer after high-school graduation when she'd vacationed as usual at The Briarcliff with her family. Russ had been the skinniest busboy working in the dining room, and he'd always smiled at her if he happened to pass by their table. She'd felt none of his attraction then; Leigh had been enamored of one of the lifeguards, and she and her friend Katrina, who had accompanied the Richardsons to The Briarcliff that year, had ignored the restaurant help completely.

Then in January of their junior year at Duke, Leigh and Russ happened to be sitting next to each other at one of the campus hangouts, and he'd remembered her. They struck up a lively conversation which they couldn't conclude on the spot, so he escorted her back to the dorm. She was taken by his engaging personality as well as his angular good looks. By that time, though he was still a bit gangly, his spare frame had filled out. For Leigh, the awkward look only added to his charm.

He'd worn his fraternity sweatshirt under a warm wool jacket, and she'd worn a black-watch-plaid pleated skirt and a demure white blouse beneath her winter coat. He'd tried to kiss her good-night at the door of the dorm, and she had surprised him by letting him, but that was only because she'd known before they'd walked half a block that this was the man she wanted to marry.

Russ had been her first lover, just as she had been his. His room at the dorm, his car parked on a deserted lane, the apartment of married friends who often went out of town on weekends—all were pressed into service for their rendezvous. They had been so young and so much in love, and their passion had seemed boundless. In April of their junior year, when Russ had dropped out of school to return to his hometown of Charlotte after his father's heart attack, Leigh had ached with loneliness.

After he left college that spring, Russ pitched in with his mother to run the family furniture business. On weekends he'd make the three-hour drive from Charlotte to Durham, and he and Leigh would have two precious nights together. Every time he left, she had felt the pain of his leaving anew; it never became any easier, especially since she needed all the moral support she could get.

Most of Leigh's friends at Duke were doves, and with unrest on college campuses increasing that year due to the government's failure to bring the war to a close, she had taken a lot of flak for her hawk stance.

"My brother is in Vietnam," she would say quietly when pressed, and then her antagonists would usually back off. If Russ were present, he'd fervently defend her, which made her quietly proud. She'd never guessed in those days that Russ would make a complete about-face and begin to speak out against the war.

In June, Leigh went home to Spartanburg to stay with her family. Her sister, Bett, who was only eight that summer, was away at camp. Since her brother, Warren, had recently left for Vietnam, Leigh thought her parents needed her.

At the beginning of the summer she sensed a change in Russ, but she'd ignored it at first. It was easier that way; after all, her parents were often visibly upset by the constant television coverage of antiwar demonstrations, and they made no secret of their prowar sentiments.

Her father often said, "I'd like to know what kind of mess this country would be in if we'd all decided not to fight Hitler." He had enlisted in the army with pride at the beginning of World War II.

And once when a small group of antiwar protesters appeared on the local TV news to explain their views, Leigh's mother burst into tears.

"I can't bear it when they make it sound as if Warren is fighting for nothing," she said, her voice muffled by her handkerchief. Leigh tried to comfort her, but her soothing words had little effect. After that, her mother always left the room when the network news was on.

Leigh's father, fervently outspoken, declared several times that the government should round up all the protesters, give them guns, and send them over on the first ship bound for Vietnam. "That'd show those jokers what's what," he said grimly.

Aside from Warren's participation in it, the war meant little to Leigh. She spent more time thinking about Russ than about the war, which was half a world away. Their own primary problem was getting together, and she spent most of her time and energy trying to figure out ways to bring it about.

After suffering through the long spring at Duke without Russ, Leigh had looked forward to weekends during the summer when Russ could visit her in Spartanburg. She'd also thought that he could drive over from Charlotte, less than a hundred miles away, a couple of times during the week, as well. Before the month of June was half over, however, she began to see that these plans were hopelessly unrealistic.

On the second night that Russ visited her in Spartanburg, she walked him out to his car to say goodbye at the end of the evening. She was delighted to have him to herself after sitting in the same room with her parents for two hours. The night was peaceful; there was no moon, but the stars were out in force and she was crazy with wanting him. It had been torture to be able to look at him but not touch.

"I can't stand it when your father talks that way about the war," Russ said unexpectedly through clenched teeth.

Her father had been particularly vocal about his belief that the President should bomb Vietnam out of existence.

Leigh drew closer and hugged his arm. "My brother, Warren—" she began. It was her stock answer.

"Don't tell me about your brother again," Russ said wearily. "Why can't any of you see that it's precisely because of Warren that you should be against the war?"

"Mother says that to speak out against the war is to demean what our men are doing there," Leigh replied self-righteously.

"'Mother says, Dad says'—Leigh, what do *you* think about it?" He pulled away from her embrace and swiveled so that he was looking her square in the face.

"Why, I think we should fight to win," she answered slowly, wondering how anyone could think otherwise. In any case she was bored with the topic and considered it irrelevant now that they were alone for the first time since Russ had arrived.

Russ's eyes searched hers. "We should bring the troops back home," he said abruptly. "It's a dirty, rotten war, Leigh. We never should have become involved."

Russ could be so exasperating. "Why are we talking about the war?" she asked playfully, slipping her arms around his neck and stretching to kiss the corner of his mouth. "Let's talk about you and me instead."

He had surrendered to her urgency, pulling her into the front seat of his car and kissing her so passionately that after he drove away she had to wait on the front porch until her flushed cheeks cooled and her racing heart slowed to its regular pace before she could rejoin her parents.

It had all happened such a long time ago.

Unbidden tears sprang to her eyes when she thought about how innocent they had both been. Innocent and in love. It was a bad combination.

When the front doorbell chimed, the sudden noise startled Leigh back into the present. She had a headache; she didn't want to talk to anyone, and she didn't want to see anyone. But her visitor was persistent, and so finally, limping slightly because her right foot was asleep from sitting so long with it curled beneath her on the window seat, she went to the door and recognized her friend Katrina through the sidelight.

She threw the door open without hesitation and was instantly enveloped in Katrina's hug.

"I thought I'd missed you," Katrina said. "I hope I didn't interrupt anything." She studied Leigh in the glow of the overhead light in the foyer.

"No, I was just—drinking tea," Leigh said.

"I'd have called, but I got stuck in a huge warehouse with this funny little guy who insisted on pulling out bolts of fabric, and since I wanted to find exactly the right print for the DeRuiters' bedroom draperies, I—but, Leigh, is anything wrong?"

Leigh sighed, blowing the air out of her mouth so that it ruffled her bangs. "That depends, I guess. I'm glad you're here, Katrina. I missed seeing you last month."

Katrina grinned. "Me, too, you. I couldn't get away because my assistant quit, and I didn't want to leave my studio without someone to oversee current projects. Speaking of which, how are you doing on that pansy painting for the Caldwells' cottage? And have you eaten? You look ghastly."

"I'm doing fine on the painting, but I think the pansies need to be more yellow, and I haven't eaten, and thanks for the compliment. I needed to be told I look ghastly, I really did.''

''Well, I suppose you merely look tired. You never did say if anything is wrong, by the way.''

''You didn't give me a chance, and why don't we go in the kitchen?''

''Great idea. Again, have you eaten?'' Katrina slung her shoulder bag onto an antique rocking horse that was stationed at the foot of the stairs and trooped after Leigh, the heels of her boots echoing loudly as she walked.

''I haven't had dinner, but I'm not especially hungry. We could heat up some lentil soup. You like it, and one pot seems to last forever with only me in the house.''

''You heat the soup, I'll set the table. Nice place mats. Are they new?''

''New since you visited in October,'' Leigh said. She was glad for this activity; spooning the soup into a casserole dish and sliding it into the microwave oven gave her something to do. While the soup heated, she automatically felt in the pocket of her jeans for Russ's letter, and it crackled against her fingers. She shot a surreptitious look at Katrina to see if she'd noticed, but Katrina seemed oblivious.

''And then Mother said, 'Let's go out to lunch,' and I agreed, and after we ate I hurried to the warehouse, and there's never a phone handy in those places, so that's why I didn't call,'' Katrina explained as she set out bowls and spoons. She spared Leigh a keen look. ''Have you been paying attention to anything I've said?'' she asked in exasperation.

The microwave oven beeped, signaling that the soup was hot. Leigh avoided answering Katrina's question by tossing a plastic-wrapped loaf of pumpernickel bread on the counter and asking her friend to stack slices on a plate, which Katrina did while talking nonstop.

Katrina Stimson had been Leigh's best friend since they'd found themselves sitting next to each other in a ninth-grade art class. They'd roomed together in college, and Katrina had served as maid-of-honor at Leigh's wedding. Katrina, who had never married, was now a successful interior designer with her own studio in Florida, where she catered to a rich and exclusive clientele. She returned to her hometown of Spartanburg once a month both to visit her elderly mother and to make rounds of the local textile factories in search of unique fabrics for her customers.

This evening Katrina was full of plans to design the interior of a mansion in Palm Beach. After they ate, she pulled out preliminary sketches of bedrooms and guest houses galore, and although Leigh had always enjoyed acting as Katrina's sounding board, this time she knew that she was merely sounding bored.

Just when Leigh began to wish that she could pull out Russ's letter and read it one more time, Katrina impatiently swept her materials into a portfolio and hitched her chair closer to Leigh's.

"All right," Katrina said. "Something's up. What's going on, Leigh? You're not acting right."

"Well," Leigh said, taking a deep breath. She studied the fringed edge of her place mat and avoided looking at Katrina.

"Why, Leigh, you have tears in your eyes! Leigh, for heaven's sake, what's wrong? It's not Wendy, is it? Is the wedding off?"

Leigh lifted stricken eyes to Katrina's. She shook her head mutely, unable to trust herself to talk. And yet she wanted Katrina to know.

She reached into the pocket of her jeans and withdrew the yellowed envelope, staring at it for a long moment before passing it to her friend, who looked totally perplexed.

"Read this. It arrived today," Leigh whispered. Katrina, after all, knew the whole story involving Russ and David; she might as well be party to this, too.

The room was quiet except for the rustle of the paper as Katrina withdrew the letter. Leigh sat unmoving, her hands clenched tightly in her lap.

Katrina read quickly. "He wanted to marry you?" she asked incredulously.

Leigh nodded and bit her lip, her eyes anguished.

Slowly Katrina held the letter out to Leigh, who accepted it and stared at the all-too-familiar handwriting with blurred vision.

"Why—why wasn't the letter delivered back in 1969 when it was written?" Katrina asked.

Leigh shook her head. "Your guess is as good as mine."

"But this is downright criminal!"

"There's certainly nothing we can do to change things now."

"You and Russ, though. Oh, Leigh, you were so perfect together."

"I thought so at the time. But I married David, and we had a good life. A happy life. And everything that happened with Russ was just—just—" She had started to say that it was inconsequential, but she couldn't possibly deny the importance of their relationship. It had been wonderful and warm and real, and she and Russ had shared a love such as few people are lucky enough to experience during the course of a lifetime. No, there had been nothing inconsequential about it.

"What are you going to do?"

"Do?"

"About this letter. Russ must have thought your answer to his proposal was no when you didn't show up at the park that Sunday."

"I'm still reeling from the shock of this. I don't think a plan of action is necessary," she said.

"The draft evaders who went to Canada rather than serve in the war were granted amnesty in 1977," Katrina said gently. "Many of them came back to the United States."

"I haven't heard anything about Russ Thornton in years, Katrina," Leigh said.

"Neither have I. But you could ask around. You could—"

"I couldn't," Leigh said firmly.

"Leigh, for heaven's sake. The man asked you to marry him back in 1969, and you never got his letter. He has a right to know."

"That's ridiculous. He got over me a long time ago, just as I got over him. He's made a good life for himself since then, I'm sure."

"Maybe not," Katrina said thoughtfully.

"I wouldn't have been exactly overjoyed if Russ had shown up a few years back when David and I were content and carrying on with our lives. I have no desire to stir up this particular stew, Katrina, believe me."

"What if Russ has never been happy without you? What if he's still in love with you?"

"It's been twenty-two years, and few torches burn that long. Grow up, Katrina. You're too old to have stars in your eyes."

"And you're too young to sit around here brooding. Your husband has been dead for over two years, and you need to get out and see more people. You've gone out with some duds since you started dating, I'll grant you that, but maybe Russ Thornton is what you need to make you smile again."

"Ah, Katrina. You're nice to be concerned, but no thanks. Anyway, let's go up to my studio and take a look at that painting. I have an idea that you can tell me exactly what it is that I need to do to make those pansies look more lifelike."

"Aren't we going to clean up the kitchen first?"

"Nah. Pansies first, pans later." Leigh stood up and led the way upstairs.

"You could at least send him a Christmas card," Katrina said as they walked through the door of the studio, but Leigh pretended not to hear as she turned her easel toward the light.

Katrina suggested a paler shade of yellow on the outer edges of the pansies' petals, admired another of Leigh's works-in-progress, and departed early in order to catch up on her sleep.

"I'll call you before I head back to Florida," she promised as she waved goodbye.

Leigh stood shivering on the porch until Katrina was gone, missing the easy companionship of their hours together. She always thought that she was adjusting beautifully to the empty house until Katrina came and showed her how much fun it was to have someone who understood your thoughts before you even voiced them, who shared private jokes of long standing, and who liked to laugh. For Leigh, the hardest part about living alone was not being able to share laughter with a kindred spirit.

On the way back to the kitchen, she passed the boxes of Christmas cards she had bought earlier in the week. They were sitting on the hall table; Katrina must have seen them. That must be why she suggested sending one to Russ.

A crazy idea, for sure. Anyway, Leigh had no inkling where to send it. And what would he think?

Send Russ a Christmas card? No. Absolutely not. But still, she found herself imagining how surprised he'd be to get it, and she knew for certain that he wouldn't be half as stunned as she'd been when she'd opened his long-lost proposal of marriage.

Chapter Two

The next day when Leigh sat down at her desk to address Christmas cards, she couldn't stop thinking about sending one to Russ. The cards were simple—large and white with an embossed message. *Peace and joy,* the cards said. They seemed particularly apt, since peace was what Russ had worked to achieve in Canada.

If—and only *if*—she sent the card, she could send it to the Charlotte furniture store. Russ Thornton was the only child of doting parents, and she had no doubt that they would forward it to wherever he was living now.

But should she? Would Russ want to hear from her?

She figured he was probably married with a lot of kids. Russ had always wanted children. No "lonely onlies" for him—that's what he'd always said.

Did his marital status matter? Couldn't she wish him peace and joy in this special season even if he was a married man who had begotten a whole army of children? She hesitated, her pen poised over the card.

Of course she *could* mention that she'd never received his marriage proposal back in 1969. But how do you throw something like that at a person you haven't seen for twenty-two years? Maybe he couldn't care less. Maybe he'd forgotten all about her.

Maybe he hadn't.

Finally, still feeling ambivalent, she scribbled both her maiden and married names and stuck the card in its envelope. By this time, she wasn't doing it for him—she was doing it for herself.

Later she walked through the cool dusk to the mailbox a few blocks away. For some reason she hesitated to toss the card addressed to Russ into the box along with the others. She stared at the envelope before closing her mind to her objections. This was the season for peace and joy, and she needed to make her own peace with the past.

She tilted the door to the mailbox, sailed the Christmas card into the opening and let the door clang shut behind it.

RUSS THORNTON DIDN'T open his own mail anymore. His secretary had some kind of fancy machine that neatly slit the tops of the envelopes. This meant that he didn't spend much time on his mail, which was a good thing during the Christmas season. Here it was December 5, and already his desk at the Charlotte main office of the Thornton Furniture chain was piled high with Christmas greetings.

Thornton Furniture always received lots of Christmas cards. Cards from pleased customers, cards from creditors, cards from debtors. If you asked Russ, and no one had, Christmas was becoming entirely too commercial. It seemed as though he sent cards to a lot of people he didn't care about one way or the other; in business, it was prudent to send season's greetings.

Not that he was a Scrooge or anything, and he certainly hadn't reached the *bah humbug* stage. What he longed for was a return to the simple meaning of the Christmas season, which he believed boiled down to—

well, to the message expressed by the card he now held in his hands.

Peace and joy. That was it. Peace, both in the world and within each person. And joy, because Christmas was the celebration of the Christ child's birth.

He inspected the card more closely, trying to figure out if he actually knew the person who had signed it. Leigh Richardson—Leigh Richardson? Leigh Richardson *Cathcart?*

He felt as if all the air had suddenly exited from his lungs. He leaned slowly back in his chair, staring at the signature. The handwriting was familiar. He could never have forgotten the distinctive wide lower loop of her *L*s, nor did anyone else he knew form *G*s in precisely that way. It had to be Leigh. *His* Leigh.

No, he corrected himself, not *his* Leigh. David Cathcart's Leigh. Why in the world was Leigh sending him a Christmas card after all these years?

He turned it over, searching for a clue. Nothing on the back. No handwritten message, no explanation, no nothing. And no mention of Dave.

"Want another cup of coffee?" asked his secretary, momentarily popping her head in the door.

"No, thanks," he said, and she tripped away down the hall.

He stood up, still clutching the card in his hand, and paced from one end of his office to the other. Something like twenty years without a word from Leigh, and now this card. It didn't make any sense.

Not that he'd expected her to forget him entirely any more than he could forget her. Leigh Richardson was a name engraved on his heart. He'd loved her, and even though he'd married Dominique, he couldn't help thinking about Leigh from time to time and hoping that she had found happiness.

It had almost destroyed him when he'd heard that she'd married David only a couple of months after he went to Canada. At first he couldn't figure out what she saw in David, who was the kind of nice, all-around guy that all the girls liked but seldom dated. Dave Cathcart hadn't even been particularly handsome, at least not by Russ's standards, and he was pretty sure that Leigh hadn't thought so either.

Why she had married him Russ couldn't imagine, and at first it had made him angry. After that, the despair had set in, and in a few years he had learned to accept the fact that Leigh belonged to someone else. He threw himself into building a meaningful life for himself in Canada, and the people he had known back home, even Leigh, began to fade in importance.

He glanced at the return address on the envelope. It sounded like Leigh's parents' address in Spartanburg, and he was curious. Did Leigh and her family live with her parents? Hadn't he heard that David had become a successful businessman? What was it—real estate? No, it had been insurance, that was it. He couldn't recall where or when he'd heard it.

Russ didn't know whether to put this card in the stack to keep or the one to throw away. Maybe he should send a card to Leigh at the address on the envelope and wait to see what happened.

No, there was a quicker way. He turned to his desk and picked up the phone. Then he just as quickly replaced the receiver in its cradle. He couldn't call her. He wouldn't know what to say.

But even after twenty years there must be things they could talk about. His mind tested an imaginary conversation.

"Hello, is this Leigh Richardson Cathcart? You may not remember me, but—"

No. If she hadn't remembered him, she wouldn't have sent the card. Maybe he should aim for a chattier tone.

"Hi, Leigh, I got your Christmas card. How's things? How's the husband and kiddies?"

That definitely wouldn't do—much too casual.

"Leigh? You won't believe who this is. No, you'll have to guess. Ted Quincy? Well, uh, no. Actually, it's Russ Thornton."

No way. Ted Quincy was the fellow from Chapel Hill that Leigh used to go out with before they met. Russ wondered if she'd sent Ted a Christmas card, too.

"Hello, Leigh, Russ Thornton here. I was wondering if you have a happy life. Me? Well, it's been an experience, I'll say that for it. Yeah, I worked to bring the war to an end, and after a while I married this girl in Canada who is beautiful and brainy, but, no, she doesn't look a bit like you. We're divorced now. What do you say we get together sometime? Can you bring David along? Why, uh, sure. We'll have a great time, the three of us, talking over old times. Your husband would probably like to know all about how I used to sneak you into my room at the dorm, and not only that—"

His mind was veering away into dangerous territory, and he'd better nip this train of thought in the bud. Thinking about Leigh lying in the narrow bed in his room at the dorm, her auburn hair glowing in the light of a forbidden candle, was enough to make him catch his breath. She had been so beautiful.

"If you don't have anything else for me to do before I go, I'll drop this deposit off at the bank," his secretary said from the doorway.

Russ wheeled around, embarrassed to have her catch him with such complex emotions visible on his face. She homed in on him with a penetrating look.

"Sure, Gail, go right ahead. Take your time," he said.

"It'll be about twenty minutes, the same as always," she said.

"Fine," he said abstractedly, sitting down and shoving Leigh's Christmas card under a pile of invoices.

"Is everything all right?" she asked.

"Yes, of course. When you come back, will you bring me the Henry file?"

"You want it before I go?"

"No, later will be fine." He tried to look as though he was busy with the papers on his desk.

With one last meaningful lift of her eyebrows to express doubt, Gail hurried away, and when Russ was sure that she was gone, he pulled Leigh's card out again. Peace and joy, peace and joy. She was wishing him peace and joy.

On impulse he dialed Information and asked for the telephone number of a David Cathcart in Spartanburg, South Carolina. The number stated by the mechanical voice on the telephone line sounded familiar, yet Russ found it hard to believe that Leigh would have the same phone number that her parents had had after all these years.

His heart said to go ahead, but his hand hesitated. Then, feeling slightly unnerved by the rapidity of his decision, he was punching out the South Carolina area code followed by the phone number in rapid succession. His mouth grew dry when he heard the phone ringing, and he almost hung up. He had no idea what he would say to her.

"Hello?"

It was Leigh's voice, and her hello ended on the same cheerful lilting note as always, although perhaps she sounded a bit huskier. He thought he would have recognized her voice anywhere.

"Leigh, this is Russ Thornton," he said.

She made a sound that could have been a gasp, and he thought she muffled the receiver. Perhaps there was someone with her; he'd better make this quick.

"Russell," she said, recovering quickly. "What a pleasant surprise." She was the only person in the world who had ever called him Russell.

"I received your card in the mail today," he said, hoping he sounded casual. "It was good to hear from you."

"Well, I—I—" She seemed unable to go on.

He decided to act as though he hadn't noticed her confusion. "Your card reached me at my office. My father died back in 1980, and Mother died a couple of years ago. It's been a challenge to take on the responsibility of a chain of furniture stores, but I enjoy it. How about you? What are you doing now?"

She spoke rapidly, and he sensed that she was as nervous as he was. "I taught art in the public schools for ten years, but now I'm painting full-time. My friend Katrina—remember her? Well, she's an interior designer, and she commissions paintings from me for her clients. It gives us a chance to work together," she said.

"That's nice, Leigh. You've always been so talented. I'm glad you're working in your field." He hesitated before taking the plunge. "And David—how is he?"

A long pause. "He died, Russ, a little over two years ago."

"I'm sorry. I didn't know. Do you have children?"

"Yes, a daughter. Wendy. She's a student at Duke. And you, Russ? Do you have a family?"

"I wish I did," he said. "Unfortunately, my wife and I were divorced several years ago, and we didn't have any kids."

Leigh sounded surprised at this. "You always loved children," she said softly.

"And still do. Like I said, I wish—but wishing won't make it so."

An awkward silence. Perhaps they had said everything there was to say. He had the inordinate desire to ask her if she looked the same, but of course, none of them did. He had put on some pounds, and a few gray hairs had sprouted at his temples. He couldn't imagine Leigh Richardson's rich auburn hair turning gray.

"Isn't this the same phone number your parents had?" he asked.

"Yes, I live in their house. After Dad died, we moved in with Mother so she wouldn't be lonely. She died about five years ago, which left me and David and Wendy. I live here alone now, but I love this house."

"It was a pretty Williamsburg-style house, wasn't it? Yellow, with white trim?"

"It's blue now instead of yellow."

"You always did like blue. I'll bet you painted the shutters green."

Leigh laughed. She had gone through a blue-and-green phase in the days when she knew Russ; her trademark had been blue oxford shirts worn with dark green skirts, and she had painted a green stripe on her blue Volkswagen Beetle.

"Actually, the shutters are white. I got over the blue-and-green thing a long time ago."

"That's too bad," he said, because the combination had brought out the myriad blue-green shades in her eyes.

Suddenly there seemed to be nothing else to say. "Well," he said reluctantly, and "Well," she said simultaneously, so that they both laughed in embarrassment.

"It's been good to talk with you," he told her.

"Thanks for calling," she said. He wondered if she felt the way he did. He would have liked to talk with her longer, but he'd be embarrassed to say the things he was really thinking. He felt as though they knew each other so well, and yet they had been strangers for the past twenty-two years.

"Have a merry Christmas," he added, knowing that his would be less than merry but trying to sound upbeat. He didn't want the conversation to be a downer.

"Merry Christmas to you, too, Russ."

"Goodbye," he said.

"'Bye," she replied softly, and then he heard the click of the broken connection in his ear.

Gail stopped at his office door. "Heidi wants to know if you've checked on those oriental rugs," she said.

He stared at her, drawing a blank.

"Oriental rugs?"

"From that dealer who stopped by last week. The one from New York."

"Oh, *those* oriental rugs," he said.

"Heidi said you were going to place the order. The woman she was working with—the one who bought a whole houseful of furniture from us—wanted to know how long it would take to order one."

"It only takes a few minutes to order it, but it could take weeks to get it. I suppose she wants it by Christmas," he said wryly.

"You guessed it," Gail said.

"Tell Heidi I'm checking," he said as he picked up the phone.

Gail went away again, and Russ called the oriental-rug dealer, concluded the conversation and decided to go out for lunch instead of ordering in.

"I'll be back in an hour," he said on his way past Gail's desk.

He walked out into the sunshine and got in his car. It was a warm day for the season, with the temperature in the seventies, which didn't help to put him in the mood for Christmas. He slid open the sunroof of his BMW and turned onto the four-lane highway fronting the store. The whole world seemed brighter than it had been earlier today, but then his life had taken an unexpected turn since then. He had never in his wildest imaginings dreamed that he would ever speak with Leigh Richardson again.

Leigh *Cathcart,* he reminded himself. He had liked David Cathcart, and he certainly hadn't known that David was dead. Leigh was so young to be a widow, and he felt a pang of sadness on her behalf.

He was no stranger to sorrow himself. His divorce had almost devastated him. He realized now that he had married Dominique with such unrealistic hopes that he would have had to come down to earth sooner or later, but he had never imagined that she would become totally dedicated to her career to the exclusion of almost everything else, including him.

A line of orange caution cones appeared on his left, warning him of a road-construction job ahead, and as he slowed his speed, a convertible with the top down passed him on the right. The driver was a woman with reddish hair whipping in bright tendrils around her face. It was almost the exact auburn shade of Leigh's hair.

Stop it, he told himself. Leigh's hair was probably not the same burnished copper that it had been when she was twenty. She probably had wrinkles. But her eyes, those incredible wide-set eyes, the irises the palest blue-green, they couldn't have changed much. He had never known anyone with eyes as beautiful as Leigh's.

And what was Leigh like after twenty-two years? Was she as much fun as she had always been? Had marriage lived up to her expectations? He wanted to see her again. But to what purpose? After that last day together before he left for Canada, the tenderness of their lovemaking, the terrible quarrel that tore him apart, his desolation when she hadn't shown up at their special place in the park on the following Sunday—why would he want to recall those memories?

Ah, well, they were both older now, and it had all happened such a long time ago. Maybe they could reminisce about the good times. He hadn't maintained a relationship with many people who had known and understood him when he was young. There was something special about old friends, and although he and Leigh had been lovers, they had also been the best of buddies.

His other friends from that time period were scattered. Sam lived in Chicago with his wife and children, Phil had moved to Arizona, and Terry, poor Terry, had been seriously wounded in Vietnam and never left the veteran's hospital in California. Leigh was the only one who lived in this area of the country.

He braked at a stoplight and squinted at the woman in the convertible. If you blocked out the details, she could have been Leigh. Then she turned her head, and disappointment washed over him. Her nose was long and hooked; Leigh's nose was short, straight and dainty.

He turned at the corner, but his mind was made up. He wouldn't go see Leigh. But he would call her again. He'd wait a few days so he wouldn't appear too eager. And he'd think of an excuse for calling; he wouldn't pick up the telephone and then find himself with nothing to say like he had this morning.

Interesting that she still had the same phone number. He wouldn't even have to look it up. It was engraved on his heart, just like her name.

USUALLY LEIGH DIDN'T retire for the evening at nine o'clock, but tonight she was so tired. Another marathon phone call with the supervisor of catering at The Briarcliff had taxed her patience, and then there had been the call from Russ this morning, which had knocked her for a loop. Now she switched off the light to go to sleep, but when the ring of the bedside telephone jolted her to attention, she sat up straight and reached out to pluck the receiver from its cradle.

"Leigh, this is Russ Thornton," said the familiar voice.

She was so surprised to hear from him again so soon that she couldn't make her tongue separate from the roof of her mouth. She groped for the switch on the lamp beside the bed, and when the light came on, she blinked. It was several seconds before she could speak.

"Why, Russ," she said, struggling to get her bearings.

"Have I reached you at a bad time?"

"No, not at all," she said, but she couldn't keep the amazement out of her voice. She hadn't expected him to call again.

"Something you said earlier today when we talked interested me," Russ said. "You mentioned that Katrina incorporated your pictures into the houses she designs. It occurred to me that we could do the same thing at Thornton's."

"Why, perhaps you could," she said, grasping at this bit of reality.

"We have two decorating consultants who advise our customers on what furniture will go in which room, things like that. They're always looking for accessories. If you'd like to bring some of your work over to the store, we'd like to see it."

Her mind raced. Was he serious? Did he really want to use her paintings or was this an excuse to see her?

"Well, I've never thought about increasing my output. Katrina keeps me busy," she said. She didn't want to see him again.

"Oh, if you're not interested, that's fine," he said, his disappointment evident.

Leigh tried to sound brisk and businesslike. "It's just that with the holiday season and everything, there isn't much time. Perhaps after the first of the year...." She let her voice trail off.

"Oh. I see."

He sounded so curt. She fought to regain her equilibrium. She hadn't meant to hurt his feelings.

"You know, there's always so much to do for Christmas," she added. She couldn't tell him about the wedding because then she'd talk about Wendy.

"I always leave my shopping until I can't possibly put it off any longer," he said.

"Not me. I like to be organized. I can enjoy the holiday so much more if I don't have a lot of things to do at the last minute."

"You always were good about that. For instance, the way you kept your class notebooks with neat sections where everything was labeled."

"I could never understand why you used to throw all your notes from every class onto the back seat of your car. You'd have to dig through all those papers before you could study for a test." Too late, she realized that she had been drawn into conversation.

He laughed. "I'm better now. I have a secretary who takes me to task if I don't keep things in the proper folders. It's done wonders for me. Anyway, that wasn't so much a car as it was a filing cabinet."

His car had been a two-door white Corvair Monza. Leigh could even remember the way it smelled—like Old Spice after-shave mixed with lemon drops. Russ had always carried a pocketful of lemon drops in those days. Whenever he thought she needed cheering up, he'd give her one.

"Whatever happened to that car?" she asked. She couldn't help her curiosity; she had felt a certain affection for that Corvair.

"A guy hit it broadside when he ran a red light, and that was the end of it."

"Oh," Leigh said, disappointed. "That's too bad. Were you hurt?"

"No, but Dominique—my wife—was in the hospital for a week or so."

Leigh wanted to ask what year that had been. How long had it taken Russ to marry? Instead she said, "Dominique—was she French-Canadian?"

"Yes, from Montreal." He wasn't sure how much else to say about Dominique, so he said nothing.

"Did you live there?"

"No, we lived in Toronto. She owned a boutique and—but this can't possibly be interesting to you."

Leigh sank back into her pillows. She was trying to imagine Russ with this woman, this Dominique. She tried to picture her. Oh, Leigh was interested all right, curious to know what kind of woman Russ would have married.

"Leigh?"

"I am interested, it's just hard to imagine your living in Canada for so long. Did you mind the cold?" He had always been so sensitive to cold weather; he'd claimed it made his teeth hurt, although she had never been sure that she believed him.

"I came back to Charlotte as soon as I could. I was sick of snow tires and snowshoes and snow shovels. Especially snow shovels. The winter is very long in Toronto."

"But at least you had white Christmases," she said. Spartanburg, South Carolina, with its mild climate, was not conducive to snow.

"Oh, lots of white Christmases," he agreed with a chuckle.

"Every year I've dragged boxes of ornaments out of the attic to decorate the house, and every year one of us would say, 'It's sure to snow this Christmas,' and almost every year we were disappointed. And after the holidays we'd carry the boxes of decorations back upstairs again, and we'd say, 'Maybe next year,' and next year we'd go through the same thing all over again. There's something so special about snow at Christmas."

"Those sleigh bells jing-jing-jingling," Russ agreed.

"Snowflakes that stay on your nose and eyelashes," she said.

"Walking in a winter wonderland," he added, and they both laughed, borne along momentarily on the same wavelength.

Leigh reflected with stunning clarity that she felt so comfortable with him. Had *always* felt comfortable with him, dating from that first night that they'd met in the little off-campus coffeehouse.

"Well," he was saying, "I've enjoyed talking to you, Leigh, but it's getting late. I wish you could bring some of your work into the store soon, but I understand. Why don't you call and set up an appointment when you're ready?"

"I will," she said. "Actually, I have some things that are almost finished. They just need a bit more work."

He sounded encouraged. "Good. That's great. And, Leigh," he said, hesitating, "would you mind if I phoned you again? Just to chat? I've enjoyed talking about old times with you."

Now she was wide-awake. "If you want to," she said, wondering if she dared to encourage him.

"I do want to," he said firmly. "I'll call you soon."

"Thanks," she replied, but that sounded silly. "I mean, I'll look forward to it." She wasn't sure he actually would call; perhaps he was only being polite.

"Goodbye, then," he said.

"Goodbye, Russ," she answered, and then hung up.

She switched off the lamp and lay staring up at the soft pattern of light reflected on the ceiling from the bathroom night-light. He sounded exactly the same. A voice that wound itself softly around the syllables of the words; a voice still sweet enough to make her tremble when she heard it. She pictured him in her mind as he had been then, but then she canceled the image. He wouldn't look the same after twenty-two years. She certainly didn't.

This morning when he called, she'd been so tongue-tied at the thought of him on the other end of the phone line that she hadn't said any of the things she would have liked to say. Nothing, for instance, about Vietnam or about Warren's not returning from the war. Nothing about their love affair, nothing about the letter she had just received, and certainly nothing but the most basic information about Wendy. They'd covered none of these topics tonight, either, but it was probably just as well.

She wondered lots of things about Russ, like if he still wore Old Spice, and if he still liked lemon drops, and if he was one of those guys who had more hair in their ears than on their head after the age of forty.

But she couldn't make an appointment to see him now, not before the wedding. Because no matter how much she wanted to see him, it wasn't worth the risk. The wedding had to be perfect for Wendy's sake, and the last thing Leigh needed was for Russ to show up and realize that he was her real father.

Chapter Three

It was December 24, two days before Wendy's wedding, and she and Leigh were on their way to The Briarcliff. Afternoon traffic was heavy on I-26 because of the holiday, and Leigh, suffering a case of wedding burnout, had declined to drive, so Wendy was driving Leigh's Cadillac. In the trunk reposed Wendy's wedding dress in all its white satin splendor, and in the back seat was stacked a precarious pile of Christmas presents.

Wendy glanced across the front seat of the car at Leigh. "You were up awfully late last night, Mom. Who were you talking to, anyway? Katrina?" she asked.

Leigh faced front so Wendy couldn't see her face. "For a while," she said, which was true. She had been chatting on the phone with Katrina when her call-waiting beeped, and after Katrina hung up, she'd talked with Russ for over an hour.

"I'm sorry Katrina can't come to the wedding. It won't be as festive without her," Wendy said. She checked the rearview mirror and pulled into the passing lane to overtake the next few cars.

Leigh held her breath. Wendy was a competent driver, but Leigh would have felt more comfortable if she didn't drive so fast.

"Katrina's mother won't be able to put her full weight on her broken foot for six or eight weeks, and Katrina can't leave her alone," Leigh said.

"Katrina is such a good nurse. Remember when she came and stayed with you after your hysterectomy?"

"I'll be eternally grateful for Katrina's kindness in those days. I was still grieving for Grandma, and having a hysterectomy on top of it was almost too much. And Dad was so busy at work—wasn't he in the process of moving his office?"

"Yes, and I was a bratty fifteen-year-old and no help at all. How did you ever put up with me?"

"Katrina and I managed to grin and bear it. We remembered how we were when *we* were fifteen. I was awfully glad when you grew out of that stage, though. You have no idea how pleased I am that you've become a kind, caring human being."

Wendy laughed. "That's exactly why I'm worried about Katrina. I know she was looking forward to my wedding, and Christmas certainly won't be the same without her. Are you sure she'll be all right in Spartanburg alone?"

"She's with her mother and the rest of their family, so that's hardly alone. Anyway, last night Katrina mentioned the possibility of taking her mother to Florida for the holidays."

"Florida for the holidays? No white Christmas? Oh, that's too bad. I hope it snows at The Briarcliff on Christmas Day. That would make my wedding perfect, just perfect."

"There's certainly much more chance of snow in the mountains, but snow or no snow, your wedding will be perfect," Leigh said firmly. It ought to be; she had worked hard enough making those tedious satin roses and firming up plans for the wedding and reception with The

Briarcliff's catering staff and running from bridal shop to bridal shop at the last minute trying to find a blue garter for Wendy, who had misplaced the one she'd borrowed from a friend.

"A perfect wedding," Wendy said dreamily.

"Watch the pickup truck behind you on the right," Leigh said sharply. "He's speeding."

Wendy let the pickup pass her before easing back into the right-hand lane. "Was your wedding wonderful, Mom?" she asked.

Leigh focused her eyes straight ahead on the undulating blue mountain range in the distance. Wonderful? She wouldn't exactly put it that way. Her wedding had been a relief more than anything else, but at least David had been happy. And sweet. And gentle.

"Well, was it?"

"Oh, yes," she said, and thought of Russ. Last night he had tried to convince her that they should see each other over the holidays and she'd continued to put him off, telling him once more that she was too busy, that she had a lot to do to get ready for Christmas. She'd been telling herself that where Russ was concerned, it was best to let bygones be bygones, to let sleeping dogs lie, to leave well enough alone.

When it seemed as if he wasn't going to take no for an answer, she had sought to end the conversation with an exasperated, "I'm not even going to be home for Christmas," followed by his incredulous question, "Well, why not? Where would you go at Christmas, anyway?"

"To The Briarcliff," she'd said, none too gently, and then she'd regretted it. They'd met there, after all, and the name would bring back more memories than she wanted him to have at the moment.

"The Briarcliff?" he'd repeated in mystification.

"For a family gathering, a whole bunch of us. I'd better hang up and get some sleep."

"You're going to The Briarcliff in winter? I thought you only went there in the summer."

"We've always wanted to celebrate our family Christmas at The Briarcliff. There's more chance of snow in the mountains," she replied.

"Oh. Snow. Well, merry Christmas," Russ said lamely.

"Merry Christmas to you, too, Russ."

"I'll give you a call afterward," he'd said, sounding miffed, and then they'd hung up.

Not that she hadn't enjoyed his frequent phone calls over the past couple of weeks, but after Wendy arrived home from college Leigh had been frantic with trying to answer the phone at times when she thought Russ might call. Wendy, enthralled with being a bride, knew nothing about Russ or his phone calls, and Leigh didn't want her to hear Russ's voice. She didn't want Russ to hear Wendy's voice, either. All she wanted to do was to keep them away from each other.

"Let's stop and grab a hamburger, okay?" Wendy said, steering onto an off ramp that led to a pair of golden arches, and Leigh nodded in assent.

Maybe Russ would stop calling her, she thought. She had been so prickly and cross during the past few days that she wouldn't blame him if he did. Especially since she had refused to see him over and over again.

LEIGH AND WENDY arrived at The Briarcliff ahead of a winter storm front, and the wind was already blowing mightily when they drove between the two stone pillars that marked the entrance to the inn's grounds. Ahead of them they could see golden light spilling from the windows, and Wendy leaned forward in excitement.

"The inn looks beautiful. I knew it would," she said in satisfaction.

"It looks like a fairy-tale castle," Leigh said, and Wendy laughed.

"There's something elegant about The Briarcliff, all right, but it's homier than a castle; it reminds me of one of those châteaus in the wine country of France," Wendy said. They drove around the sweeping driveway circle at the front entrance, where a uniformed attendant whisked away their luggage and promised to park the car.

After a few check-in formalities, Leigh looked around the lobby for their family group. She didn't have to look for long, because her sister Bett called to them immediately.

"Leigh! Wendy! Oh, I'm so glad to see you!"

Bett and her three children swarmed across the crowded great hall of the inn to greet them. In the background the fires in The Briarcliff's massive four-sided fireplace leaped and danced. Carson, Bett's burly good-natured husband, ambled over and embraced Leigh first and then Wendy.

"How's our bride doing?" he asked, holding Wendy at arm's length.

"Great," Wendy answered, her eyes sparkling up at her uncle.

"Are you sure you still want me to give you away? I'm worried about this wedding-march business. You know I've got two left feet. Bett says I'm the worst dancer she's ever experienced."

"Follow me, I'll lead," Wendy assured him, and everyone laughed.

Bett's children were stair steps: Darren, Billy and Claire-Anne, ages eight, six and five respectively. All of them had inherited their mother's pale red hair and freckles, and all of them were built like their father. They flocked after Carson and Wendy, who went to bask in the glow of the fire.

A sharp and biting wind was tossing the tops of the trees outside the mullioned windows. Early winter darkness had already closed in upon the picturesque inn on the top of Briarcliff Mountain, but the inn was cozy and warm and echoed with the pleasant sounds of conversation and laughter.

"We're in luck—the weatherman is forecasting snow tonight," Bett said, linking her arm through Leigh's as they moved toward the fire.

"Thank goodness. Wendy will be disappointed if it's not a white wedding in every way," Leigh said. She noticed a group approaching from the other end of the hall. "Oh, there's Andrew and his family," she said happily.

The Craigs—Andrew, his parents, Nancy and Jim, and his grandmother, Vera—met them in front of the Christmas tree. Andrew was tall, much taller than Wendy, with a thick thatch of brown hair and warm brown eyes. He and Wendy threw their arms around each other, much to the delight of Bett's brood.

"The inn is so beautiful when it's decorated for Christmas," Nancy Craig said, as she looked approvingly at the garlands of greenery looped from the ceiling.

The huge stone chimney, erected by Italian masons in the late 1800s when The Briarcliff was built as a mountain retreat for a wealthy philanthropist, was situated in the middle of the great hall of the inn and divided it into four distinct areas, each with its own hearth flanked by huge pots of poinsettias. Every area was dominated by its own enormous Christmas tree, and each tree was decorated in a different style. In their section, small unblinking topaz yellow lights twinkled from the branches of the tree; gilt balls of various sizes swung amid ribbons of silvery tinsel. Frothy golden garlands swooped from branch to branch, clasped with tiny angels made of papier-mâché.

Andrew brought Leigh and Bett cups of eggnog from one of the bustling waiters who crisscrossed the hall periodically bearing laden trays. He and Wendy stood close together, gazing raptly into each other's eyes. As the mellow tones of Christmas carols played on hand bells wafted in from the adjoining music room, Leigh felt an emotion that seemed ridiculously close to envy. Wendy looked so very much in love. *Oh, to feel that way again,* she thought with a stab of longing. Then Wendy turned and smiled at her, and envy melted into pride. Andrew was a fine person, and though Leigh had originally wished they had waited until after graduation to be married, she approved wholeheartedly of her daughter's choice of him as a husband. Impulsively she leaned over and kissed Andrew's cheek.

"I'm so glad you're the one Wendy is going to marry," she whispered, and he beamed with pleasure.

"Everyone gather in front of the Christmas tree for a picture," Carson called, fiddling with the adjustment of his Minolta as though he meant business.

They crowded close together, and Carson enlisted a hotel employee to do the honors.

"Say 'cheese,'" called one of the children.

As she faced front and arranged her expression for the camera, Leigh caught a startling glimpse of a tall man on the other side of the chimney. He was wearing a blue sweater with a wide red stripe across the chest and standing with his hands in his pockets, watching them intently. Her jaw fell; there was something about his utter immobility, something about the way he was studying their group.

"Don't say 'cheese,' say 'wedding,'" insisted Wendy, inspiring a burst of laughter, and the flash went off.

Leigh could have sworn—but it was impossible. She had been thinking about Russ Thornton so much that she was beginning to see him everywhere. She blinked rapidly until the man was gone.

"One more picture," Carson insisted, while they were all still seeing floating blue spots as a result of the last one.

"Let me straighten Billy's collar," Bett said.

"Oh, Mom," groaned Billy.

"He's chewing gum," Darren was only too happy to point out.

"I'm not. It's candy."

"Well, get rid of it," Carson ordered.

Billy spat into a napkin while Bett rolled her eyes in exasperation and stepped back into place. Leigh, distracted by the byplay, noticed with a start that the man who had been watching them was edging around the corner of the fireplace again.

She squinted her eyes, trying to refine his image, and decided that he wasn't as thin as Russ. Of course, she hadn't seen Russ in twenty-two years. It *could* be Russ. Or could it? If only she could observe him walking, she'd know. The way Russ's shoulders swung would have given him away.

"Leigh, stop scrunching up your forehead," Carson ordered. "All right, everybody, say 'wedding.'"

"No, say 'happy,'" Wendy said, and she was smiling up at Andrew when the shutter clicked. Leigh had barely managed to rearrange her face in time, and she was relieved when Carson called a halt to the photography session.

"Okay, that's enough pictures for the present," he said, tucking the camera back into its case. "But be warned—

I'll be taking plenty of candid shots by order of the bride and groom."

They began to drift away in clumps of two or three people, and Leigh was about to ask Andrew's grandmother if she would like another cup of eggnog when she saw him again, the man in the blue-and-red sweater. Leigh refused to blink this time. She forgot about Andrew's grandmother and summoned all her concentration to study his face, paying special attention to the shape and line of it. It could be Russ. It *could* be.

But why? *Why?* She felt a sudden chill when she realized that he knew she would be at The Briarcliff because she had told him so herself. The recollection of this oversight on her part sent cold ripples of anxiety up her spine.

"Oh, here's Jeanne," Wendy cried, running to meet her college roommate, who was to serve as her only attendant. Jeanne was breathless from the cold, and introductions had to be made all around, which kept Leigh from watching the man who was so intently eyeing their group. A waiter appeared with trays of cake and cookies. In the general confusion, Darren chased a squealing Billy around the room, and Carson took off in pursuit. When Leigh managed a quick glance toward the corner of the fireplace, the man was no longer there.

Leigh decided that she definitely needed a few minutes to pull herself together. During a quiet moment, she separated herself from the group as if to inspect the fragrant cascades of greenery adorning the mantel and stood for a long moment inhaling the sharp, pungent scent of fresh-cut blue spruce.

It's natural to feel keyed up, she told herself. *My daughter is going to be married the day after tomorrow.* She stared into the fire's golden depths, thinking that she should get back to the group. She felt suddenly thankful for social obligations; they would keep her securely anchored to reality for the next few days.

As she moved away from the hearth, she glanced over her shoulder. In front of the neighboring fire, a young couple on the couch were totally absorbed in each other. There was no sign of anyone else, and her knees felt rubbery with relief.

She briefly considered asking the couple if they'd seen a man in a blue sweater with a red stripe across the chest, but she thought better of it. Of course, there were the other two hearths, but there seemed to be noisy family groups on those sides. No, there was no sign of a man alone.

I was only seeing things before, she told herself. *I must be more tired than I thought.*

Her face felt so hot. She tried fanning herself with a paper napkin, which did absolutely no good. The corners of the room looked cool and shadowy, and she drifted toward one. She noticed that the Christmas tree in this section of the hall was decorated differently from the one where her family was congregating. The ornaments on this one seemed to be tiny wood folk carvings, and they looked handcrafted. She gravitated toward the tree for a closer look, and then, as if in a dream, she heard his voice.

"Leigh?"

She whirled around, suddenly wary. The wide skirt of her simple red dress flared against her knees. The man in the blue-and-red sweater was silhouetted against the fire, but because he stood so close, she saw his face distinctly. She would have known him anywhere.

Her breath caught in her throat. "Russ?" she whispered.

He strode forward, and in that moment there was no one else around. No family, no couple on the couch, no waiters bearing trays—just the two of them, their uncertain faces illumined by the twinkling white lights on the huge Christmas tree.

She drank in his face; it was so much the same, yet different. His eyes, dark and lustrous, with a web of fine lines at their corners that hadn't been there before; the straight planes below the cheekbones squaring off at the jawline; the broad shoulders so much the same; and he was tall, but not as thin as she remembered him. She had forgotten the tangle of his curly eyelashes. Her heart swooped down to her toes, then up again. She couldn't speak.

For a moment she dreaded that he was going to throw his arms around her in enthusiastic greeting. But somehow she had extended her hands involuntarily toward him, and he reached for them as if for a lifeline and clasped them between his. Her fingers fluttered and were still. She was locked in his gaze as she tried to comprehend his presence. Behind her the noise of the group diminished; they could have been strangers, not members of her family and Andrew's.

"Leigh," Russ said, his voice grating under the force of suppressed emotion. "I had to see you."

"No," she whispered. She spared a wild-eyed glance at the family party, looking for Wendy. He mustn't see her; he mustn't guess.

"I knew you were going to be here, you see, and I didn't want to spend Christmas alone. I flew up here this afternoon—"

"Flew?" she repeated distractedly. She would have flown if she could, but she was incapable of movement. Besides, he was still holding her hands.

"In my plane. A four-passenger Beechcraft—I use it for business. Another Christmas spent with my aged uncle and aunt and all their children and grandchildren would have given me the willies. I'll try not to interfere with your plans, but I *had* to see you."

In desperation, Leigh squeezed her eyes shut and opened them again. He was gazing down at her with an expression of such bright expectancy that she wanted to cry. Why couldn't he have waited until later, until after the wedding when Wendy would be safely away on her honeymoon?

"You shouldn't have come," she managed to say.

"I hoped you'd understand. I know I'm putting our relationship in jeopardy by doing such a crazy thing, and I understand your obligations to your family. If you only have ten minutes, I'll take that. Or five. Anything at all, Leigh."

Russ had never begged her for anything before, but it sounded suspiciously as though that was what he was doing now. She tried to summon her anger from the ample reservoir that had fed her past hurts, but at this moment she could find none. Instead she only felt bewilderment. She had no idea what she was going to do about him.

She swallowed and inhaled deeply. "I can't think. I don't know what to say. I didn't expect this," she said.

"Can we meet later tonight?"

This is awful, she thought. *I can't let Wendy see him. Or Bett. She might guess—well, something.* Which was probably a ridiculous thought. She didn't think that Bett had ever met Russ, and even if she had, she'd only been eight years old in 1969.

"We could meet in the library," Russ said urgently. "Just to talk. You're still so lovely, Leigh. I can't believe it's been twenty-two years."

Leigh shot a worried look toward Wendy. She and Andrew stood with their arms linked around each other, holding court for the admiring group of children. Claire-Anne, the five-year-old, was yawning. Everyone would go to bed before long; the kids had been reassured that Santa Claus could find them here at The Briarcliff, and they would be up at the crack of dawn to make sure that he really had.

"I—I—" She saw that Bett was looking around, and probably she was trying to figure out where Leigh was.

"Meet me for a few minutes," Russ urged. She pulled her gaze away from the group; Russ's determined face filled her vision.

She mustered the strength to yank her hands away. "In the library, then. Around eleven o'clock," she said quickly. She turned on her heel and fled—no, floated—toward the other side of the fireplace, leaving him staring after her. She felt his eyes on her back; her cheeks suffused with rising warmth. Embarrassed, she pressed ice-cold hands into the hollows beneath her cheekbones.

Russ was here. How in the world was she going to handle it?

Bett's voice broke through the fog surrounding her. "Leigh? We're going to gather around the piano at the end of the hall and sing a few Christmas carols," she said. Despite Leigh's flaming face, she seemed to notice nothing amiss.

A limp Leigh let herself be carried along with the group. They had begun to sing "The First Noel" when Russ quietly approached the other side of the piano and began to sing, his eyes never leaving Leigh's face. The words to the carol died in her throat.

Russ had always been a terrible singer, she remembered, and the thought brought a smile to her lips. In mid-song he smiled back, that wonderful lopsided smile that had always endeared him to her.

Leigh felt as though everyone around the piano must see that Russ was looking at her. He sang gustily, his voice ringing out over the others, and she lowered her face to hide her expression. From the sound of it, he didn't sing any better than he ever had. When she lifted her head he was grinning at her and his eyes were dancing, and she knew that he knew what she was thinking.

Leigh bit her lip and looked away. Russ had always been able to read her; why should it surprise her that he was doing it now?

Because it's been twenty-two years, she told herself vehemently. *Everything is different.*

She stole a look at Wendy. Her daughter was singing softly, her eyes alight, her hand nestled trustingly in Andrew's. Wendy had dark, wavy hair, its texture remarkably like Russ's. And she had broad shoulders and a pointed nose, a square jawline and small, even teeth—in short, she looked so much like Russ that anyone who saw them together would have to know that they were father and daughter. Except for her eyes; she had Leigh's sea-blue eyes.

A faint queasiness made it difficult for Leigh to go on singing. For all these years she had kept the secret, and now Katrina was the only living person besides herself who knew the truth about Wendy's paternity. No matter how much Leigh wanted to renew her relationship with Russ Thornton, her daughter's well-being was paramount. Leigh could not let Wendy find out here and now about her real father. A possessive ferocity arose in Leigh's chest, and she moved slightly forward so that her body blocked Wendy and Russ's view of each other.

This is insane, she thought as the pianist played the introduction to "Silent Night." *Silent in the night,* Leigh thought, *how apt.* Never telling anyone but David and

Katrina about Wendy; keeping the secret so that Wendy wouldn't be hurt. And now here was the one person who could destroy the world she'd made for her daughter, *their* daughter, and she was actually planning to meet him in the library later. Worst of all, she was still attracted to him.

When the last strains of the carol faded, Leigh turned away so that she wouldn't have to look at Russ, although she felt his probing eyes on her back. She covered her confusion by bending down to kiss little Claire-Anne good-night. When she straightened, Russ was gone.

Relief made her garrulous, and she found that she was overdoing her good-nights. Finally, after bidding the Craigs an effusive farewell, she helped Bett shepherd the children toward the elevators. Wendy, Andrew and Jeanne followed.

"I guess it'll be an early morning," Jeanne said, once the elevator doors had closed and they were headed upward.

"We're all going to meet in Bett and Carson's suite to open presents at eight o'clock, and then it's down to brunch with the other guests in the dining room. Everyone will be free to pursue various activities throughout the day before the wedding rehearsal at seven sharp, followed by the rehearsal dinner in the Balsam Room," Leigh said. She felt as if she were speaking by rote; no one seemed to notice.

"I don't know about everyone else, but I'm ready to pack it in," Andrew said.

"Me, too," Wendy replied as they stepped out of the elevator. "I hope you're not up for any late-night chats, Jeanne."

Jeanne laughed. "Today I helped my brother put together a bicycle for my nephew, a chore which had to be accomplished at five in the morning so my nephew wouldn't see it. No, I think I'll sleep early and well."

Andrew kissed Wendy good-night in front of the room she was sharing with Jeanne, and he escorted Leigh to the single room that she was occupying alone.

"Good night, Andrew," she told him.

"Is there anything you need? Anything I can get for you before I leave?" he asked.

Leigh smiled and patted his arm. She couldn't believe how normal she managed to look and sound. "Thanks, but I'll be fine. In fact, I'm going to read a bit before I go to sleep."

"See you in the morning, then," he said.

Leigh went into her room and pressed her back against the closed door. She felt a wild, nervous impulse to laugh hysterically. Or cry. Or something.

What if Russ had looked into Wendy's beautiful face and had seen the resemblance? What if, during those moments when they were all gathered around the piano, he had guessed?

Wendy didn't have a clue, she was sure of that. Wendy was so wrapped up in Andrew that she had no thought of anything else. But Russ—he could have put two and two together easily. For that matter, anyone could have. Wendy was so clearly her father's daughter.

The red digits of the clock on the round table beside the bed indicated that it was now ten-thirty, which meant that she had time to call Russ's room to tell him that she wouldn't meet him in the library as planned. To tell him that he'd better leave The Briarcliff now, because she didn't intend to talk to him at all. The telephone stared up at her from the table beside the bed.

She had no idea whether Russ would honor such a request even if she summoned the strength to make it. Certainly Russ was every bit a gentleman; he would probably depart quietly and without a fuss. Although hadn't he said he'd flown his plane here? A snowstorm would keep him from leaving.

She brushed aside the folds of the long blue velvet drapery at the window. There was no moon and no stars, and the wind had died. It wasn't snowing, though. If she met with Russ for a few minutes—he had asked for five or ten—perhaps she could convince him to go back to Charlotte where he belonged.

She went to the mirror over the big double dresser and stared at her reflection. Her face was thinner than it had been when she was twenty; her laugh lines showed, and her freckles did not. Her hair was worn in the same flowing style, reaching almost to her shoulders with wispy bangs across the forehead. And it was still the same copper color, thanks to the skills of an excellent hairdresser.

No, she didn't look the same. Russ was only being kind when he said so. And he didn't look the same, either. He had changed. But she liked the changes. Even though he posed a threat to her peace of mind, she couldn't help admitting that Russ Thornton looked better than ever.

LEIGH'S FEET MOVED soundlessly and reluctantly along the thick carpet in the hallway. A pause at Wendy's door assured her that her daughter and her roommate were serious about getting a good night's sleep, and she was sure that no one else in her family or Andrew's would be up and about. She rode the deserted elevator to the first floor where she halted outside the paneled library door and fought to surround herself with an air of detachment. She was determined that he would leave. Tonight, if possible.

Russ stood when she entered the library. On the way downstairs in the elevator, Leigh had prepared a fine speech. Now, however, facing his serious, unblinking scrutiny, all the words deserted her. His eyes searched her face, looking for something he had hoped to find; whether he found it or not, she couldn't tell. He smiled, a warm smile of welcome.

"We're lucky," he said, moving forward to take her hand. "There's no one else here. Come sit beside me on the couch. There are still coals in the grate."

In the face of his obvious pleasure, she caved in. She let herself be led to the leather couch and sank down beside him, halfheartedly planning her escape. She could say the words now. The words refused to come, however, and she gazed helplessly at Russ Thornton, understanding completely in that moment of looking deep into his dark eyes how she had fallen in love with him in the first place.

The only light in the room was a small lamp on the table beside the chair where Russ had been sitting. The walls were lined with the books that inn guests were encouraged to take to their rooms and read; the fireplace was small, and the embers within it lit their faces with a golden glow.

He held one of her hands. "I was afraid you wouldn't come," he said. His hopeful expression brought back so many feelings of loss and longing that she turned her head away.

"I almost didn't," she said faintly, keeping her face carefully averted.

"I'm glad you did," he said.

She forced herself to lift her head and look him in the eye. "You have to leave," she said as sternly as she could manage, but she realized too late that her forcefulness had only piqued his curiosity. "I mean, I wish you'd leave," she amended, pulling her hand away from him.

He looked suddenly deflated. "That's not what I wanted to hear," he said.

"This situation isn't easy for me," she said. "Here I am celebrating Christmas with my family, and you show up unannounced."

"You seem to enjoy our phone conversations," Russ pointed out.

"Phone calls, yes. But this—" and she shook her head in despair.

He let out a deep, lingering sigh and slid down on the couch so that his long legs extended toward the fire. He folded his arms across his chest and stared moodily into the fireplace.

"I wouldn't have thought you'd come here at Christmas," she said after a moment. "Doesn't your family expect you?"

"Now that my parents are gone, I often spend the holidays alone. When I was watching you in the great hall with your family, I realized how much I'd been missing. Was that your sister in the gray dress? Are those her children?"

"Yes, that's Bett," she said, and when he looked interested, she haltingly told him about Bett's whirlwind of a family.

"Does she live near you?" he asked.

"Less than an hour's drive away," she told him.

"And Warren?" he asked.

"Warren was killed in Vietnam, Russ," she said.

She swiveled her head in time to see the color drain from his face, but he recovered rapidly and shook his head. "I'm sorry, I hadn't heard," he said.

"Anyway, we're not a big family now, but we are close," she said.

"I figured out that the girl with the dark hair was your daughter," he said. "But I was mostly looking at you."

He doesn't know, Leigh thought in a moment of amazed revelation. *He hasn't guessed!* Wendy's resemblance to him, so obvious to Leigh, seemed to have escaped Russ completely. Her relief was instantly diluted by her sense of responsibility toward Wendy. Russ couldn't stay here. He *couldn't.*

She faced him squarely. "Russ, I meant it when I asked you to go. My daughter is getting married here the day after tomorrow. I'm very busy. I don't need this."

He seemed taken aback. "She's getting married? To whom?"

"To Andrew Craig, a boy she met at college. The point is, this isn't a good time for this—this reunion of ours."

"You seem glad to see me," he said after a moment.

"Do I?"

"Well, aren't you?"

"No. Not now."

"When? Next week? Next year?"

Leigh averted her eyes. He was so earnest. So genuine. If only—but she couldn't live the "if onlies." She'd learned that long ago.

"You've upset me so by showing up like this," she said in a rush.

"I figured we had a lot to say to each other," he said.

"We do, but not now. It's—it's—" She felt hysteria rising within her, but she pushed it away.

"If I'd known your daughter was getting married," he said with the utmost sincerity, "I probably wouldn't have come. But I didn't know, and I did come, so I want to make the most of it. I told you I won't interfere with your family plans, but any time that you have left over—"

"I won't," she said firmly.

His eyes were rueful. "Perhaps you could make time?" he suggested.

Leigh shook her head. "It's doubtful," she replied, feeling sad.

Russ stared at her for a moment before standing abruptly and walking to the shuttered window. He pushed back the shutters with one hand. "I can't fly in this weather," he pointed out. "It's a snowstorm." With his free hand he drew her close, so close that her hair brushed his shoulder, and she didn't have the heart to resist.

Then she looked out the window and saw that Wendy would have her white Christmas. Snow swirled in eddies around a post light near the path outside; it drifted into billowy mounds in the sheltered angle of the low wall defining the courtyard beyond. Dancing, whirling, sparkling magical snow—and somewhere a clock chimed the hour.

Leigh counted twelve silvery chimes. When she looked up at Russ, he was smiling down at her, and the rapt expression on his face was her utter undoing.

"Merry Christmas, Leigh," he whispered, and then he inclined his head slowly, so slowly that her heart stopped beating, and kissed her.

Chapter Four

The next morning Leigh awoke abruptly, and the first thing she thought was, *Russ is here.*

She had no idea what she was going to do about him. Last night he'd made it clear that he had no intention of leaving. She'd repeated her point that he couldn't count on her for company; he'd insisted that he didn't care. He just wanted to be near her, he said.

With her lips still warm from his kisses, she had asked him—no, begged him—to leave her alone today. Not that she thought he would. She was all too well acquainted with the stubborn spark she'd seen in his eyes last night. She only hoped that he'd have the good sense to time his approaches so that no one else in her party noticed him among the throng of people who had chosen to celebrate the holidays at the well-known Briarcliff.

At least he hasn't guessed about Wendy, Leigh thought thankfully. She slid out of bed and padded as soft-footed as a cat to the window to see the new-fallen snow. How he could have seen Wendy and not suspected, Leigh couldn't imagine. The features that they shared were so familiar to her that she thought they should be obvious to anyone. She had to admit that Russ's sharp nose was softened a bit in Wendy's face and that the similar texture of their hair might be a characteristic that only she would notice. But the squared jawline—wasn't that unmistakable? And the broad shoulders—weren't they a sure giveaway? Maybe not. Maybe it was her guilt that made her catalog resemblances that were not really as striking as she thought.

When she raised the shade, she saw that the grounds of The Briarcliff seemed silvered in misty light; the fresh snowfall blurred the shadows of the mountain ridges and unfurled around the inn like a glistening white bridal train. The scene was so quiet and peaceful, a direct contrast to Leigh's complicated emotions.

As she dressed, she wondered if she really wanted Russ to leave. On her mothering level, where she instinctively wanted to protect her young, she believed that he must go. If he stayed, he might guess about Wendy. On another level, the one where she operated like any other woman who hoped for an all-encompassing relationship with a man, she wished that things could be the same between them as they had been twenty-two years ago. Or was she merely overwhelmed by Russ's sudden presence in her life at a time when she was bound to be sentimental, anyway? Leigh was smart enough to recognize her own vulnerability.

After the wedding, if Russ stayed around that long, and Leigh had no doubt that he would, she would figure out what to do about him. Before she could think this through, Wendy and Jeanne burst laughing through the connecting door to their room, shouted "Merry Christmas!" and swept her up on a wave of enthusiasm and hilarity that effectively ended Leigh's reflections.

The three of them gathered up their presents and arrived breathlessly with the others at Carson and Bett's suite where they were greeted by the excited squeals of the children, who had been awake since the first tentative rays of sunlight crept over Briarcliff Mountain. There were repeated jovial exclamations about the appropriateness of last night's snowfall, and Wendy and Andrew seemed wrapped in their own particular bliss, which was exactly, Leigh thought, as it should be.

After much oohing and aahing over presents, they all trooped downstairs to brunch. The dining room had been draped with red velvet ribbons for the occasion, and a sculptured-ice Santa presided from his spot in the middle of the buffet table. All the while Leigh was tending little Claire-Anne and watching Wendy, who was glowing with happiness, her eyes were darting into the corners of the room and past the garlanded entrance searching for Russ. She saw no sign of him. Well, what had she expected? She had asked him to leave her alone, hadn't she?

By the time brunch was over, the great hall of the inn was abuzz with children trying out their new toys; a quartet of carolers moved from one section of the hall to another singing Christmas songs.

"This is the kind of Christmas I've always hoped for," Wendy said, swooping up behind Leigh during a lull.

"Isn't it lovely," Leigh murmured in agreement.

"Mom, is anything wrong? You look—well, so *removed.* It isn't like you." Wendy regarded her with mild concern.

"I'm just being a bit reflective," Leigh replied.

"I was thinking earlier how much Dad would have loved all of this," Wendy said softly, her gesture taking in the decorations, the smiling faces of their family and the glittering snowscape beyond the wide windows.

"Yes," Leigh agreed wistfully.

"If only he could have lived long enough to meet the man I'm going to marry. Dad would have loved Andrew, wouldn't he?"

"I'm sure he would have," Leigh said. Suddenly her heart ached with a pang of disloyalty to David. All this thinking about Russ meant that she'd given David no more than a passing thought, and this at a time when she should have been thinking about David more than ever. David had, after all, embraced Wendy as his own. No man could have done more than that.

"Don't cry, Mom. This is the happiest time of my life. Dad wouldn't want you to be sad," Wendy said. She drew a lacy handkerchief out of her pocket and passed it to Leigh.

Leigh dabbed at the tears threatening to overflow her bottom eyelids, and as she returned the handkerchief to Wendy, she saw Russ standing unobtrusively at the other end of the hall. His smile was tentative, and, her heart laden with sadness, she let her eyes meet his for one long moment.

He was struck by the pain he saw and stunned by the rawness of her need. The droop of her head, which she tried to disguise when her daughter approached; the strained expression around her eyes; she touched him to the very core of his being in some indefinable way. In her, Russ saw all the uncertainty and disillusionment that he felt about his own life. In that moment he felt more than an attraction to her, he felt a kinship. In the twenty-two years that they had been apart, they had both suffered. Now they had the opportunity to come together again, if that was what they both wanted, and to comfort each other, if that was in their power.

Leave her alone—hell, he thought fiercely. Today was Christmas Day. No one should be as much alone as he sensed Leigh was, even in the rush of activity surrounding her family. He knew all about keeping busy so you wouldn't have time to let the feelings surface. He knew what it was like to pretend to be happy and cheerful so that other people wouldn't feel concerned about your own sadness. And that was what Leigh was doing—she was pretending. The Leigh he saw this morning wasn't the spontaneous, happy-go-lucky girl he had known. And yet that girl was somewhere inside her, and perhaps he would be the one to set her free.

He wheeled abruptly and went back to his room. He had a card up his sleeve, and he sensed that this was the time to play it.

LEIGH REALIZED, when she looked up and saw that Russ was gone, that he had pulled another disappearing act. At least he was respecting her wishes so far. He wasn't embarrassing her in front of the family. She would embarrass herself, however, if she didn't keep up a cheerful front.

"Anybody want to build a snowman?" Carson wanted to know, and Leigh, feigning a gaiety that she didn't feel, quickly took up the cause. They all bundled up in their warm coats and woolly mittens, flocking outside to join several other families in the construction of an immense snowman in the circle created by the grand loop of the inn's driveway.

Once Leigh looked up to see Russ watching her intently through a window of the great hall. She made a wry face at him without thinking as she helped the boys roll a large snowball for the snowman's head. The next time she sneaked a covert glance at the window, Russ waved. She shook her head slightly in disapproval, but she couldn't help smiling at him. He grinned back.

After the snowman had been built and Carson had taken pictures of all of them gathered around it, Nancy, Andrew's mother, said that she felt like spending the afternoon napping. Vera said that sounded like a good idea, and Bett soon followed them into the inn, insisting that a protesting Claire-Anne lie down on her bed for a while so that she wouldn't fall asleep in the middle of the rehearsal dinner that night. Carson, Jim and the boys wandered toward the creek, where a snowball fight was in lively progress.

Andrew threw one arm around Wendy and one around Leigh. "It's a fine snowman," he said expansively. "Look at everyone inside the inn admiring him."

Leigh glanced at the window where Russ had stood. She didn't see him, but a couple of children standing there with their parents were applauding. Andrew swept a comic bow in their direction, and one of the children mimicked him.

"I'm so cold that my feet feel like blocks of ice," Wendy said, stomping her boots in the snow.

"Come up to my room," Leigh said. "I brought a hot-water bottle."

Wendy darted a hasty glance in Andrew's direction. "Andrew and I thought we'd warm ourselves in front of the fire in the library," she said apologetically.

"Of course," Andrew hastened to add more out of sense of duty than a desire for Leigh's company, "we'd love for you to come with us."

Leigh, stung by her own insensitivity, realized immediately what she should have understood before she spoke—that Wendy and Andrew would naturally want to spend time alone together.

"No," she said briskly, "I'll be perfectly okay on my own. *My* feet are cold, too, and a hot cup of tea in my room sounds more than inviting. You two run along."

Wendy looked indecisive, torn between wanting to be alone with her husband-to-be and her obligation to her mother.

"No, I really mean it," Leigh insisted. She started to walk toward the inn.

"Mom," Wendy said, still unsure.

"You worry too much," she said, going back to where Wendy stood and slipping her arm through her daughter's. Leigh turned to Andrew for support. "Andrew, how about helping me out?"

"Come along," he said, appropriating Wendy's other arm. "We'll have those feet of yours warm in no time."

Wendy followed, knowing when she was outnumbered, and in the lobby Leigh bade them a cheery goodbye. Once in the elevator, however, she let her determined smile fade and rubbed her eyelids with a cold thumb and forefinger. Of course Wendy would disdain a hot-water bottle in favor of Andrew; Leigh should have known better than to offer it. Somehow she must learn to let go of Wendy, little by little, bit by bit, even though she knew it would be one of the hardest things she had ever done. She and Wendy were closer than most mothers and daughters, perhaps because they had depended so heavily on each other for comfort ever since David's death. It would be a real challenge to back off in the months ahead, because she was already feeling shut out.

Leigh's room was an oasis of quiet after the hubbub everywhere else at the inn; it was a good place to nurse her rejection. The bright sunlight penetrated into all the corners of the room, bringing out the glow of the cherry furniture and casting rainbow reflections from the prisms of the light fixture onto the cream-colored walls of the room, and Leigh immediately felt better.

She hung her coat in the closet, draped her muffler over a doorknob, and only when she was about to pick up the receiver to order a cup of tea from room service did she notice that the red message light on her telephone was blinking.

She knew that there was only one person who could have left her a message. Everyone in her party had been outside with her for the past couple of hours.

Common sense advised her that to ignore the winking red light would be the utmost folly. Leigh had absolutely no doubt that Russ Thornton would appear knocking at her door if she didn't respond to his message. And that simply wouldn't do.

She picked up the phone and telephoned the desk. As she waited for the clerk to answer, she felt a hundred misgivings.

"Yes, Mrs. Cathcart, we do have a message for you," observed the desk clerk. "I'll send a bellman to deliver it."

"Please read it to me on the phone," Leigh said.

"I'm sorry, but we can't do that. The sender asked specifically that it be delivered."

"But—"

"The bellman will be there shortly" was the firm answer, and Leigh suspected that the wheels of this particular Russ Thornton gambit had been greased with a liberal tip. Impatiently she hung up and awaited the inevitable knock. When she opened the door, a uniformed inn employee handed her not only a white envelope but a small green-and-gilt-wrapped box. After he disappeared down the hall, she stared at the tiny package and let her apprehension give way to dismay. Why was Russ giving her a gift?

The wrapping paper fell away to reveal a white box. *Jewelry,* she thought with foreboding. *But why?*

She lifted the box's lid and removed a layer of cotton. A golden glimmer... a familiar shape. Her eyes blurred for a moment when she saw the heart-shaped locket against the black velvet lining. As she lifted the locket on its chain, it winked seductively in the gossamer rays of sunshine filtering through the snow-laden branches of the oak trees outside her window.

On the back were engraved their initials, L. R. and R. T. *Just the way we'll engrave our wedding bands someday,* Russ had whispered on that spring night so long ago when he'd given her the locket to reassure her that their separation because of his father's illness was only a temporary interruption of their relationship; that night neither of them had thought that anything could come between them.

Leigh remembered that the locket's chain had broken sometime during that last summer when they lay together in their secret green glade in the park, and Russ had scooped the locket up from where it had fallen amid the pine needles and he said, "I'll take it to the jeweler's and have it repaired for you." Later, in the heat of their disagreements, they had both forgotten the locket, although Leigh had thought about it many times since, wondering if it was still waiting unclaimed in some Charlotte jewelry store after so many years.

Russ had kept the locket all this time. How incredible, and how crafty of him to present her with it now. He knew that it was the one gift that she wouldn't send back to him, the one gift that would touch her more deeply than any other.

Clutching the locket in her hand, she picked up the phone, hesitated, and then dialed Russ's room.

"Russ," she said when he picked up the phone. "I don't know what to say."

"How about Merry Christmas for starters?" he said.

"Merry Christmas, then, but—oh, Russ, thank you for the locket. I—I often wondered what became of it." She held it at eye level and watched the gold heart twisting on its chain so that their two sets of engraved initials blurred into each other. *I am you and you are me,* she thought, the words surfacing from somewhere in her subconscious. It was what they used to say to each other all the times that they felt inseparably close. She folded her fingers around the heart until she felt her own pulse.

"I meant to give it back to you, but the opportunity never arose. Now I think you should have it," he said. "Anyway, Christmas is a most appropriate time for gifts, if you consider something that was always yours a gift. Look, I don't know what's on your agenda this afternoon, but would you like to join me for a walk? Now?"

"I'm supposed to be drinking a cup of tea," Leigh told him. She set the locket carefully on the table beside the bed; having it back was one thing, but wearing it was another.

"You don't sound the least bit thirsty," he pointed out, and she smiled.

"Actually, I wasn't," she admitted.

"How about it? Doesn't a walk seem like the perfect way to spend such a beautiful afternoon?"

Leigh glanced out the window. The sky was a bright crystal blue, and sunlight fairly bounced off the blanket of snow covering the mountain. She really didn't want to coop herself up inside the inn. She did, after all, have a life of her own.

"I'll put on my coat and meet you somewhere away from the inn," she said, feeling her heart lighten with joy at the very thought of seeing him.

"I'll be waiting beside the stone pillars at the main entrance to the grounds. Can you be there in ten minutes?"

"Seven," she said, and he laughed.

"That's even better. Bye," he said.

Leigh caught a glimpse of her reflection in the mirror as she hung up the phone. She was smiling, and who could blame her? After all this time, she and Russ were planning to go somewhere together again, and it was just as it had been in those long-ago days when they took each other's presence in their lives so much for granted. Twenty-two years seemed to melt away in the force of their attraction to each other; in some ways, it was as though they had never been apart.

She threw on her coat and literally ran from her room, feeling furtive and yet exhilarated as she traversed the great hall as unobtrusively as possible, and finally she breathed a sigh of relief as she escaped the confines of the inn without seeing anyone she knew. She drew long drafts of air into her lungs, heady with her freedom.

Russ was waiting, and he waved and bounded toward her across the snow when he caught sight of her approaching from the direction of the inn. When they met in the middle of the driveway, he caught both her mittened hands in his; she could feel his warmth through the thick wool.

"I'm so glad you decided to join me," he said, his eyes sparkling as they took in the sight of her. He looked boyish and carefree and unabashedly happy to see her. She smiled up at him, a dazzling smile, and clung to his hands for a few seconds longer than necessary before releasing them.

"Race you to the road," she said, flinging the words back over her shoulder, and he laughed and said, "Be careful! There may be ice in the drive!" but there wasn't, and Leigh skimmed past two startled parents who were pulling their bundled-up baby on a small sled in the snow alongside the driveway. The incongruity of it amused her: a few years ago, she would have been one of those totally responsible parents who was looking askance at any crazy adult who wasn't acting her age. And now she didn't even care how she appeared to these people or to anyone else as long as she was having a good time. She laughed with the sheer delight of it.

When she breathlessly skidded to a stop on the narrow path bordering the highway, Russ was beside her. "As someone who runs every day, I'm ashamed to admit that you almost beat me," he said.

"Almost? I *did* win. I was a whole nose ahead of you on the straightaway."

"I won't quibble. Want to run with me tomorrow morning? I usually go before breakfast."

"Tomorrow I'll be busy," she said, reminding him.

"Ah, that's right. Well, for now you're mine," he said lightly, taking her hand as they started their downhill walk.

The gesture surprised her in a way, although it seemed perfectly natural. He grinned at her and reached in his pocket with his other hand. "Want a lemon drop?" he said, offering her the package.

"You still have lemon drops," she said softly, feeling a tiny pang at the sight and scent of them.

"Of course," he said. She held out her mittened hand and he slid one out of the bag and into her palm. She put it into her mouth before it could stick to the wool of her mitten. The sour-sweet taste brought back so many memories, all mixed up with the way Russ's car had always smelled, the way *he* smelled, even the way he tasted. Last night when he had kissed her, she had marveled that he tasted exactly the same and had been amazed that she actually remembered.

Leigh shivered slightly as a cold wind blew through the stand of trees on the slope, and Russ squeezed her hand. She might remember the taste of him, but this was something she had forgotten—they had communicated so much to each other through touch in the old days; Russ had liked to punctuate conversations with meaningful little squeezes of her hand, and she had often squeezed back in agreement. She had never done that with anyone else; how could that have escaped her memory?

Maybe too many things had slipped her memory, after all. Oh, she remembered the big things, like the seriousness of the moment when he had first slipped the chain of the heart-shaped gold locket around her neck and the pain on his face when she left him that last day in the park. She'd *thought* she remembered the little things, too, such as the lemon drops. But in fact she only recalled the obvious—for instance, the way the lemon drops smelled and tasted. She wasn't ready for the emotional response she was experiencing. She wasn't ready at all.

"The craft village is down the hill. The stores won't be open because it's Christmas Day, but we can window-shop. Heidi, one of my decorators, told me to be on the lookout for colorful quilts, and she also said that if I can find any authentic antiques, I should buy them. I don't know how to tell if they're authentic, that's the problem."

"My mother owned an antique store for a few years after Bett left home," Leigh said. "Maybe I can advise you."

"You'll be busy with the wedding tomorrow," Russ reminded her.

"Oh. Yes, that's true," she said, pulling herself up short. For a moment she had been thinking that she would be at The Briarcliff longer than she actually was. Time had a way of warping when she was around Russ.

"As for quilts, Heidi says they're great for the country style of decorating that's so popular now," Russ said.

"Katrina knows this little old lady who lives deep in the mountains and who makes the most marvelous quilts. I'll see if I can get an address for you."

"That would please Heidi no end," Russ replied.

They heard a shout from the top of the hill and stopped short as a boy riding an upside-down garbage-can lid swooped in front of them, barely avoiding their toes. He tumbled sideways and rolled in the snow, then sat up with a jaunty grin, picked up the lid, and ran downhill to meet his friends.

"That looks like fun," Russ said, glancing up the hill. "I wonder if we could do it."

"If we had a couple of garbage can lids, maybe we could. I remember when Wendy was little and it would snow, the kids would use anything to slide down the hill on the next street over. Pizza pans, cafeteria trays, all sorts of things became toboggans for them."

"It must have been fun raising a child," Russ said wistfully.

"Oh, it was," Leigh began before remembering that she didn't want to talk about Wendy. And yet Wendy had been such an important part of her life that it was almost impossible not to inject her into the conversation.

The boy with the garbage-can lid and his friends ran noisily past them up the hill. One boy hollered an invitation to the others to come over to his house to play a new video game. Their voices fairly crackled in the crisp cold air.

"At Christmas, I really start feeling down sometimes," Russ said. "That's when it's painfully clear to me that I've missed out on so much by not having a child. Or children. I'd always thought I would have a family."

She shot him a curious look. "I was surprised when you told me you hadn't," she said, knowing full well that she was treading on dangerous ground.

"It never seemed to be the right time to have a child. At least for Dominique." He tried to keep the bitterness out of his voice, only partially succeeding.

"She didn't want children?"

"I thought she wanted them when we got married, and maybe she did at the time, I don't know. Later, when she told me that kids didn't fit in with the kind of life she wanted to lead, I tried to accept that. I thought I had come to terms with our childlessness until we divorced; afterward I had to realize that probably I'd never be a father."

Leigh held her breath; what if she were to tell him flat out, right this very moment, that he *was* a father? That his daughter was smart and beautiful and that she was everything anyone could hope for in a daughter? What would he do? What would he say?

They walked on in silence, which she hoped he would interpret as sympathetic. He could have no idea of the pain she was feeling at this moment, and yes, of the terror. She had kept the secret so well; even thinking of telling it made her mouth go dry and her knees feel weak.

"So, now I'm resigned to not having kids," Russ said. He kicked a pinecone out of the path and it rolled downhill, giving Leigh time to think. What she thought was that she didn't want to think about it, and with the craft village looming in the distance, she was able to manage a quick change of subject.

"Look," she said. "The craft village looks so beautiful under its blanket of snow."

It *was* lovely. Bare snow-frosted tree branches arched through the wintry blue sky to shelter the little rustic stone cottages arranged neatly along the sides of the highway, and snow glittered from the windowsills and in the niches between the stones. It could have been a Christmas-card scene depicting a small New England village, but in fact the Briarcliff craft village was something quite different.

A hundred years ago, the wife of the philanthropist whose retreat this was had sought to extend her good works to the impoverished mountain people who lived nearby. She had been entranced by the folksy crafts of the mountain people; the wood carvings, the weaving and the sturdy furniture would, she was sure, find a ready market in the North. And so she had built a village where the mountain artisans could work, and the craftspeople had formed the Briarcliff Crafts Cooperative, which had sold handmade items to some of the most exclusive shops in New York, Chicago and Philadelphia.

Now that The Briarcliff was an all-season resort, the cooperative sold most of their crafts on the premises, functioning as a series of gift shops for the inn. Today other guests enjoying the bracing mountain air browsed among the shops as they admired the window displays, and as she and Russ joined the crowd, Leigh recalled how during past summers spent here with her family, the craft village had always been a treat.

In the window of the first house, an old loom built of woods native to the mountains dominated the setting. Soft homespun cloth spilled over the weaver's bench, and several bedspreads and tablecloths in different patterns were knotted loosely and draped artistically around a basket.

In the next shop, Russ found the antiques he had been looking for. "What do you think about that handcrafted pine shaving stand?" he asked, shading the glass from the reflection of the sun and peering inside.

"Very nice," Leigh said approvingly.

"I don't know. I have no imagination about decor. I should send Heidi up here to look at some of these things," Russ said as they moved on.

"Heidi—you've mentioned her a number of times," Leigh observed.

Russ slowed his steps. "I suspect I know what you're thinking, and no, she isn't. She is twenty-four years old, has worked for me for six months and lives with her boyfriend in a house decorated with old Coca-Cola signs and curtains made of mosquito netting dyed army green. I have absolutely no interest in her at all. Anyway, she's practically young enough to be my daughter."

Leigh felt her face flush. "I wasn't implying that you had an unusual interest in her," she said, wishing the subject had never come up. It struck too close to what she didn't want to think about, to what she didn't want Russ to know.

"You were wondering about Heidi. You might as well admit it," Russ said good-naturedly.

"I couldn't help but be curious about someone you mention often," she said in a small voice.

"For your information, there isn't anyone else in my life at the moment. How about you?"

"No," she said slowly, "there's no one."

"Then let's have a lemon drop. To celebrate," he said solemnly. He handed her one and ate one himself. "Now, we might as well check out the wood-carving place. And I promise I won't mention Heidi again."

Feeling chastened and on edge, Leigh kept a considerable distance between her and Russ as they walked across the street. She was annoyed to feel tears sting the inside of her eyelids. She blinked, willing them to go away.

They stood in front of the wood-carver's house, and Russ said something, the words sounding to her ears like a blur. She fought to recover her composure.

"Leigh, what's wrong?" he said, all concern.

"Nothing," she said, rolling the lemon drop from one side of her mouth to the other. "Nothing."

"I looked down at you and all of a sudden you weren't there," he said, half to himself.

"I'm here," she said, forcing brightness.

"Just for a moment—"

"Just for a moment perhaps my attention wandered," she said as briskly as she could manage. She focused her attention on the objects in the window, which consisted of carved chipmunks and elves that seemed to have cornered the market in cute. They were definitely not her type of thing nor did they fit her mood, and she turned and began to walk back up the hill.

Russ followed her, catching up with her in a few steps.

"I know you've got a lot on your mind with your daughter getting married," he said.

"Yes," she admitted.

"If you want to talk about it, I'll be glad to listen."

"There's not much to say," she said tersely.

"Where's Wendy going to live after she's married?" Russ asked.

Leigh's mind raced. If she didn't talk about it, she would be upset. If she did, she might say too much. Leigh decided to take the latter course and to keep her remarks brief.

"She and Andrew are both still juniors at Duke, and they found a lovely apartment not far from campus."

"Does it worry you that they haven't graduated from college yet?" he asked.

"I'd hoped they would finish college before they got married, but they didn't want to wait."

"Well, they're young and in love. That can make up for whatever material things they're lacking."

"Yes. I suppose it can," Leigh said, and she was thinking, *Young and in love. The way she and Russ had been twenty-two years ago.* She sped up her step, unwilling to pursue the topic. She hoped Russ wouldn't either.

"Leigh, wait. You're walking so fast," he said.

She reluctantly slowed her step, and he caught up. He slid an arm around her shoulders, sensing her mood. "I guess some things are still too difficult to talk about. Right?"

She didn't know what irritated her more, his chatty tone of voice or the fact that he always had been able to read her. Now, as much as she wanted to renew their relationship, she felt on very shaky ground with him. She couldn't figure out the guidelines, hadn't managed to establish any boundaries. She was used to dealing with him as though they were both still twenty, and yet they had each lived a lifetime, a *separate* lifetime, in the intervening years. She still felt the same magic when she was near him, but it wasn't enough to carry her safely through the mine field of her emotions. And right now the mines were exploding all around her.

She turned to face him, her hands stuck deep in the pockets of her coat. They were clenched into fists.

"Look, Russ, I'm completely at a loss right now. One minute I'm glad you showed up at The Briarcliff, and the next minute I think it was the biggest mistake in the world.

And I've got this wedding on my mind and—oh, I don't know. It's a really emotional time for me, as you can surely imagine. This on top of it—well, it's crazy, that's all." She lifted her shoulders and let them drop, then resumed walking.

Russ, his mouth clamped in a tight line, was right beside her. "Crazy? Yeah, I guess you're right. I'm crazy, you're crazy, the whole world is crazy. So let's make a little time in our lives for something real and warm and happy—like getting to know each other again. Like spending part of Christmas Day together and enjoying it."

Leigh forged ahead, walking faster now. "I don't think I'm enjoying it," she said.

His face fell. "You *were*. *I* was. Until you started thinking about things that don't have anything to do with us."

"Oh, don't they?" she muttered under her breath. She didn't think he heard her.

"All right, I'll butt out of this picture. I'll get away from The Briarcliff as soon as I can, leaving you to get on with the wedding. That's what I did twenty-two years ago, and I can do it again," he said.

Stricken, Leigh lifted her head and gazed at him. He was staring straight ahead with an anguished expression.

She stopped, saw a stone bench that had been brushed free of snow. "Wait," she said, reaching out blindly.

"Wait? Oh, that's funny. *You* didn't wait, did you, Leigh? You married David Cathcart as soon as I left for Canada. Now you expect me to wait? I told you, I'm out of here."

She hadn't expected this. He had always been calm in the face of chaos. Now she knew that his mental state was as agitated as hers was; the difference was that he held his feelings inside. Suddenly his pain was real to her, and she knew in that moment how much she had hurt him.

It was then that he noticed the tears welling up in her eyes, saw that she was struggling to maintain her composure. He swept aside his own anger long enough to caution himself that he didn't want her to become as frustrated as she had been on that last day they had met in the park before he fled to Canada, and from the looks of things, she was well on the way. He exhaled in one long breath, and all the fight went out of him.

"All right," he said heavily. "All right. I didn't mean it. Or at least I don't mean it anymore."

She took his hand and led him over to the bench, stumbling once and righting herself by clinging to his arm. He sat down, barely conscious of the high laughter of the children playing nearby.

She clasped her mittened hands together in an effort to keep them from trembling, and she struggled to find the words. They didn't come easily. Finally she lifted her head.

"Russell, I have something to tell you. Your letter—the one in which you asked me to marry you, the one you sent to me right after our last argument that day in the park—I never received it, Russ. I never knew you wanted to marry me. I didn't find out that you had proposed to me until the letter was delivered early this month." The tears spilled over now, sliding down her pale cheeks.

This information sent him reeling; he was thunderstruck.

"I thought you had refused me when you didn't show up at the park," he managed to say.

"I didn't *know,*" she said, the words extracting themselves with the utmost pain. "I didn't know."

He stared at her helplessly, hardly able to believe it but knowing, from the tormented expression on her face, that he would *have* to believe it because it was, God help him, the truth. He was numb, and she looked more wretched than he had ever seen her. He could only imagine how heart-wrenching it had been for her to find out now that he had wanted her to marry him.

"Leigh," was all he could say. "Oh, Leigh." Nothing he could do or say about the past would make things right after all this time, so he did what he could about the present. He pulled her gently into his arms and kissed away her teardrops one by one.

Chapter Five

That evening Leigh moved woodenly through the wedding rehearsal. She entered the chapel at the appropriate time, sat alone in the first pew and watched Wendy and Andrew practice the ceremony. She felt as if she were only going through the motions, because telling Russ about the letter had left her feeling drained and devoid of energy.

He had taken it hard. She had expected bewilderment and perhaps even anger, but she had not been prepared for the raw expression of grief that sprang to Russ's face before he pulled her into his arms. Sitting on that bench, lost in their private sorrow, they had clung together for a long time, oblivious to passersby.

During those moments, splintered images eddied through her mind; the heat of her anger on that day so long ago when he told her that he planned to leave for Canada, his face contorted by grief when she told him to get out of her life. She'd meant it.

She'd never meant it. All she'd really wanted was to be with Russ forever.

Finally the memories had receded and the cold had seeped through to their consciousness, and shivering, they had reluctantly forced themselves apart. Still shaken, Russ had walked her back to the inn, where they had separated before they came within sight of the windows and where Leigh had proceeded zombielike to her room and gone through the motions of bathing and dressing for the rehearsal and the dinner that would follow.

The proceedings at the altar forced Leigh to pay attention. This wasn't the time to be thinking about Russ's reaction to her revelation; she was a key player in Wendy's wedding, and she'd better shape up. She riveted her gaze on the scene being played out in front of her.

The minister, a relative of Andrew's who would officiate at tomorrow's ceremony, said, "I'll ask, 'Do you take this man to be your lawful wedded husband, to have and to hold from this day forward, for better, for worse, for richer, for poorer, in sickness and in health for as long as you both shall live?' Then, Wendy, you will reply 'I do.'"

"I do," Wendy said softly as though trying the words on for size.

Leigh thought of how proud Russ would be of Wendy and how he also deserved to share this day. Suddenly it didn't matter that he hadn't been able to be part of Wendy's life; he had been part of her begetting, and as her real father, he should be present for her wedding. Their love for each other in those long-ago days was the reason that Wendy existed. Yet Leigh knew that if he showed up at this small wedding, his presence would surely be noticed.

No, Leigh could not invite him. It was impossible. She made herself stop thinking about it and forced herself to listen to the minister's instructions about the recessional.

When the practice ceremony was over, Wendy and Andrew stopped to consult with the leader of the string quartet that was to play at the wedding in lieu of an organist.

"Shall we go in to dinner?" asked Jim Craig, offering one arm to his wife and the other to Leigh.

Leigh pulled herself together, and with the Craigs, led the procession into the small private dining room that the Craigs had reserved for the occasion. Dinner seemed interminable. Leigh caught herself barely responding to questions that were put to her and feeling as if she were operating on the fringe of reality.

Other scenes flashed through her head; she was thinking of Wendy as a teenager, with braces on her teeth; she was thinking of Wendy as a young, gap-toothed girl in a Girl Scout uniform and as a toddler trying to learn to ride a tricycle.

"Coffee?" asked a waiter at her elbow, and she shook her head. Try as she might, she could not clear her mind of scenes of Wendy growing up, parts of Wendy's life that Russ had missed and from which Leigh had, by her marriage to David, effectively shut Russ out.

Even so, now Leigh was at a loss to know what else she could have done under the circumstances. Alone and pregnant, she hadn't known Russ's address in Canada, and she had been too dazed by her plight to think clearly. The only thought that had penetrated her consciousness at the time was that she and Russ had parted in anger and that she had never heard from him afterward. Her pregnancy had capped off a summer that had been miserable from the beginning. She remembered; she remembered it all.

During the summer of 1969, Russ, who was caught up in the anti-Vietnam-war movement full-force by that time, refused to accept her family's hospitality after the first few uncomfortable visits to her parents' home. Leigh had been secretly relieved when he stopped coming over. She was unhappy with her position between opposing camps, and she was sure that she'd soon coax Russ back to her way—and her family's way—of thinking.

Her persuasion hadn't worked, of course. Soon Russ joined a group to send out flyers protesting the government's actions in Vietnam, and subsequently he organized a protest march on Raleigh, the North Carolina state capital, on the Fourth of July.

Because of Russ's awkward antiwar stance, Leigh had let her parents assume that the romance was winding down, and when, flabbergasted, they recognized Russ on television burning his draft card in front of the North Carolina capitol building, her father had erupted from his recliner chair with an oath.

"What the hell is this country coming to?" he had asked angrily. "Who do those people think they are? Who does Russ think *he* is?"

"He has a right to speak out, if that's the way he feels," Leigh said.

Her father's keen look pierced through her. "If you ask me, you need to give that boy the old heave-ho. I'd better not see him around here again."

Leigh thought about defending Russ, but she realized that it wouldn't do any good, especially when her father stomped out of the room. She knew her father well enough to know that once he had taken a stand, he would not back off. That afternoon she crept away to her room and cried, knowing that as long as Russ held his radical views, he would not be welcome in her parents' home.

She loved Russ as much as ever, of course, but in view of the growing tension between Russ and her family, they had begun meeting secretly on weekends in a state park halfway between their two cities. When they met on the weekend after the Fourth of July, Leigh attacked Russ viciously.

"How was I supposed to explain to my parents when they saw you burning your draft card? Why did you do it, anyway? What good did it do? When I saw you on television, I didn't even know who you *were* anymore!" she said, tears streaming down her face.

"Leigh, calm down," Russ said, attempting to take her in his arms. They were standing on a small arched bridge in the woods in a secluded area of the park, and the only sound other than their own voices was of the creek below singing against the stones.

"I can hardly wait until this fall when we're back at school and things are normal again," she said, because it seemed to her that all their troubles had started once they left the college milieu, but Russ grabbed her wrist and twisted her around so she'd have to look at him.

"I'm not going back to Duke," he said softly. His eyes were dark and liquid, flecked with green glimmers of light from the sun filtering through the trees overhead.

"Not going back?" she replied incredulously. "I thought your father would be well enough to return to work in September."

"He will, but this doesn't have anything to do with him. Leigh, I can't conscientiously continue to accept a student draft deferment. I want to work against the war, to do something positive, something that will make a difference. I met this guy when I was in Raleigh, he knows about an organization in Canada—"

Russ was serious. He wasn't joking. Leigh knew all about draft resisters and how they were leaving in droves for Canada; she knew a friend of Warren's who had skipped the country instead of waiting for his army induction. Her parents had called him a coward and worse.

"Don't you see, Leigh? This is something I *have* to do." Russ cupped her face gently between his hands, and as always when he looked at her with that expression of love and openness, her knees went weak and the palms of her hands grew damp.

"I thought you loved me," she said, her voice quavering with uncertainty.

"I do. Oh, you know I do," he said softly.

"Then how can you go? How can you possibly leave me?"

"Because I *do* love you. What's happening in the world scares me, Leigh. I can't think about planning a future the way things are now. Look at the mood of the people in this country—it's ugly. I want to work to make it better for us."

"The war will be over soon, you won't have to go anywhere, there's no need, don't you see, Russ? Don't you?" She was babbling now, and crying, and her damp cheek was pressed so hard against his shirt that the buttons bit into her flesh.

"I have to go," he said, and that was all he said, but she knew he meant it and that there was no point in arguing.

She needed his reassurance, needed to know that he cared. In their secret green glade she drew him down on top of her, and they made desperate love. Afterward, spent and shaking, they clung to each other, each terrified of the future.

"What will happen to us?" she had asked fearfully. She couldn't imagine life without Russ.

"We'll be together," he told her, but she was not so sure.

As he slowly walked Leigh back through the leaf-filtered light to her little blue Volkswagen, Russ said uncertainly, "Next week?"

"Next week," she'd answered dully, and he'd bent down to kiss her through the open window, his lips warm and tender.

No matter how much she had thought about it, no matter from what angle she considered it, she couldn't figure out how to change Russ's mind about going to Canada. He was sure that he was doing the right thing, and nothing would persuade him otherwise. He had always been stubborn.

"Going to Canada to evade the draft is illegal," she had said forcefully in continuation of their argument when they met in the park the next weekend. "If you leave, you'll never be welcome in this country again."

"Someday I'll come back," he said with a faraway look in his eyes.

"And what about me in the meantime?"

"You could go to college in Canada."

"It's so far away, Russ! Why, I've never been north of Durham, North Carolina! It gets too cold in Canada. Besides, we don't know anyone there!"

"Ontario is right across the border from Detroit. There's a university in Windsor, I checked it out. I'm going to get my degree there, and you could, too. As for the cold—we could keep each other warm. If we have each other, we won't need anyone else." He'd smiled at her so engagingly and with so much charm that she'd almost capitulated before she realized it, and the fact that Russ would use his charm to get around her made her even more angry.

She'd beaten her fists against his chest, and she'd ranted and she'd raved, but nothing she said seemed to make the slightest difference.

They kept meeting at the park that summer; her parents thought she was out with friends on those lazy summer weekend afternoons, and she had no idea what Russ's parents thought. If she'd had the strength to do it, she might have broken up with him. She couldn't stand the agony he was heaping on her, but the overriding factor was that she knew it would be worse, far worse, not to have him at all. He was leaving soon enough, and she wanted to hold him and kiss him and make love with him as much as she could now. She lived in the Now, she wished that Now could last forever, and she tried to memorize every look, every touch, every gesture, every word to take out and examine later. Later, when she would be alone.

Their last day in the park together had been a nightmare.

It had started out pleasantly enough; Leigh had brought a picnic lunch, which included Russ's favorite brownies. They had walked in the woods, dabbled their bare feet in the creek, and in their glade after lunch they had made love slowly and languorously in the somnolent mid-August heat.

It was after they dressed that Russ pulled her on top of him in what she had thought was a playful mood. When he captured her face between his hands so that her long hair curtained both their faces, hers above and his below, something had changed in him and she had known with growing fear that what he was about to say was momentous.

"I'm leaving for Canada over Labor Day weekend," he said quietly before lifting his head from the blanket to kiss her, and at first she had been so stunned that her lips remained motionless against his. Then she had been overwhelmed with rage.

She rolled away from him, off the blanket and onto the cushion of pine needles, and she had scrambled to her knees.

"You coward," she said, venom dripping from her every syllable.

He sat up. "Leigh," he began, but she was determined that he would not talk her out of her anger.

"Men are dying in Vietnam, Russ. They're fighting for what they believe."

He looked as though she'd punched him in the stomach. "I'm doing what *I* believe is right," he said, his eyes beseeching her.

"You believe it's right to run away? To let someone else fight your battles for you?"

"Vietnam is not my battle," he said unhappily and with an aloofness that only angered her more.

"It isn't my brother's battle, either, but he's doing his duty. *He* didn't head north; he saw a job that needed to be done and he's doing it, and he's fighting for people like you who look down on him and his fellow soldiers."

"The way I see it is that there's a job that needs to be done, but it's certainly not the job of killing people. My duty to my country is to make people see what an immoral war we're conducting, so that eventually we can put an end to it." Russ seemed imperturbable, which only intensified Leigh's fury.

"There'll be an end to it, all right, no thanks to people like you. The war will be over because of Warren and others like him, not because of guys who tucked their tails between their legs and ran out of the country."

"Leigh, sweetheart, listen to me. You're entitled to feel any way you like, but this isn't as easy for me as you seem to think. I'm leaving everything I know and love to carry on this work, and I'd like your support."

She stared at him. How could he be so calm and levelheaded? How could he think that anything he could do in such a faraway place as Canada would help at all? He was stupid, stupid!

"Russ, you're making a terrible mistake! Classes at Duke start the day after Labor Day. Please come back to school. We were so happy before you left," she pleaded. It was all she could do to keep from throwing her arms around his neck and begging him.

He eased himself up onto his knees so that he was facing her. His face was solemn, and he slowly raised one finger to caress her cheek. "I can't," he whispered. "Don't you see?"

All her pain and anger beat against the inside of her head until she couldn't think or reason; she only knew that Russ was determined to proceed on this foolhardy course and that nothing she did or said made any difference. She threw herself at him, sobbing and screaming in frustration.

"I hate you! I hate you! How can you do this to me, to us? Oh, God, go! Get out of my life! I never want to see you again as long as I live!"

He had grabbed her wrists to hold them immobile against his chest, and she had the satisfaction of watching his face turn chalk-white beneath his summer tan. In his shock he relaxed his grip so that she was able to pull away, and she held his gaze triumphantly for one long moment, grimly satisfied that she had finally hurt him. For far too long she had been the only one suffering.

She left the picnic basket and the blanket behind, running like a fury to her car and starting it with keys left earlier in the ignition. She jammed the gearshift into reverse, hardly looking where she was backing and barely missing a tree. Russ stood at the edge of the woods staring, but she was gone like a bat out of hell before he could run after her.

She thought she heard a muffled shout as she rounded the curve onto the main road, but she couldn't be certain. The only thing that she was sure about was that there had been tears gleaming in his eyes after she told him to get out of her life, and she told herself that she should be happy that the awful things she'd said had found their mark.

But she hadn't been happy; she'd only been sad. And although she'd hardly strayed from the telephone all week, Russ hadn't called, not even to say goodbye before he left the country.

The only good that had come out of that day was that it was, by Leigh's obstetrician's calculation, the day that Wendy had been conceived.

Of course, Leigh knew now that Russ had written her that long-lost letter. But little good that did either of them now; they had lost so many years. Wendy had never known her real father. And tonight, instead of rejoicing along with everyone else, all Leigh wanted to do was go back to her room and cry.

"Join us in the lounge for a drink?" Andrew's father suggested after the rehearsal dinner.

Leigh managed a smile. "I'm really very tired," she said. "I think I'll go upstairs."

"We'll see you tomorrow," Nancy told her. Wendy and Andrew said that they were going out to the great hall to sit in front of the fire and listen to a folk group singing Christmas carols with the rest of the party except for Bett and Claire-Anne.

"Honestly, I've lugged Claire-Anne around so much today my arms are aching," Bett complained as the three of them crowded into the elevator.

And my heart is aching, Leigh thought involuntarily.

Bett and Claire-Anne left the elevator on the second floor, leaving Leigh to ride to the third floor alone. Gala New Year's Eve Celebration—Make Your Reservations

Now, urged a bright red-and-green poster on the wall of the elevator. Leigh turned her face the other way. New Year's Eve? She would be doing well to get through Christmas.

She left the elevator and hurried to her room, closing the door behind her with a relieved sigh. She really did want to go to bed, though she felt so keyed up that she had scant hope of sleeping. She ran hot water into the tub for a bath and doffed her clothes, leaving them lying where they fell. Once in the tub she lay back, succumbing to the soothing steam rising against her face and smoothing out the tired lines between her nose and mouth with her fingers. She had smiled so many false smiles tonight that her face hurt.

Russ didn't know and hadn't guessed that Wendy was his child. She was thankful for that. If he hadn't guessed by now, she didn't think he would. Time was growing short, and Wendy would soon be married and gone, leaving her and Russ to—well, what? Say their goodbyes and return to their respective cities?

Leigh didn't know how Russ was feeling, but she couldn't easily forget the moments of tenderness they had shared earlier. Later she'd call Katrina and tell her all about it. She needed to talk to someone, she needed a shoulder to cry on and—

The unexpected trill of the phone startled her. The caller wouldn't be Wendy, and it probably wasn't Jeanne or Bett. Russ. It had to be Russ.

She stood up, flipped a towel around her, jumped out of the tub and raced for the phone.

"H-hello?' she said.

"I hope I didn't wake you," Russ said.

"No, I just got back from the rehearsal dinner."

"How did it go?"

"It was lovely." She would have liked to tell him the truth, that she had been overcome by her memories, but this didn't seem like the time.

"Will you meet me somewhere? In the library? The lounge?"

She thought for a moment. She wanted to be with him. "Not the lounge. Andrew's parents are there having a nightcap. And not the library—anyone could walk by the door and see us there."

"Must we be a secret? Can't you tell your family that we ran into each other and are old friends?" He sounded hopeful.

"I'm too exhausted to do any explaining tonight," Leigh said in a strained voice.

"I hope I'm not disturbing you, Leigh, but I've been pacing the floor ever since we came back from our walk. I couldn't eat dinner and I know I won't be able to sleep. I'm so—oh, I suppose you'd call me distraught. What you told me today has my mind jumping around on several different tracks. I—I just want to talk about it."

"Me, too, but right now I'm dripping water on the floor. I got out of the tub to answer the phone," Leigh said. "I'll call you back as soon as I get my robe on."

Russ squeezed his eyes closed, and a picture of Leigh wearing nothing but a towel appeared on the inside of his eyelids.

"I was hoping you'd come to my room for a while. Will you, Leigh? For, say, an hour?"

"I'll have to get dressed," she said doubtfully. She hadn't bothered to pin her hair up before getting in the tub, and the back of it was wet and clung damply to her neck.

"Throw something on—anything," he urged. "It doesn't matter how you look."

"Okay," she said. "I'll come for an hour. Maybe less."

"Good, I'll be waiting. My room's on the third floor in the old wing. Walk right in—I'll leave my door unlocked."

After they hung up, Leigh slowly unwrapped the towel and studied her reflection in the cheval mirror in one corner of the room. Now there was no makeup hiding her tiny facial flaws; no eye shadow brought out the complex blues and greens of her eyes. No clothes covered her figure faults, and she conceded that there were a few. Her hips had spread a bit too wide, and her abdomen bore faded stretch marks left over from her pregnancy with Wendy. Her breasts, which had once been firm and had needed little support, now sagged slightly. Russ remembered the way she had looked when she was twenty. If their relationship became sexual, and she knew that this was an option if they continued to see each other, how could she bear the look of disappointment in his eyes if he saw her the way she was now?

With one last despairing look into the mirror, she threw open her closet door and pulled out a sweater and a pair of jeans, which she pulled on as quickly as she could. She fluffed her hair with a warm stream of air from the blow dryer and tucked the still-damp strands behind her ears. Then she remembered that she'd better do something about makeup, so she dabbed on a bit of foundation, some blusher and lipstick.

She navigated the familiar hallways of The Briarcliff as quickly as she could, and when she arrived in front of Russ's room, she paused with her hand on the doorknob. Did she really want to do this? Was it *wise* to do this? No matter; she needed to be with him. To talk it over. To set her mind at ease.

When she pushed open the door to his room, he was lying on the bed leafing through a magazine. As the door opened, he tossed the magazine aside and leaped to his feet, hurrying to greet her.

She closed the door gently behind her. He stopped in front of her and hesitated, then held her firmly by the shoulders as he leaned down and kissed her cheek. She swayed for a moment, staring up at his handsome features. She thought quickly and irrelevantly that he no longer used Old Spice, and she thought he would smile if she told him she'd noticed. But he was gazing at her so soberly, his dark eyes illuminated by such a serious expression, that she said nothing. Without a word, he led her to a small love seat in one of the window alcoves and pulled her down beside him.

"I didn't want to be alone after you told me about the letter. I thought I would go out of my mind blaming the postal service, the government, anybody. Then I began to understand that I was to blame. Not anybody else. *Me.* I didn't try to contact you before I left. I was so shaken when you didn't show up that all I wanted to do was get out of town and get on with my life," he said.

"Don't blame yourself," she said gently. "I was wrong, too. I told you to get out of my life, and then I foolishly waited to hear from you because I was young and silly and thought you owed it to me to apologize for all the pain you had caused me by what I considered your stupid antiwar stance. Please forgive me for the things I said, the things I did—"

"There's nothing to forgive, Leigh. I could have handled it better. Maybe if I hadn't been in such a hurry to leave for Canada, we could have figured out a plan to be together. And as for writing you a letter to propose, that has to go down as the all-time dumbest idea ever. I should have come to your house and asked you properly."

"You weren't exactly welcome," Leigh reminded him.

"So what? I should have broken down the barriers, carried you off on my white charger—"

"White Chevrolet Corvair," she reminded him. "With red upholstery, and scented with lemon drops and Old Spice after-shave."

He smiled for the first time since she'd arrived. They were both quiet for a moment, and then he slid an arm around her and pulled her close. She rested her head against his shoulder and felt his breath against her hair. It seemed so fitting and right to be together like this, and she closed her eyes, savoring the moment.

He rested his cheek against her hair. Pensively he thought of the pain and emptiness of his life. During his marriage, he had needed something he didn't get from Dominique, and the strange thing was that he hadn't even known it was missing until they split up for good. Then he had realized how barren their relationship had been right from the first, not only as far as having children was concerned, but in all the intimate ways, too. For a long time he had doggedly tried to repair the relationship over and over, and it had never worked. Now, here was Leigh. And remembering what the two of them had together in those days so long ago made him hope that somehow they could recapture it.

She stirred, and her hair, still damp from her bath, brushed against his cheek. He raised his hand to stroke her head, and she lifted her face to his. He gazed soul-deep into her eyes, those beautiful eyes he remembered so well. Her eyelids fluttered downward like butterfly wings, and he saw her pulse beating at her temples. He was overwhelmed with tenderness for her.

He lowered his face to hers, their cheeks grazing momentarily, and he felt her catch her breath. She shifted so that she was able to slide her arms around him, and he held her close, feeling the rise and fall of her ribs as she breathed, getting used to the rhythms of her again. Without a warning, he felt a lump rise in his throat. She meant so much to him, even now. She was an important part of his past, a memory that he had held dear for so long, and now that she was part of his present he was electrified by the possibilities.

His lips found the hollow of her cheek and rested there before seeking her mouth. He resisted the impulse to touch her breasts, to trace the curve of her hips with his fingertips. Instead he concentrated on the sweet sensation of her kisses, losing himself in the nearness of her even as currents of impatience threatened to displace all his rational thoughts.

When his mouth found hers, she was amazed at how hungrily she returned his kisses. Despite her growing physical excitement, she felt comfortable and easy with him, much like the way she had felt with David.

David. Even though Russ's kisses were nothing like her husband's, the thought of David and all he had meant to her sent a chill rippling through her. She pulled away, interrupting the silken flow of kisses and closing her eyes against the expression on Russ's face.

Russ kissed her eyelids one by one. "What's wrong?" he asked.

She opened her eyes and sat up straight. "I'm not feeling comfortable with this," she said. "It doesn't have anything to do with you."

Russ smoothed her hair back behind her ears, his eyes twinkling with amusement. "I'm glad to hear that," he said. "For a moment, I thought I was somehow lacking."

She caught his mood and couldn't help smiling back. "No, um, I'd say you were pretty much up to your old standards," she said. "As I remember them, that is."

"Maybe sometime you'll let me refresh your memory," he said.

She didn't know what to say. It wasn't as though her memory needed refreshing. She remembered everything all too well.

"Look," he said, "I know you have a busy day scheduled tomorrow. Are you planning to go back to Spartanburg after the wedding?"

"I'd planned to drive back tomorrow night."

"Stay, Leigh. Let everyone else go home, and after they've gone the two of us can spend the following week alone together. The Briarcliff is famous for its New Year's Eve party. I'll make reservations for two. You'd like that, wouldn't you?" His eyes searched her face eagerly.

She answered slowly. "Oh, I'd like it, all right. But—"

He laid a finger across her lips. "No arguments. Let's just do it and figure everything else out afterward."

Leigh's thoughts raced. She wasn't looking forward to returning to her big, empty house alone. If her memories of David made her uncomfortable here, they'd be even worse there.

Of course, staying on at The Briarcliff might raise some questions, but then again, who would have to know about it? Only Wendy, because Leigh would want her daughter to know where she could be reached in case of emergency. Everyone else would leave for their respective homes as soon as Wendy and Andrew departed on their honeymoon.

Russ seemed to be holding his breath as he waited for her answer. His uncertainty was written all over his face; clearly, he thought she might refuse. She lifted her hand and touched his cheek, then swiftly bent forward to kiss him.

"I'll stay until New Year's Day, Russ. I want to."

He stood when she did and took her into his arms. "It'll be terrific," he whispered close to her ear. "You'll see."

She still felt shaky about giving her assent, but maybe if they took things slowly she would feel reassured, not only about David but about all the rest of it.

He walked her to the door. When she turned to face him, every detail about him seemed clearer than ever. The dark eyes shadowed by tangled eyelashes, the clean, spare line of his jaw, the long curve of his neck. Everything about him seemed precious to her in that moment. She swallowed, her mouth suddenly dry. There was one other thing she wanted to say now that she was sure that he didn't suspect anything about Wendy. She knew of no other way to go about it but to ask him straight out. She drew a deep breath and plunged ahead.

"I'd like—I'd like you to come to Wendy's wedding, Russ. She's being married at two o'clock tomorrow afternoon in the inn chapel." As soon as she spoke the words, she stopped breathing.

She had taken him by surprise, she knew, when his brow wrinkled in mild concern.

"You're sure my presence wouldn't cause any problems for you?" he asked.

She managed to meet his eyes but kept her expression casual. "I'll explain somehow if it becomes necessary. But I really want you to attend. It would make me very happy." She tried to read his expression, but if he sensed anything amiss, he gave no sign.

"If it means so much to you, Leigh, I'll be there," he said, bending to kiss her cheek before she left.

She returned the kiss, mostly to hide the rush of relief that she knew would show on her face. And then she fled to her room, hoping she hadn't done something unbelievably stupid.

Chapter Six

The next day, Leigh's daughter's wedding day, Russ arrived at the chapel where the wedding was to be held as the last of the guests were being seated. Even so, he managed to get an aisle seat on the groom's side. He estimated that there were only about fifty guests, none of whom he knew. He recognized Bett, Leigh's sister, but she didn't show even a flicker of acknowledgment when she passed him. That wasn't surprising. To his recollection, they had never met when he was dating Leigh.

The small chapel glowed with candlelight; candles were everywhere—at the altar, flanking the entrances to the pews, even in the window alcoves. Decorations consisted of red and white poinsettias in keeping with the season, and the pungent green scent of spruce and balsam hung in the air.

He sat back and listened to the string quartet, which was a nice touch, he thought. He wondered if that had been Leigh's idea or Wendy's. He didn't think it was something Leigh would have thought of, yet he didn't know Wendy and so had no clue as to her tastes.

It was hard to think of Leigh as a mother. Not that he had any doubt that she was a good one, but it was a whole segment of her life about which he knew very little. They used to talk about the family they planned to have—two boys and two girls. A big family, they both had decided. But the way things turned out, he had no children and Leigh only had one. He wondered why Wendy was an only child. Perhaps Leigh and Dave had decided to limit their family. There was nothing so unusual about that, and yet Leigh had been so fervent in her wishes to have "a whole houseful of kids," as she had put it.

Dave might not have shared Leigh's wish for a big family, and maybe he had been the one to say that one child was enough. The early years of their marriage could have been financially difficult, with Dave building up that insurance business of his, or—well, maybe either Dave or Leigh had been physically unable to have any more kids after Wendy for some reason.

Now Leigh, as mother of the bride, glided past on the arm of one of the groomsmen, her face slightly flushed, her long hair folded into an intricate smooth twist at the back. He caught his breath when he saw the gleam of the gold locket in the sleek hollow of her throat. He was surprised that she had chosen to wear it for the wedding of her daughter.

He didn't stop to ponder the meaning of the locket. Leigh, wearing emerald-green wool crepe with a wide satin cape collar, looked beautiful, more like a bride than the mother of one. He noticed a strand of hair fluttering at the nape of her neck and resisted the urge to go to her and tuck it into the twist.

Leigh reached the front pew where she sat down and composed herself, looking as though she couldn't be happier. Russ wondered, though. From some of the things Leigh had told him, he thought she might have mixed feelings about her daughter's marrying so young.

But is twenty-one really so young? he asked himself. When he and Leigh were twenty, they had known with the conviction of the very innocent that their love was enough to last a lifetime. Maybe they had been wrong. It hadn't sustained them even through the bitter battle over his leaving the country.

He still thought their love would have weathered any circumstance if it hadn't been for the lost letter. Leigh wouldn't have refused his marriage proposal, he was sure of that. Thus they would have been engaged when he went to Canada, and she could have followed him there at the earliest opportunity. If her parents, because of his anti-war stand, hadn't gone along with their plans, Leigh could have dropped out of school for a semester to earn money for her plane fare to Ontario. Or she could have joined him the following summer, and they could have been married in June and both worked for a while before finishing college. So many plans he had worked out in his mind, and it had all come to nothing in the end! If only Leigh had received the letter before he left.

If only, if only...

The door swung open behind him, and at this cue that the bride was about to enter, Leigh stood. The rest of the guests followed her lead, and he stumbled to his feet. First the little flower girl, who magnanimously scattered red rose petals by the handful, her brow furrowed in concentration. She was dressed in long-skirted red velvet with a wide velvet hair bow trailing past her waist. Then the maid-of-honor, Wendy's only attendant, wearing red satin. She carried a lighted candle wreathed with holly leaves instead of the traditional bouquet.

Finally, with all eyes upon her, Wendy began her walk down the aisle on the arm of a male relative—probably Bett's husband, Russ figured. As Wendy passed, he studied her, searching for resemblances to Leigh, and he was immediately struck by her sea-blue eyes, Leigh's eyes. He was stunned, because they were *exactly* like Leigh's, and he hadn't been prepared to see those eyes in another woman's face, even her daughter's.

Wendy was a beautiful girl. *Woman,* Russ reminded himself. She had long, dark hair, and that was nothing like Leigh's, although she wore it long and loosely curled the way Leigh usually did. Instead of a veil Wendy wore a white fur circlet clasped in the back by a spray of pearls; her gown was a sleek sweep of white satin with a deep V-back edged in beaded flowers. She swayed slowly down the aisle, holding her head like a princess, her hand resting lightly on her uncle's arm.

Russ would have liked to have a daughter like that; a lovely child who, when she was little, liked to sit in his lap and listen to him read stories about poky puppies and marching ducklings and little engines that could. A daughter to ferry back and forth to school dances as she giggled over boys with her girlfriends in the back seat of the car. A young woman who would seek his advice about her choice of career and whether she should marry the man of her dreams before they both finished college.

In answer to that question, Russ would have said yes, he thought, without any qualms about it. He would have advised Wendy to hold on to her love, hold on tight and never let it go. To fight for it unto the death, because although he was a pacifist, he knew from bitter experience that the only thing in the world worth fighting for was love and love alone.

IF SHE TURNED her head ever so slightly, Leigh could barely glimpse Russ out of the corner of her eyes. He was standing in the last pew of the tiny inn chapel, his face angled toward the door as they waited for the bride to appear on the arm of her uncle.

The string quartet was playing a classical piece that Wendy especially liked; she had decided to forgo the traditional here-comes-the-bride wedding march in favor of something softer. Andrew stood at the altar with his best man, smiling broadly.

And then, an auspicious pause in the music, and Wendy appeared on Carson's arm, wearing the gown that, by a laborious and often stressful process, she had selected for what she called "the most important day of my life."

She looks so beautiful, Leigh thought in a burst of well-justified maternal pride. The gown, with its delicate embroidery and fur cuffs to match the circlet on Wendy's head, her satin shoes with the high, high heels chosen because Andrew was so much taller, the dewy smile that might have been only for Andrew. As Wendy passed, she blew a kiss toward Leigh. And then there she was standing before the minister, Leigh's little girl, all grown up and about to be married.

Leigh was so absorbed in her own thoughts that she almost forgot to sit down. Bett leaned forward and touched her shoulder, and then she remembered. Following her lead, the guests resumed their seats in a rustle of movement.

"Dearly beloved," the minister began, and as Leigh listened to the words, she thought of the many other weddings she had attended, including her own. She could think of no other couple who evidenced so much love for each other as Wendy and Andrew. Andrew couldn't take his eyes off Wendy, and she was smiling up at him so sweetly that Leigh felt suddenly confident that this marriage was absolutely right for both of them. And to think that she had tried to talk them out of marrying right away;

well, it was what most parents would have done under the circumstances.

Leigh shifted slightly in the pew so that if she cast a sidelong glance, Russ would be in her line of vision. When she allowed herself a peek, she saw that he was staring squarely at her. Her eyes shot front again, and she felt the color rising on her neck. She prayed that Bett, who was sitting behind her, wouldn't notice.

Leigh wanted to telegraph to Russ, *Don't keep looking at me! Look at Wendy.* But there wasn't any way for her to get the message across to him; she could only hope that he would realize that he was embarrassing her by his avid and obvious stare.

"I wish Wendy's father could be here," Bett leaned forward to whisper suddenly as Wendy and Andrew embraced and kissed at the conclusion of the ceremony, and Leigh's heart skipped a beat.

She wanted to cry out, *He is here,* but she only whispered, "Yes." As if to reassure herself, her hand rose quickly to touch the locket at her neck.

FROM WHERE RUSS SAT on the aisle, he had a good view of the ceremony. Wendy Cathcart was a looker, all right, but his critical eye told him that she would be even more beautiful in five or ten years. She looked so young. So unformed. Like a blank slate. And the groom—he seemed, well, nice enough, but *callow.* Had he, Russ, ever been like that? He had no sense of himself when he was younger.

Wendy and Andrew stood in front of the minister now. Russ couldn't help seeing Leigh, because she was within his field of vision when he looked at the young couple standing at the front of the chapel. He willed Leigh to turn her head and look at him. Briefly he thought he saw her eyes slide sideways before facing front again. He supposed it was the most he could hope for at present.

"Do you, Wendy," began the clergyman, and Russ forced his attention to the couple standing before the altar. When the minister had finished, Wendy spoke a clear "I do." The minister addressed Andrew, who gazed lovingly at his bride and said his "I do" so forcefully that the married couple in front of Russ exchanged amused but understanding smiles.

Russ had to admire Andrew. If he, Russ, had been speaking those same vows to Leigh at the height of their love for each other, he might have shouted them.

For a moment he allowed himself to imagine that Wendy was Leigh and that he was Andrew, that they had somehow found themselves in front of the altar in this little chapel and were being married. In his imagination, twenty-two years had disappeared without a trace, they had never been separated by Russ's antiwar activities, and they were marrying with the blessing of both sets of parents. If he were standing before the altar at this very minute, he would hardly be able to take his eyes off Leigh's face as she spoke the words that would make her his.

He yanked himself back to reality. Why was he thinking this way? The truth was that Leigh had married David Cathcart only a couple of months after he, Russ, left for Canada. It had been David into whose eyes she had adoringly gazed when she repeated those all-important vows, David who had left on his honeymoon with Leigh in a flurry of rice, David who had signed the hotel register on their honeymoon as husband and wife, and it was Leigh *Cathcart,* not Leigh Richardson, who was sitting so primly in the first pew.

He sat back and tried to study Leigh dispassionately. Why was he so hung up on her? Why had he never been able to get over her? If she had loved him, *really* loved him, she would have waited for him. Never mind that his letter proposing marriage hadn't been delivered. The truth was that she had married another man almost immediately after he, Russ, left the country.

And despite his hardheaded pursuit of her, he was beginning to realize that he was going to have a hard time forgiving her for doing it.

THE CEREMONY seemed so short, Leigh thought as Wendy retrieved her bridal bouquet from Jeanne and the string quartet struck up the recessional. Wendy and Andrew started their triumphant walk up the aisle, but here Wendy defied tradition and flew directly to Leigh, enveloping her in a big hug.

"Thanks, Mom," she whispered, her eyes bright with joyous tears, and after Andrew hugged Leigh, the happy couple were on their way out of the chapel.

With the eyes of the other guests on Wendy and Andrew, Leigh allowed herself to look Russ full in the face, hoping in that moment to share with him a silent communion. She was expecting a look of recognition, a meaningful glance or maybe even a smile, but when she saw the expression on his face, it was enough to make her heart clench in her chest. His eyebrows were drawn to the middle of his forehead and he was staring at her as if she were a fly under a magnifying glass. She hadn't expected this from him—not here and not now, anyway.

She felt as if someone had stuck a pin into her and let all the air out. As she waited for Andrew's cousin, who was supposed to retrieve her after the ceremony, she steadied herself against the back of the pew. Russ's look had rocked her to her foundations; there was something dark and foreboding about it, and it was a side of him that she didn't recognize.

She could have looked away immediately, but she was so stricken that she found it impossible to pull her gaze away. She was barely conscious of the reflexive upward tilt of her chin as a proud defiance surfaced from her subconscious.

I raised my daughter entirely without your help, she found herself thinking. *And I—no, David and I—did a wonderful job. You missed the chicken pox and the broken front tooth when she fell off her bike, and that awful boy she said she was in love with when she was in the tenth grade. You can't even imagine the sacrifice involved in being a parent; how dare you look at me like that!*

At that moment Andrew's cousin arrived and offered his arm, and Leigh swept out of the pew and past the guests. When she passed Russ, Leigh's smile froze on her face, and she refused to look at him. She wished she hadn't invited him. He didn't belong here—didn't deserve to be part of Wendy's life.

As for staying on at The Briarcliff, it was not too late to change her mind.

THE RECEPTION TURNED out to be a sit-down dinner in the Timberlake Room for about fifty people, and Russ found himself sitting beside a garrulous grand-uncle of the groom on his right and a little girl on his left who kept hiccuping. The conversation on both sides left a lot to be desired, and he tried in vain to catch Leigh's eye. She was definitely avoiding looking in his direction, so he resigned himself to listening to his dinner partner's tiresome monologue about municipal bonds.

The little girl finally stopped hiccuping, and Russ turned his attentions to inquiring politely about her

Brownie troop activities. Across the table, two college friends of Wendy and Andrew's were flirting outrageously. He doubted that he and Leigh had ever gone about getting to know each other in such a silly fashion.

He felt so out of place that he was enormously relieved when the tiered wedding cake, adorned with swags of spun-sugar filigree, was wheeled in.

Wendy and Andrew cut the cake, drank a toast, and the cake was served.

"'S bad for the digestion," said Russ's male dinner partner, who proceeded to consume three slices, anyway.

"Excuse me," Russ said, getting up as his companion was quaffing his third glass of champagne. Russ had every intention of bolting for the men's room and thence to the peace and quiet of his own room. He had been unsuccessful in catching Leigh's eye and now she had disappeared altogether. Furthermore, no one seemed interested in cultivating his acquaintance, and he wished he had turned down Leigh's invitation. He was even beginning to question whether this wild-eyed flight to The Briarcliff in search of Leigh had been a good idea in the first place.

The rest rooms were in a short corridor just outside the door to the Timberlake Room, and as he was going in the men's, he met Leigh coming out of the ladies'. He automatically stepped to the right to let her pass, and she dodged in the same direction. He moved to the left; so did she.

"Shall we dance?" he said, and he was unexpectedly rewarded by the reluctant upturn of the corners of her mouth.

Clearly neither of them had expected to encounter the other in this narrow passageway, but Russ knew immediately that something was wrong from her point of view.

Her ruffled feathers surprised him. He'd thought he owned the rights to all the misgivings.

"I shouldn't have come to this wedding," he blurted.

"I invited you," she said uncomfortably. He wished she would smile again.

Too long a pause, and then, "It was a beautiful wedding," Russ said.

"I think so, too," Leigh answered. Two women unconnected with their party pushed past them into the ladies' room, one of them stepping on Russ's toe. He winced.

"We shouldn't stand here," Leigh said.

Russ remembered a pantry that opened off this corridor; when he used to work here during summer vacations from high school, he and his buddies had used it when they wanted a break from the headwaiter's strident demands. Since then the door had been wallpapered so that it was barely discernible, but he nudged it with his foot and much to his surprise it swung open. "In here," he said, pulling Leigh in after him.

The space was a broom closet now; they found themselves standing amid a bristly forest of mops, brooms and assorted brushes hanging from hooks.

Leigh struggled to prevent it, but she couldn't help laughing.

"You always did take me to the nicest places," she said. "How did you know about this closet, anyway?"

"During the summer when I met you and was lusting after you as you ate in the dining room with your family, I used to dream of being alone with you. Some of the other guys used to bring girls in here."

"In *here?*"

"It was a pantry then, and slightly cleaner. As I understand it, there were these large sacks of flour and cornmeal that could be pressed into use as an instant couch."

"Pressed?"

"Messed?"

"Undressed in a little love nest?"

"And after that they'd need a rest," he said, and whatever had been wrong between them evaporated and drifted away on the low notes of her laughter.

He grasped both her hands in his. "How long until this wedding is over?" he asked her.

They smiled at each other, old friends, their pleasure in each other's company illuminated by the harsh electric light bulb overhead.

"Not long," she replied. She wished that she could stay angry with him, but how could she when he made silly jokes and smiled that comical crooked grin that had always been her undoing?

"Your daughter is quite lovely," he said in all seriousness. "In fact, she looks a lot like you."

"Do you think so?" she said, but she was thinking, *Take another look. Haven't you guessed? Can't you see?*

Any resemblance must have gone right over Russ's head, because he said, "I've only known two people with eyes that exact shade of sea blue. And that's you and Wendy," he said.

"We've got all the genes for that shade locked up," Leigh said lightly.

"Can we get together after everyone leaves?"

"I don't know. I'll think about it."

"Why couldn't you tell everyone you need a rest?" he said. "You could go to your room, and I'll call you."

"I said I'll think about it," she said firmly. She pulled her hands away from him as two female voices receded in the hallway. Leigh looked distracted. "I wish I knew of some way to get out of this closet without anyone seeing us," she said.

He opened the door a crack. "The coast is clear. You go first, I'll wait a respectable minute or two and follow you."

"Okay," she agreed.

He held the door for her, and she slipped past him. Someone outside spoke to her, and he smiled at the effusiveness of Leigh's greeting. Whoever it was would never guess that she had spent the last few minutes in a broom closet.

After a decent interval had passed, he stepped outside and closed the closet door firmly behind him. It seemed to him that he had no choice but to return to the wedding reception and try to press his case with Leigh.

When he reentered the Timberlake Room, Wendy was circling the room, bidding goodbye to her guests. Russ edged toward Leigh, determined not to let her get too far away from him.

"You wouldn't have to follow me around the room," she pointed out in an undertone.

"I'm not," he said. "I'm only waiting for you to tell me when and where we can meet."

At that inopportune moment, Leigh's sister, Bett, hurried past with one of the boys in tow.

"I'm taking Billy upstairs," she said to Leigh. "Can you believe he spilled a glass of water all over his new suit? It was a full glass, too. Oh, I'm sorry, I didn't mean to interrupt." Bett's eyes flashed from Leigh's face to Russ's in clear mystification.

Leigh drew a deep breath. "Bett, this is Russ Thornton. We're old friends, and when I ran into him here at the inn I invited him to the wedding."

Bett stared at her for a moment, taking in the red spots high on Leigh's cheeks, but Leigh had to give her sister credit for recovering quickly. Bett offered her hand and said cordially, "How do you do, Russ. I'm glad you could come. Now if you'll excuse me, I really must get Billy into some dry clothes. I'll see you later, Leigh. And it was nice meeting you, Russ." With one last quizzical lift of her eyebrows in Leigh's direction, Bett hurried off in pursuit of her offspring.

"Your sister hardly batted an eyelash. I suppose she wouldn't really remember me, would she?" Russ asked.

"I doubt it. She was only eight that summer, and she was away at camp when—when—"

"When we were in love," Russ supplied.

"Exactly," Leigh said in a small voice.

They stopped talking when they noticed the photographer heading their way, and they unfurled pleasant smiles across their faces when he paused to take their picture. Afterward, knowing that Leigh could be called upon to pose with the bride at any moment, Russ said, "I'm making things awkward for you, and I'm not so comfortable myself. I really do think I should leave, but not before you tell me where we can meet."

"I haven't said I would," Leigh said distractedly. "I can't even think about it now because Wendy and Andrew will be going soon."

As if to underline her statement, Jeanne hurried past. "Wendy is going to throw her bouquet," she told Leigh. "She wants all eligible females to gather at the end of the hall. You included."

"Not *me,*" Leigh said with a vigorous shake of her head.

"Yes, you," Jeanne said, urging her forward. Leigh sent a helpless backward look at Russ, who was smiling a bemused smile.

"You're supposed to stand with your back to the crowd," someone called out from the knot of people surrounding Wendy as she prepared to throw her bouquet.

"Don't be silly," was all Wendy said, and then, with a mischievous wink and no preamble, she lofted her bridal bouquet into the air. Leigh, speechless, knew in that moment that Wendy had deliberately tossed her bouquet in her direction, and she instinctively put out a hand to catch it.

Everyone laughed and clapped at Leigh's obvious astonishment when she looked down in confusion at the bouquet of white roses in her hands.

"That's not fair!" Leigh exclaimed, as she looked at the disappointed faces of several young women, friends of Wendy's, who might have caught the bouquet.

Wendy smiled broadly and hurried to put her arm around Leigh. "I'm the bride, and this is my special day. If I want to throw my bouquet to my mother, I will! Anyway, who was that handsome man who was talking to you?"

"Why—why—"

"Mom, you're blushing! For goodness' sake, I must meet him," Wendy said, craning her neck to look over the heads of her wedding guests as she tried to spot Russ in the crowd.

"I don't think that's such a good idea," Leigh said tightly, but Wendy had already spied Russ, who was edging toward the door at the other end of the room. Wendy took Leigh's hand and tugged her, protesting all the way, in Russ's direction.

"Now," Wendy said peremptorily as they intercepted him at the door, "introduce us." She smiled up at Russ, completely unaware that her smile was almost his smile.

Seeing the two of them side-by-side unnerved Leigh so much that she could hardly speak. Suddenly she felt totally irresponsible; what an impetuous idea it had been to invite Russ; how foolish she was!

Russ, seeing how flustered she was, stepped in. "I'm Russ Thornton," he said smoothly. "I'm an old friend of your mother's. We ran into each other in the inn library, and she was kind enough to invite me to the wedding. You are a beautiful bride, Wendy, and your mother is justifiably proud of you. I wish you and Andrew every happiness."

Wendy smiled. "Thank you. And I'm glad you could come to the wedding. Are you here alone?"

"Yes," Russ said, but he leaned almost imperceptibly closer to Leigh, who thought that this conversation had gone on quite long enough.

"Oh," she said, touching Wendy's arm. "There's Andrew, and I believe he's looking for you."

"I'm sure he is. He's eager to get on the road. Goodbye, Mr. Thornton, I'm glad I got to meet you," Wendy said.

"Call me Russ. And I hope we'll meet again." He smiled.

"Excuse me, Russ," Leigh said. She was still holding the bridal bouquet; she felt ridiculous. Whoever heard of the bride's mother catching the bouquet? She felt irritated at the idea, but there seemed to be nothing she could do but hang onto it and follow in Wendy's wake as Wendy hurried to Andrew's side.

"Come upstairs with me," Wendy urged, turning to Leigh after a whispered consultation with her new husband. "Andrew wants to leave right away, and I'm going to need some help getting out of this dress."

Leigh felt absurdly grateful to Wendy for providing her with a chance to leave, but in the spirit of letting go of Wendy, she felt that she should protest. "Perhaps Jeanne should go with you," she said.

"Jeanne is deep in conversation with Andrew's cousin, and since he's hinted that he'd like to see her again, I have no intention of breaking up their little tête-à-tête. Come to think of it, I wish I hadn't interrupted your conversation with Russ Thornton."

"Wendy, you're stepping on your train," Leigh said.

Wendy paused to give the train an impatient twitch. "Andrew will be livid if I prolong this any longer than necessary," she said. "He wants to get to—well, our honeymoon hideout is a secret, but it's a long drive from here."

"Not too long, I hope," Leigh said, following Wendy's train out the side door through which they could reach the service elevator.

"Too long to suit Andrew," Wendy said with a laugh. "Sometimes I think the bridegroom feels left out of things. Oops," she said once they were in the elevator, "the door's going to close on my skirt!" But it didn't, and they were both quiet on the ride to the third floor.

In Wendy's room, Leigh set the bridal bouquet in a vase of water and unbuttoned the slippery satin-covered buttons at the back of Wendy's dress. When Wendy had slipped the gown over her head and stood in front of Leigh in her lacy underwear, Leigh thought, *That's how I used to look. Slim. No stretch marks. No cellulite. And that's how Russ remembers me.*

Wendy hurried around the room, unself-conscious as she kicked off her white satin pumps, shimmied into her going-away suit and pulled on matching hose.

Leigh heaved a shaky sigh, mourning her own lost youth.

Wendy mistook her expression. She slipped her foot into one leather shoe and stood uncertainly on her left foot, frowning slightly. "Aw, Mumsie, don't take it so hard," she said. "I'll call you tonight to make sure that you've reached home safely. Andrew and I will be back in Asheville with his parents by January 3. And you haven't lost me, you've gained a son. I know it's trite, but it's also true." Wendy hobbled across the room and hugged her.

Leigh returned Wendy's hug. There was no point in telling Wendy how far off the mark she was. How could she tell her daughter that the thing that was really worrying her was the possibility of going to bed with a man?

Much to Leigh's embarrassment, it was almost as though Wendy could read her thoughts. "That man I met—Russ," Wendy said, retrieving her other shoe and perching on the edge of the bed to put it on. "How long have you known him?"

"Oh, quite a while," Leigh said as she turned away to arrange a helter-skelter pile of what must be Jeanne's cosmetics on the dresser top.

"How long? He looks kind of familiar."

Leigh's head shot up. She used the mirror to eye Wendy's reflection; behind her, Wendy seemed calm and matter-of-fact. No, Wendy didn't suspect anything, didn't realize that the reason Russ looked familiar was that every time Wendy looked in the mirror, she was confronted with the selfsame features.

"Dad and I knew him at Duke," Leigh said carefully.

"How nice that you happened to run into him here. He said he was alone—does that mean he's not married?"

"He's not married."

Wendy shut her purse with a snap. "He seems to like you. I think you should try to see him again," she said. She looked around the room. "Where have I put the car keys? You'll need them for the drive back home."

Leigh found them on the dresser. "Here they are. And actually, Wendy, I'm not going home yet." She slid the keys into the pocket of her suit.

Wendy's eyebrows flew up. "Not going home? You mean you're staying here at The Briarcliff? Whatever for?"

Leigh drew a deep breath and tried to look nonchalant. "Well, Russ asked me to stay on. I said I would. Until New Year's Day."

Wendy stared at her, speechless. "Why—"

"Don't look so surprised. You *said* I ought to see him again," Leigh said, unexpectedly amused at Wendy's amazement.

"I didn't expect it to happen so suddenly," Wendy said, but she was grinning.

"At any rate, when Russ suggested that I stay, I thought it might be a good idea. I wasn't relishing the idea of going home to that big empty house," Leigh said, tracing the marquetry pattern on the dresser top with one manicured fingernail.

"Of course you weren't. And I'm delighted. Honestly, Mother, I would feel so much better if you weren't all by yourself. You *need* someone."

"Hey, who's the mother here? I'm the one who is supposed to be worrying about you. You're the one who just got married."

"Which is why I recommend it. If you could just find someone nice, someone as much like Andrew as possible—"

"Speaking of Andrew, he's probably pacing up and down the corridor wondering what happened to you. Don't you think we'd better go downstairs?"

"I certainly do. I think I've got everything. My bags were stowed in the trunk of Andrew's car this morning, and I don't need anything but my purse, and—"

Jeanne burst into the room. "Andrew is having fits wondering where you are, Wendy. My, don't you look fantastic! Come on, I've been deputized to make sure that you arrive in the Timberlake Room posthaste," and Jeanne made an exaggerated bow toward the door.

"I *was* going to hang up my dress. . . ." Wendy said.

"That's what maids-of-honor are for, and I'll do it later. Shall we?"

Wendy hurried out of the room, turning to Leigh for one last hug before she appeared before their guests for the run to the car.

"Bye, Mom," she murmured to Leigh. "I'll call you. Promise."

"I love you, dear. And don't worry about me."

"I love you, too, and I promise not to worry about a thing," Wendy said. She looked radiant as Leigh followed her into the elevator.

Guests lined up on the sidewalk under the portico outside the reception room and Wendy and Andrew, hand in hand, ran the gauntlet as people called "Goodbye!" and pelted them with birdseed from the satin roses that Leigh had so painstakingly made.

"Birdseed," sniffed Vera, Andrew's grandmother. "In my day we threw rice."

"It's because of the birds," Darren said importantly. "Wendy explained all about it. If you throw rice, the birds eat it and it makes the birds swell up and pop open. Then they spill their guts all over the—"

"Darren!" said Bett in horror, as she clapped a hand over her son's mouth.

"The birds in winter appreciate the birdseed so much," Leigh said, tactfully drawing Vera away from Bett's family. Bett was rolling her eyes, and Billy said plaintively, "I didn't think birds *had* guts," before Carson popped a candy cane in his mouth.

Wendy, happily oblivious to this discussion, blew a kiss to her guests out the window of Andrew's small car, and then the newlyweds were off, rolling down the driveway in front of a plume of exhaust.

"Brrr! It's cold out here," Claire-Anne said, despite the furry white cape and muff she wore over her velvet dress.

"Let's hurry back inside, then, before we all catch cold," Bett said, as she shepherded her brood. "Leigh, the wedding was perfect."

Leigh, who had been borne along on a crest of emotion all day, felt a sudden letdown. The wedding that she had planned carefully for so many months was over; Wendy was married.

"I was happy with the way it turned out," she admitted, her eyes searching for the familiar shape of Russ's head over the heads of the other guests. She didn't see him; she wondered where he was.

"Carson and I are all packed to leave, and we're going to head home right away," she said. Bett lived in Shelby, a little over an hour's drive from The Briarcliff.

"Thanks for everything. It was a wonderful Christmas," Leigh said, stooping to kiss Claire-Anne goodbye.

"I'll call you one of these days after I've rested up," Bett promised.

After Bett, Carson and family had gone, Leigh lingered in the lobby of the inn to bid farewell to some of the other wedding guests. When the last one had driven away, she walked slowly through the great hall, wondering where to find Russ. To tell the truth, she was exhausted. Her feet hurt. She could use a nap or a hot bath or— "How about joining me for a drink?" asked Russ as he stepped out from behind a pillar, and when she saw the certain pleasure that leaped into his eyes at the sight of her, she thought involuntarily and with a shiver of happiness, *At last we're alone.* She thought no more of weariness, and then the room darkened and receded so that the two of them with their bright faces might have been the only people in it.

Chapter Seven

"Well, it's over. Wendy is married," Leigh said with relief and more than a little regret. Somehow it didn't seem possible; in many ways, Leigh still thought of Wendy as her little girl. It would be hard to think of her as a grown-up, mature and sensible married woman, although Leigh had no doubt that Wendy was indeed all of those things.

"Wendy was a beautiful bride, and Andrew seems like a fine young man, but they seem so young," Russ said, meeting her eyes over the little table in the lounge where he had steered her after their meeting in the lobby.

"That's what I thought when Wendy and Andrew first came to me and said they wanted to get married. I have to admit that I tried to change their minds; I told them how hard it would be to deal with the pressures of the first year of marriage while worrying about college grade-point averages and final exams—but no matter what the Craigs or I said, they wouldn't listen."

"At that age, I suppose they aren't so much deaf as they're blinded by the stars in their eyes," Russ observed.

"Spoken as one who knows," she said.

"Yeah, I suppose so," he said ruefully, and they were quiet for a moment, each lost in thought.

Leigh used this lag in the conversation to study him; Russ looked so suave and urbane in his dark suit—like a man of the world from head to toe. She supposed he was. He seemed so *finished*. When she had known him before, he'd had many rough edges. Katrina used to refer to Russ as "Mr. Knees and Elbows" until Leigh persuaded her to stop. Now Leigh smiled at the memory.

"What's so funny?" he asked.

She shook her head. "I can't tell you."

"Why not?" he asked in a bemused tone.

"Secret," she said, and smiled again. She wished Katrina could see Russ now. She decided she could tell him that, so she did.

"I expected Katrina to be at the wedding," he said. "I looked for her among the guests."

Leigh quickly told him how Katrina would have come to the wedding if her mother hadn't fallen and broken her foot during the week before Christmas.

He leaned across the table. "I always liked Katrina a great deal. Not as much as I liked you, of course, but a lot. And as much as I'd like to see her again, I'm not as desperate to see her as I was to see you."

"You didn't tell me you were desperate," she said.

"I wanted to see you. Nothing less would do," he told her.

"And now that you have?" She wondered if her voice sounded as small to him as it sounded to her.

"I'm bowled over. Knocked out. You're as lovely as ever, Leigh. I was prepared for—well, something different."

"Different?" She felt a certain tightness in her chest, as though she were beginning to have trouble breathing.

"So many people our age are tired, bored, jaded. You're not. You're energetic and vibrant, and very refreshing."

"When I see my sister Bett I feel—oh, somehow passé. Bett's so involved in her children's lives, and I feel old when I'm around her. Now, with Wendy gone..." She shrugged, and a shadow fell over her features.

She's feeling Wendy's flight from the nest more than she's admitting, Russ thought to himself when he saw that momentary sadness flit across her face. He decided to steer the conversation down another path.

"I like your sister, Bett," he said. To his relief, Leigh smiled.

"Bett and I are very close," she told him. "There's such an age difference between us that we didn't really know each other until we both grew up."

"I envy you," Russ said. "I always wished I'd had a brother or a sister."

Leigh became reflective. "I missed my brother, Warren, today, Russ," she said. "He always enjoyed family gatherings so much."

"I suppose it's at times like this that you can't help thinking about him," Russ said.

"Warren and I were pals when we were kids, mostly because we were only a few years apart. After he died, it was hard for me to believe that he'd never walk through the front door of our house and toss his jacket over that rocking horse at the foot of the stairs, never sneak up behind my mother and distract her while he reached around and stuck his finger in the bowl of frosting for a forbidden taste, never chase Bett around the house threatening to skin her alive for disturbing things in his room."

"I wish I'd met him."

"He was a likable guy. There will always be a terrible emptiness inside me where Warren is supposed to be, but I came to terms with his death long ago, Russ." She paused, choosing her words very carefully. She had wanted to say them for so long, and now that she had the opportunity she didn't want to botch the job.

"In the course of accepting it," she said slowly, her eyes boring into his, "I realized that you were right and I was wrong. About Vietnam, I mean. Our troops had no business being there."

At first he froze, his features an unreadable mask, and then his eyes clouded over with sadness. "You know," he said, his eyes never leaving hers, "there's no satisfaction anymore in knowing I was right. I wish that none of us had ever had to concern ourselves with that war."

Russ paused to sign for their drinks. "This is supposed to be a happy day for you," he said ruefully as the waiter retreated. "I didn't mean to make you sad."

"Sad? I'm not sad. And Wendy's wedding has made me see that life goes on. No matter what." She was thinking about David now, something that Russ intuited immediately. His heart ached for Leigh; she seemed, in that moment, very forlorn.

"You've had a hard life, haven't you, Leigh? It hasn't been easy," Russ said. He touched her hand, which was resting on the edge of the table.

"Is anyone's?" she asked him, turning her hand over so that their palms touched. "Was yours?"

"Not very," he admitted.

"Things haven't turned out as either of us expected, yet neither of us has wasted time wallowing in self-pity," she pointed out, her tone upbeat now.

"We're survivors," he said.

"Survivors," she agreed, seeming to take heart. "We accept reality and go on."

"Today's reality may not be tomorrow's," he said.

"But today's reality is the only important one," she said softly, searching his eyes to see if he understood.

"Yes," he said, squeezing her hand. "And tonight's."

He held fast to her hand as they walked out of the lounge, and she was aware of heads turning as they passed. She caught a glimpse of them in the mirror on the wall; they *were* a handsome couple. They always had been.

In the great hall, the sounds of people having a good time swept over them in waves. A large awestruck group was clustered around a storyteller in front of one of the hearths. From the dining room sounded the clatter of cutlery, and behind them in the lounge they heard a shrill peal of feminine laughter.

So many sights, so many sounds. Leigh hesitated, thinking that she didn't want to be around so many people after being on display all day. She was reluctant to put on her public face again. Yet where could she go? She didn't feel as though she could invite Russ to her room; Jeanne might still be in Wendy's room straightening up before she left to spend the night with relatives.

Lights from the nearest Christmas tree played across Leigh's features, illuminating the uncertainty she was feeling. Russ felt helpless to banish that hint of shadow from Leigh's eyes. He could understand her sadness, but he didn't want to accept it. Perhaps he could change it—but he immediately admitted to himself that that was an arrogant assumption on his part, because what he was really thinking was that if only she'd go to bed with him, she'd be all right.

Don't think that making love will be as wonderful as it was before, he cautioned himself. It was as close as he had come to admitting to himself that he had a few reservations about resuming a sexual relationship with her. He wasn't twenty years old anymore, and he knew now that sex wasn't the all-important cure-all for relationships that he used to think it was in his younger years. This time around he was more interested in Leigh's head and heart than he was in other parts of her anatomy.

Yet there was no dodging the issue; they would have to confront it eventually if they continued to see each other. *If* they continued to see each other! Maybe they wouldn't. But how could they *not?*

If *he* decided that sleeping with each other wasn't in their best interests.

If *she* said she didn't feel like going to bed with him.

However: If they didn't feel like going to bed together, *he* would never know if that part of their relationship would have worked. And he had to know.

Therefore: He would make love to her tonight.

Damn. Maybe they didn't know each other well enough for him to initiate lovemaking yet.

This is Leigh, he reminded himself. Of course they knew each other. She was probably as curious as he was to know if the sexual part of their relationship could still work.

"Maybe—maybe you'd like to come up to my room?" he said, his voice low.

She nodded silently, her lower lip caught between her teeth. She wasn't at all sure that she was ready for what Russ probably had in mind, but she'd deal with that later. She knew him so well that all she'd have to do was tell him she wasn't ready and he'd back off quickly, perhaps too quickly. What she probably needed was a little persuasion.

A little persuasion? No, a lot of persuasion. Tonight she was still keyed up from the wedding; she was exhausted. This shouldn't be the first time they made love after so long. It would be better to wait.

They were the only ones in the elevator as they rode it to the third floor, and as they disembarked he slid his arm around her shoulders. Leigh held her breath as they passed her own door; she half expected Jeanne to pop out like a jack-in-the-box. But in a few moments they stood in front of the door to Russ's room and he was swinging it open and indicating that she should precede him inside.

The bed was neatly made; the love seat where they had sat when she paid her last visit looked inviting.

"I could order something from room service if you'd like," Russ suggested. "Maybe a light supper? Drinks?"

"I'm not hungry," she said, but she hastened to add, "If you want something, please go ahead." She went to the long recessed window and brushed the filmy casement curtains away from the glass with one hand; below, a mound of snow glistened in a spotlight and a group of children were sliding on it. A draft of cold air whistled through the sides of the window, and Leigh shivered.

Russ bent to light the fire in the fireplace. Then, as the flames caught, mingling the scent of burning logs with the fragrance of the evergreen boughs heaped on the mantel, he joined her, lifting the heavy velvet drapery so that they could both see out. As they watched the children, Leigh's shoulder brushed his chest, the emerald satin of her wide cape collar whispering against the fabric of his suit. He caught a whiff of her perfume; it was Arpège, the same as she used to wear. Once shortly after they started dating, he had spent his lunch money to buy her a small flacon of it, and he had gone hungry for a week. He had considered the sacrifice well worth it.

"Leigh," he said, and her name was a sigh on his lips. She turned to him, her eyes searching his face for one long moment. He felt a catch in his throat, almost as if he wanted to clear it, but this was entirely emotional. Her expression had taken on a softness, a pliability. He bent to kiss her parted lips.

Leigh lost herself in his kiss. With the touch of his lips, without warning, all doubt fled, and along with it, her fatigue. She didn't want to wait; she had waited long enough. It had been twenty-two long years since they had made love; twenty-two very long years. She slid her arms around him, and burgundy velvet draperies swung around them as he crushed her in his embrace.

They had touched many times since they'd found each other again, but not like this, not with this heat and urgency. They sought each other's mouths hungrily as though they could not get enough of each other, his fingertips exploring the lines of her face and the curve of her neck as if to reassure himself that it was really Leigh.

She felt as if none of this could be happening to her. Since David died, she'd gone out on a few dates, but she hadn't let the men kiss her the way this man was kissing her, with sheer male greediness, nor did she tremble within the circles of their arms or cling to them for support.

This isn't just any man, she reminded herself, *this is Russ.* And her knees turned to jelly at the thought.

She had only loved two men in her life, and Russ Thornton was one of them. Her heart filled with wonder at the odd circumstances that had brought them together again after such a long parting. That mail carrier, his long beard whipping in the wind as he walked away from her house; the Christmas card she had sent to Russ and his subsequent phone call. It seemed so unreal, like a story she had read about somebody else.

But this was no story, nor was it a dream. His lips and tongue and teeth were real, and his hands were real as they moved reverently, then more urgently over her body. She felt herself melting into him, felt clothes falling away, felt skin soft against skin, felt her hair tumbling from its twist. She had no time to worry about how she looked. She only knew how he looked: flat belly, firm thighs, broad shoulders. And he wanted her; that was apparent.

As if through a haze she saw him smiling at her, and then he was swinging her into his arms and she was protesting that someone might see through the curtains, and he laughed low in his throat and said how could they when the room was on the third floor facing the side of the mountain, and she said that was exactly the point, and he said that no one would be up on the mountain on this cold night and if they were, they could go ahead and look, and she didn't care if the whole world watched them by that time, but he turned out the lamp, anyway.

When she lay against the pillows on the bed and gazed up at him in a moment of pure, crystalline happiness, he paused to cup her cheek in the palm of one hand. The flickering firelight softened the square line of his chin and gilded the wide pupils of his eyes. His eyelashes cast feathery shadows on his cheeks.

I will remember this moment forever, Leigh thought as he studied her intently, and she lifted her arms to embrace him.

"I think I never stopped loving you," he said unsteadily.

At first she thought that such love could not be possible, but then, overcome by the tenderness she felt for him in that moment, she admitted that perhaps it was. Maybe the first love was the seed from which all other loves grew; maybe that seed could sprout again. After all, the things she had originally loved about Russ then were the things she loved about him now.

His hand lay on her breast over her heart and she covered his fingers, so familiar, with her own. And then, barely breathing, she closed her eyes so that he could tenderly kiss her eyelids one by one; she traced the tips of his curly eyelashes with one finger, and he trailed a chain of kisses to the hollow of her throat where the gold locket gleamed. She arched up to meet him as he settled himself over her, and she opened her mouth to his kisses as she opened her body to the rest of him. All of her open, letting in the warmth and the joy and the life, everything that she had been missing for such a long, long time. And it was Russ, her wonderful Russ, and it was so much the same that tears sprang to her eyes when she thought of being without him for all those years. She pulled him closer, wanting to feel all of him, the weight of him, everything. She twined her legs around his and wound her fingertips in his hair. As much as two people could be connected; that was the way she wanted to be enmeshed with him. Bodies and hearts and even souls flowing one into the other, so that she could once again say, "I am you and you are me," and it would be the truth.

The truth. The truth. The truth.

The words thudded against her brain in time with her heartbeat. Above her, Russ shuddered, and she realized too late that it was over.

His body, sheened with moisture, lay heavily upon her, crushing her against rumpled sheets. She lay wide-eyed beneath him, and she could hardly breathe.

As he rolled to one side he buried his face in her hair. His left hand rested on her thigh, and she sensed that he was reluctant to break contact with her. She felt that she needed more space but not because of anything that he had done: he'd been everything she'd expected and more. It was her own deceit that disgusted her and had curdled the act of love in its final moments.

She sat up. He reached out to her, but slick with his sweat, she eluded his grasp.

"Leigh?" he murmured, wanting her in his arms.

"I'd better get back to my room," she said clearly and distinctly, turning her head away so she wouldn't see the wounded look in his eyes.

"It's still early," he protested. A slightly panicky feeling settled over him; what was wrong?

"I've been on my feet most of the day," she answered, slipping off the bed. She walked unsteadily to the pile of clothes on the carpet and wordlessly began to sort them out. The fire had died and an icy chill had settled over the room.

Russ watched her in disbelief as she fumbled with soft tangles of lace and a pair of panty hose that seemed tied in knots.

Well. That's it, then, he thought, trying to keep his cool. *So much for retracing our footsteps. Now we can both get on with the rest of our lives.* He should have felt relieved, but he only felt numb at the way things had turned out.

Without saying a word, he got out of bed. She put on her skirt, fumbling with the clasp on the waistband, and she shrugged into the jacket and fastened it with clumsy fingers.

"If only—" he said heavily, but seeing the look on her face, he stopped. He shook his head. "How could it go so wrong when everything was so right?" he asked.

"I wish I could tell you," she said, and before he could figure out what she meant, she had slipped out the door.

LEIGH WOKE UP THE NEXT morning in her own room, her head hurting and her mouth dry. She felt as though she'd had too much to drink last night, only she hadn't. When her eyes opened, she recognized her surroundings immediately as The Briarcliff, and the memory of last night's debacle flooded into her consciousness. She sat up in bed, silently contemplating what she should do next.

Nothing, she thought, and then she proceeded to the bathroom where she filled a glass with water from the faucet. She swallowed two aspirin and headed back to bed with every intention of going back to sleep, but before she had pulled the covers up around her shoulders, the telephone rang.

"Leigh?" said Katrina in response to her groggy "hello."

"Yes," Leigh said, abandoning in that moment any hope of going back to sleep. "Where are you, Katrina? Are you in Florida?"

"No, Mother and I decided to stay in Spartanburg. I called your house a few minutes ago to see if you wanted to come over and meet my cousin, and I was worried when you weren't home yet. Is anything wrong? Why didn't you drive home after the wedding?"

"I—" Leigh said, but then she stopped. She had no idea how to tell Katrina what was going on in her life.

"You sound sick," Katrina said. "What is it—the flu?"

"Worse," Leigh said with conviction.

"*Nothing* is worse than the flu. Last year Mother made the foolhardy mistake of saying rather dramatically that she'd rather have a broken foot than the flu, and look what happened to her. Don't tell me you have a broken foot, Leigh. It couldn't happen to two people I know at the same time. Or could it?''

''Something's broken, but it's certainly not my foot,'' Leigh answered, propping herself up on two pillows.

''Well, what is it? Stop acting so mysterious,'' Katrina said.

''A broken life? A broken heart? I don't know,'' Leigh said miserably.

''I'm more in the dark than ever now,'' Katrina replied in sheer bafflement.

''Russ Thornton followed me to The Briarcliff, and I invited him to Wendy's wedding,'' Leigh said.

''You *what?*'' Katrina yelled, nearly shattering Leigh's eardrum.

''I ran into Russ Thornton and asked him to come to the wedding. He sat in the last pew and stared at me throughout the ceremony.''

Dead silence. Then a giggle of disbelief. ''Back up just a minute, please. How did he know you'd be there for Christmas?''

''I made the mistake of telling him,'' Leigh said.

''Well, that's what I call foolishness on your part and pure nerve on his. Or bravado. Or something.''

''Try insanity.''

''That's more like it,'' Katrina said. ''Whatever possessed you to invite him to the wedding?''

Leigh massaged her eyelids. ''I wanted him to see Wendy being married. He's her father, and I figured he had a right.''

''He has no idea that Wendy is his, does he?'' Katrina asked in alarm.

Leigh sighed. ''No, I don't think so, although she looks so much like him that I don't see how he can miss it.''

"She resembles you, too, Leigh. Those eyes. The way she moves. I can understand why the thought might not occur to him. After all, he doesn't know when Wendy was born. As far as Russ is concerned, she could very well be David's."

"In all the ways that matter, she *is* David's, Katrina," Leigh said. "He made her his own daughter by accepting her wholeheartedly from the very beginning. I hope she never finds out differently. You know how it was with Wendy and David. They were so close."

"True," Katrina said. "So what are you going to do now? I suppose Russ has left."

"No, he's still here. We—we decided to stay over and—and spend some time together," Leigh said.

"Spend time together? As *what?*" Katrina asked incredulously.

"As friends," Leigh said, although she considered the whole plan off after last night.

"Remember I told you that you two were perfect together? Are you still?"

Leigh wasn't sure now to answer this. She had no intention of telling Katrina about the fiasco of their lovemaking, at least not now while it was so fresh in her mind.

"I told him about his marriage proposal arriving twenty-two years too late, and he was terribly shaken," she said, ignoring Katrina's question. She thought about that day—was it only the day before yesterday?—and felt her heart soften toward him. Russ had been so kind and so sweet when she told him about the long-lost letter. So accepting.

"What did he say?"

"Oh, not much. But in its way, the moment after I told him was beautiful. We reached out to each other, and then we had to part because of the wedding rehearsal, and we talked afterward, and—"

"Leigh, wait a minute! You're moving too fast! You've hashed over your whole romance except the fact that Wendy is his daughter? When do you plan to drop that little tidbit of information?" Katrina asked.

"Never," Leigh said as positively as she could. "That's a secret that no other living person knows except you and me. And no one needs to know, either."

"It's not fair, Leigh," Katrina said pointedly.

Leigh sat up and swung her feet over the edge of the bed. "Fair to whom? I have to protect Wendy, you know."

"Wendy is an adult now, my friend. She's quite mature—you've said so yourself—and stronger than you think. If you *really* want a chance with Russ, you've got to tell him about Wendy. Or else he may find out later in some way that you won't like, and the news could drive you apart. Think about that."

"I think you're borrowing trouble, Katrina," she said. She didn't want to admit that the longer she was awake, the clearer it was that she'd better pack and leave The Briarcliff before Russ came looking for her.

"Okay, okay," Katrina said, "I'll back off. But I'm always available if you need me."

"Thanks. I'll tell you all about it when I get home," she said, adding to herself, *It'll be sooner than you think.*

"Leigh," Katrina said and then hesitated. She drew a deep breath. "Be careful, won't you?"

"Trust me, Katrina," Leigh said, picking the expression out of the air, not thinking about it at all, and it wasn't until after she hung up that she realized in horror that she had just spoken the two words she had never said before, two words that had wreaked utter havoc in her life.

Chapter Eight

"Trust me."

That was what Russ used to say about so many things. It was a catchphrase for everything, from whether he would be able to pick her up at the dorm in time to hurry to a concert to letting her know that he had taken responsibility for birth control. As far as birth control had been concerned, she had trusted him and it had failed. And as always she, the woman, was the one who had paid the price.

It was in September of 1969, shortly after Russ left for Canada, that she missed her period, and she had always been so regular that she began to worry immediately. In those days, there had been no drugstore kits for determining pregnancy, and she had waited on tenterhooks for some sign that she wasn't pregnant. Instead her breasts began to swell, something that had never happened before. And on the morning when she had awakened feeling queasy, she had known immediately that it meant the worst. She was pregnant. And she was alone.

Not entirely alone, however. David Cathcart had been following her like a shadow ever since she'd arrived on campus for the start of the semester. Leigh and David had been friends ever since they were freshmen, and she had always liked him. With Russ gone, it seemed entirely natural to sit together in the library as they studied and to walk somewhere afterward for a late snack, to attend fraternity parties as his date and to call him when she felt low, which was often.

David noticed, as the days wore on, how downcast Leigh was. He had tried everything to snap her out of the depression that was so obvious from the beginning of the school year, but nothing had worked. Finally he had subsided into the perfect companion for that time in her life—one who unfailingly bolstered her spirits by merely being there and asking no questions.

One windy Saturday when everyone else had gone to the big football game of the season and the two of them were strolling rather aimlessly across the almost deserted campus, David said earnestly, "I care, you know. I know something is bothering you, and I wish I could help."

David's kind remark was more than Leigh in her wretchedness could take, and she had burst into tears. For the past couple of days she had been frantic. Katrina knew, of course, that Leigh thought she was pregnant, but outside of her best friend, Leigh had told no one. Informing her parents was out of the question, because she had no idea how they would react. Furthermore, abortion in those days was illegal, and even if it hadn't been, Leigh couldn't have aborted this baby. *Russ's* baby. And yet what was she to do? Russ didn't love her, he wasn't around to help her, and the problem was more than she could handle alone.

David found a quiet corner where a brick wall formed a shelter from the wind, and there beneath a bright pyracantha vine he had spread his jacket so Leigh wouldn't have to sit on the ground. Once she stopped sobbing, Leigh told him the reason for her misery. She didn't look at him the whole time she was explaining how it must have been the last time that she and Russ had been together in the park that she got pregnant, and when she looked up David was gazing at her with both love and tenderness.

"Leigh, I can help. I love you, Leigh, and I always have, even when you and Russ were so wrapped up in each other. I've been crazy about you since the day I met you in freshman year, but I never thought until recently that you could accept me as more than a friend."

Thoroughly confused, Leigh had stammered, "Of—of course I consider you my friend, David. But you can't love me," and she blotted at her tears with a tissue she pulled from the pocket of her skirt.

David, sweet David, had taken her chin in his hands and lifted her tearstained face so that she would have to look at him. His round face was solemn, and his eyes behind the horn-rimmed glasses were kind.

"You'd better believe I love you, because we're going to be married," he said, and then he kissed her for the first time.

It had never occurred to her before that she could marry David, and she was astonished. After he kissed her a few more times, she pulled away and clasped her hands protectively over her abdomen. "I can't marry you, David," she whispered. "It wouldn't be right. I don't love you."

"I have enough love for both of us," David said stubbornly. "In time maybe you'll learn to love me."

She had told him she would think about it, and she had walked back to her dorm in a daze. *Marry David?* How could she when she loved Russ?

But Russ didn't love her. If he did, he wouldn't have left without a word.

The more she thought about marrying David, the more possible it seemed. He was, above all, a nice person and a decent human being. Her parents had met him and liked him. His thoughtfulness and kindness in the days following his unexpected marriage proposal convinced her that he would be a wonderful husband. *Marry David?* Well, maybe.

Katrina said in disbelief, "How can you, Leigh? You don't love him."

"He loves me," Leigh replied as she thumbed through books she had checked out of the library. They illustrated the development of the embryo day-by-day; by this time, her baby was no longer a little pin dot floating in a uterine sea; it had sprouted tiny buds that would soon grow into arms and legs. The idea of the baby was becoming more real to her every day.

David had a part-time job and an ample allowance from his parents. Leigh had been offered a student assistantship in the art department, and if she took it they could just get by if they rented a cheap apartment near the campus. She had counted the days and knew that the baby would be born in May; her due date was during the week after exams and before graduation. If the baby cooperated, she wouldn't even have to miss a day of classes.

David hovered over her protectively whenever they were together, and he called her at least three times a day to ask how she was feeling. He brought her crackers for her morning sickness, and he held her in his arms for hours at a time to comfort her. He was patient in waiting for her answer to his proposal, and finally when Leigh missed her second period, she knew she'd have to do something.

She called David at four o'clock one afternoon in early October and asked him to meet her outside the dorm. As they walked in the waning afternoon sunshine, she shivered. She knew that once she had taken this enormous step there would be no turning back.

Leigh was honest. "I've always liked you, and you're one of the best friends I've ever had. But I don't love you. I think it's important for you to know that," she told him.

David sighed and looked away, but then his eyes unflinchingly met hers. "And?"

"And if you still want to marry me, I will. I—I do think we could be happy living together, you and me." She watched him uncertainly, unsure of his reaction.

He had broken into a wide smile, enveloped her in his arms and covered her face with kisses. And then they had laughed, and he had whirled her around in excitement and they had gone straight to the student-housing office to check the bulletin board for a likely apartment.

That night they called both sets of bewildered parents, and without telling them why haste was necessary, they informed them that they planned to elope. Their parents convinced them to wait until the following weekend so that they could be married properly in the campus chaplain's study with both immediate families hastily assembled for the occasion. And that was what they had done.

Truly, marriage to David was pleasant from the very beginning. Going to bed with him for the first time had seemed strange, and there had been a certain amount of inexperienced fumbling on his part, but Leigh was patient and David was a fast learner. He had delighted in her pregnancy, and by the time they had been married four months, both of them forgot for long stretches of time that the baby Leigh was carrying was not David's child.

And whenever any thought of Russ surfaced, Leigh put him firmly out of her mind. It was as though his child growing within her edged him ever so slowly and surely out of her mind and her heart, leaving only David and her memories. In time even the memories receded so that her whole world became David and Wendy, and when she thought of Russ at all, it was with a sweet nostalgia and only a passing regret for what might have been.

Yes, she had learned to love David, and she had been enthralled by her daughter, and after all was said and done, theirs had been a marriage more successful than most of her friends'. They had hoped for more children after Wendy, but unfortunately Leigh hadn't become pregnant again. David had often said how thankful he was that they had Wendy, and Leigh had echoed his thoughts. When David died, she was devastated because she couldn't imagine life without him. But she had adjusted. And now here she was, with Russ creating problems in her life again.

She headed for the shower, turning the spray to its most forceful setting. The stinging jets of water jarred her into action, and she dried herself quickly and with a sense of purpose. She'd toss everything into her suitcase, gather Wendy's belongings from the room she had shared with Jeanne and be on her way before Russ Thornton was even out of bed.

She slammed out of the bathroom, rummaged in the closet and straightened abruptly when she heard the unmistakable clearing of a throat. She looked up to see Russ, wearing a gray sweat suit, sitting on the edge of the bed.

She did a quick double take. He was the last thing she would have expected to see.

"How did you get in here?" she demanded.

"Last night you dropped the key to Wendy's room next door," he said, dangling it in front of her before slamming it down on the table beside the bed. Leigh winced, hoping he hadn't damaged the finish of the lovely cherry wood. Her eyes darted to the connecting door. It hung slightly ajar.

"You shouldn't have come in uninvited," she said. Her hair was dripping on the carpet.

"I knocked, but you didn't answer," he told her.

"Still," she said pointedly.

"All right, all right," he said. "I wanted to see you, and I was afraid you had other ideas."

"I think it would be best if I went home this morning," Leigh said with dignity.

"I don't," Russ replied, studying her from head to toe. She was thankful that it was a very large bath towel; nothing showed that he wouldn't have seen if she were wearing a dress.

"A matter of opinion," she said.

He ran a hand through his hair. Wendy had the same habit when she was upset. Leigh turned away, unable to look at him.

"I went for a run this morning and gave this matter quite a bit of thought," he said.

"Russ, I wish you would go so I can get dressed."

"Since you were in my bed and entirely naked last night, I don't see what difference it makes if I see you in the altogether now," he pointed out.

"Technically I suppose it makes no difference. But I do want you to leave," she said. She turned her back on him and walked to the closet, striving for a nonchalance that she didn't feel. Her heart pounded against her rib cage so loudly that she was sure he could hear it, too.

She found underwear in her suitcase and ripped a pair of slacks and a shirt from their hangers. She would go into the bathroom to get dressed since he refused to leave. Not that she was above calling the management and complaining if she had to, but at the moment she had everything under control.

She acted as though he wasn't even there; Russ couldn't believe it. Or maybe he could, come to think of it. She'd always had a way of distancing herself from any unpleasantness between them. That's how they'd gotten into the mess they were in when he left for Canada.

He propelled himself off the edge of the bed and grabbed her arm as she was about to retreat into the bathroom. He startled her so that she dropped the armload of clothes and almost let the towel fall, too.

"You can't do this," he said tightly.

"Have you been drinking, Russ?" she said through gritted teeth.

"I told you, I went for a run and I've been thinking. About you and me, and I can't let it end like this."

"End? It never began," she said bitterly, her eyes flashing. She twisted out of his grasp.

"Don't be a fool," he said.

"Last night was a mistake," she retorted angrily.

"It may have been a lot of things, but it was no mistake," he replied. He wrapped his arms around her so she couldn't move. Trapped in his embrace, she reminded him of a frightened rabbit tangled in a snare, ready to bolt at the first opportunity. He wasn't trying to frighten her, he only wanted her to admit what they both already knew.

"Russell," she said on the edge of a sob. "Please."

He realized how frightened she was and relaxed his arms. "It's okay, Leigh," he said with a hint of tenderness. "Whatever was running through your mind last night doesn't matter. We're a lot of other things besides lovers. Friends, for instance. That's important to me—maybe more important than the other. I don't want to lose you again."

Leigh closed her eyes and drew a deep breath. How could they be friends? There were some things she could never tell him.

But then she and Katrina were friends, and she didn't tell Katrina everything, either. About how last night had ended, for instance. Of course she would, in her own good time, speak to Katrina about what had gone wrong, but not until she, Leigh, was ready to talk about it.

When she opened her eyes again, Russ was gazing down at her with eyes full of love. *Love,* she thought in a daze. *He is still in love with me. He really cares about me,* and the thought was overwhelming. After all, who else cared about her in such an intimate, loving way? Wendy, whose husband would require most of her attention now? Bett, whose life was filled with her active family? Katrina, who lived so far away that they saw each other only once a month?

She was silent for a long time, so long that he began to chastise himself for barging in here like this. Just when he was on the verge of stammering an apology and beating a hasty retreat, she spoke.

"I just don't know how to act around you," she whispered. "I—I'm lost."

"No, my Leigh, at last you are found." Hiding his relief, he kissed her on the forehead and deliberately stepped away. "And now, to prove to you that I really am a gentleman, I'm going to leave you to your privacy. But let's meet for breakfast in the dining room in, say, one hour?"

Fifteen minutes ago, she couldn't have imagined that anything would change her mind, but then she hadn't reckoned with Russ's charm and earnestness, which she couldn't discount because he was so obviously sincere.

"I'll be there," she said, her heart lightening at the thought of looking at him over the breakfast table. Suddenly she was ravenous.

"I knew you would be," he said and smiled before he left her room, closing the door quietly behind him.

IN THE HALL, Russ released the doorknob and sagged against the wall. He wasn't nearly as self-assured as he looked or acted. When she'd told him to leave, he'd almost done it, and when she acted so distant, for a moment or two he'd thought there was no point in continuing; it was clearly a problem that could not be solved by handing her a lemon drop.

But she hadn't been able to hide her need for somebody, and that somebody might as well be him. Her loneliness was so real that he'd have to be blind not to see it.

And he wanted her in his life. He was lonely, too, and at no time was he aware of being alone as much as he was during the holiday season. This year, she had made him feel alive and hopeful again, the way he *should* feel at Christmas. She had given him joy. He'd like to continue their sexual relationship, but if she didn't want that, then it was enough to be friends. *No,* he thought, *that isn't quite right. I want her as much as I ever did, maybe even more, now that I've been around a bit and know how important it is to find the right woman.*

He actually ached to be near her. To be *with* her. No, more than that. Putting it more poetically, he longed to immerse himself in the experience of her; in doing so, perhaps he could recapture the magic of their love.

He recognized how foolhardy it was to pin his hopes on that, but he felt that he had to try. Their love had been so special. They had been good for each other, he and Leigh.

He had always regretted their being separated by circumstance; how unfair the circumstance, he had never realized until she told him about the lost letter.

A second chance seemed almost too good to be true, but here it was and he wasn't about to let it slip by. He was ready to concede that he might have to make a few adjustments in his expectations.

At first, when their relationship had begun in this, its second incarnation, he'd thought that they could pick up exactly where they left off twenty-two years ago. She looked so much the same, still the most beautiful woman in the world to him, and she smelled the same and laughed the same and smiled the same brilliant smiles.

Now the more reasonable side of him knew that nothing was really the same at all. Everything had changed. But his idealistic side told him that somewhere inside Leigh Cathcart was the Leigh Richardson he had once known. The shining core of her might have been tarnished by layers of living, of watching the world swallow up her hopes and dreams, of trying to come to terms with reality. In this she was no different from anyone else, and he of all people was well-equipped to understand. It just made what he needed to do more difficult, that's all.

He had so little time. Soon they'd each go back to their ordinary lives, living out their ordinary days, and he wanted so desperately to change that. To find the extraordinary thing that the two of them had had together and, this time, to make it work.

He shrugged out of his sweatshirt before the door of his room had closed behind him. He had fifteen minutes to meet her in the dining room for breakfast.

He usually sang in the shower, but this time he didn't. He would save the singing for later when it was time to rejoice.

BREAKFAST COMMENCED in uneasy silence and progressed in nervous fits and starts to cautious observations about their fellow diners and eventually about each other. Leigh was surprised that Russ ate so little.

"I ate earlier," he said, offering no more explanation, and she doubted that he had really eaten. He looked confident and sure of himself, but she wondered if that was only a façade to hide his real feelings. She hadn't mistaken the love in his eyes earlier; it had changed her mind about leaving. Now he seemed very quiet, withdrawn into himself. As if he were thinking things over, and she wouldn't blame him. After last night and her histrionics this morning, he was probably reconsidering. But, oh, she hoped that he'd reach the same conclusion that he'd reached before—that she was worth pursuing.

She made an extra effort to be pleasant, then wondered if she was overdoing it. She forced herself not to speak in order to give him a chance, but the long silence made her so uncomfortable that she finally stammered a request for the maple syrup, which he passed to her without comment. She desperately racked her brain for something intelligent to say, but nothing occurred to her. She began to wish that she had left the inn after all.

She could still leave. She could get up from this table and go to her room, resume packing, and be on the road in fifteen minutes. The only trouble was that it was a long road, and there was nothing at the other end.

All of her life she had been something to someone, and now she was nothing to anyone. She had been child of her parents, wife to her husband, mother of her child. Now her parents were dead and so was her husband, and her child no longer needed her. What was left?

Her work. Of course she had her work, and it was important to her. Long years of teaching art to kids who really had no passion for it and were only taking the course because they thought it would be an easy credit toward graduation had sharpened her appreciation for the freedom she had now as a free-lance artist. Her work was absorbing, but it was not as demanding as a family. Her paintings didn't *need* her.

Did Russ *need* her? She stole a glance at him from beneath lowered eyelids. He didn't look as though he needed anyone. Divorced, successful, competent—that was Russ. He had managed to get along without her or anyone else for a very long time, and although he had admitted that he was lonely at Christmas, so were a lot of other people, even some who were married.

If he needed her, he could give her life the direction it had been lacking. If he loved her—but it was too soon to be thinking about lasting love. The emotion that she had seen in his eyes was real enough, she was sure of that. But there was still last night's fiasco to be overcome, and a whole lot of other things, too.

Russ signed for their meal, and they walked into the lobby. Today it seemed that many people were checking out, and small children were running up and down the polished floor of the foyer.

"Too noisy in here," Russ said, raising his voice over the din. "How about a walk outside?" He looked unnaturally serious, and she wished he would smile. She needed some indication that he was glad she hadn't left.

She'd brought her coat with her because she had thought she might suggest a walk herself. He helped her put it on, and they walked past the crying babies in the lobby out into the frosty air, where it seemed unnaturally quiet.

"There's new snow," she pointed out unnecessarily as they set off on one of the paths.

"It fell early this morning," he said, his words a white plume in the chill air.

"Where did you run? Not outside, I gather."

"They've built a gym above the ballroom. There's a weight room, a place for aerobics classes, and a track. That's where I ran."

"Why do you do it? Run, I mean?" she asked.

He shrugged. "Trying to stave off the aging process," he said.

She looked slightly startled. "Most people say it's for the exercise," she said.

"It's the same thing. Exercise is for the purpose of feeling young. How do *you* feel about getting older?"

The question surprised her; she hadn't expected it. "Kind of sad," she admitted. "There are compensations, I suppose. Wendy, for instance." She slanted him a look out of the corners of her eyes. She had forgotten and let down her guard. She shouldn't have mentioned Wendy.

"I don't see anything remotely good about being middle-aged," he said. "In fact, last time a woman made eyes at me, I found out she was just trying to get used to her bifocals."

She looked up sharply, trying to figure out if he was joking and decided that it was at least an attempt. *We're making progress,* she thought. She stuffed her hands down into her pockets and walked slightly ahead of him down the path, which was cleanly shoveled. It wound around a stand of spruce trees and skirted a flat, snowy area which, in warmer months, was the golf course.

"Let's walk to the overlook," Russ suggested as they approached the turnoff that led up the mountain.

"Good idea," she agreed, falling into step beside him. The overlook was reached via a steep path faced with a sheer rock cliff on one side and snow-laden spruce trees on the other. Beneath the drooping spruce branches a purling stream ran headlong over a rocky bed, its edges glittering with crystals of ice. Their boots crunched through the thin layer of snow on the path, leaving dark footsteps in their wake. It seemed to Leigh that there was nothing to say, or at least nothing right. She couldn't crack jokes the way he could; maybe it would be best to center the conversation on him.

"Tell me how you ended up taking over the family business," she said. "After you became an antiwar activist, I figured that would never happen."

"It was what I originally intended to do after college, although I got sidetracked a bit," Russ told her. "Then when my parents died, I was faced with the choice of selling the business and living happily ever after on the proceeds or making a go of it myself. A life of leisure never appealed to me. I saw a chance to improve the stores and was excited by the prospect. I sold off some of the less-profitable stores, improved the main store, and added new lines of furniture. The business is in good shape now, and I'm proud of that. I'm financially secure, and now I've got a little spare time to spend doing things I like, such as flying."

"I remember that you used to think that people who were well-to-do owed something to society," she said.

"I still do. I support several worthy causes, such as Big Brothers and Big Sisters and a school for migrant children. The money I've made makes it possible for me to do these things. Oh, when I was in Canada and involved in the antiwar effort, I suppose I thought that living my life only to accumulate a lot of money would be a sellout. Now I see that having money allows me to help the less fortunate more than I could if I were poor. The realization didn't come upon me all at once. It dawned on me gradually."

"David arranged our finances so well that I'll never have to worry about money again," Leigh said, glad that they were finally managing to make something besides small talk. She glanced at him to see if he was really interested in any of this.

He didn't look bored, so she took a deep breath and went on talking. "It's a lot different now from the early years when David was struggling to establish his insurance business and I worked right alongside him," she said. "I was his secretary and his bookkeeper, his answering service and even his janitor. At this point in my life I like having enough money, but there are more important things. I often think—" and she stopped, unsure that she wanted to steer the conversation in the direction it was going.

"You think what?" he probed gently, looking interested.

"Well, that I'd be better off if I'd had to work—really work—for a living after David died." This was something she'd never revealed to anyone else.

"You work. In fact, I envy your career."

She shrugged. "It's not a big deal. I mean, I'm not a wonderful artist, only adequate. I'm certainly not under the illusion that the pictures I paint for Katrina are great art."

"They fill a need, and that's important. I still hope you'll bring some of your paintings into the store sometime, so my designers can look at them. I'd like to see them, too. To this day I treasure that little portrait you painted me for my birthday when we were at Duke together."

"You still have it?" she asked in surprise. The painting had been a self-portrait in oils. She'd always considered it one of her best.

"Of course I do," he said. "It hangs at the end of the hallway in my house."

She was unnerved by this information; the picture had been painted at the height of their love affair, and she had portrayed herself as she thought she looked after lovemaking—eyes drowsy, hair slightly disheveled, lips swollen with kisses. It seemed to her to be too intimate a painting to hang in a hallway.

"You hung the painting in the house you shared with Dominique?" she blurted.

He smiled faintly. "She never saw it. I found it at my parents' house after Dominique and I were divorced. I couldn't bear to hang it in my bedroom, so I put it in the hall. It's a lovely painting, and I'm fond of it. Always have been."

"I see," she murmured, but she was staggered by the idea that Russ Thornton had been looking at her picture every day for many years. She would have thought that he'd tossed it out in the garbage long ago.

"We're almost to the overlook," he pointed out as they rounded a curve in the path. He clasped her hand to help her cross an icy patch where water had trickled out of a crack in the rock face of the cliff, and he held on to it as they mounted the steps to the overlook.

I'm reading too much into the fact that he still has the painting, Leigh told herself. *Maybe he's just one of those people who can't stand to throw anything away. Maybe he's a born pack rat. It doesn't mean anything.*

The importance—or unimportance—of the painting flew from her mind at the sight of the panorama spread out below, when she stopped and caught her breath at the overlook. The valley stretched vast and white, the sweep of snow interrupted only by a small cabin from whose chimney a spiral of smoke wafted upward. Beyond the valley rose the Great Smoky Mountain range, cloaked in a gentle smoky blue mantle. Overhead, the sky was a blue so brilliant that it was not found on any painter's palette.

"How lovely," she breathed, instinctively moving closer to Russ. He squeezed her hand in reply, and even though he did not speak, she understood that he was as awed by the scene as she was. Gone was any discomfort they felt in each other's presence; they were drawn together by their appreciation of the scene before them.

Up here where the air was so light and cold, they seemed far above trouble and care. Last night seemed to have been a long time ago, and the world below so tiny and insignificant. Leigh felt centered in herself, her mind expanded, and suddenly she saw everything more plainly.

With luminous clarity, she finally understood. She could not merely wait for a good relationship to develop with Russ, and she couldn't expect him to do all the work. If she wanted more than they had now, she would have to take positive steps in that direction.

She saw now that nostalgia might have been enough to bring them back together again, but it was not enough to keep them together. The truth was that they could not have the kind of relationship she wanted if she continued to keep the secret that weighed so heavily on her mind—the secret that Wendy was Russ's daughter.

But how could she tell him? Did she *want* to tell him?

His arm, quite naturally and almost of its own accord, encircled her shoulders and pulled her against him. She liked being there, but she knew that if she told him about Wendy, things would never be the same. Maybe she'd lose him.

How can you lose what you don't have? asked the small voice inside her head.

We have something, she answered. *I'm not sure what it is, but there's love. And respect.*

But she didn't need that small voice to remind her that without honesty, love and respect were of little use.

Telling Russ about Wendy wasn't the only problem, and it certainly wasn't the most immediate. Leigh knew that soon she would have to face the task of sorting through her feelings about Russ, keeping some and discarding others. It seemed like a monumental task to face those feelings, and she was well aware that if she said goodbye to Russ forever after these next few days, she would never have to face her feelings at all.

But to say goodbye forever seemed unthinkable, as unthinkable as it had been when he told her that he was going to go to Canada.

The sunshine felt warm on her face, and it felt right to be standing beside Russ, looking out over the valley. She knew she didn't have to do anything right away, right this very moment. For now, there was only this—a beautiful, shining moment when the world seemed far away, a moment to treasure, perhaps as long as she lived.

But was it enough? Enough to last her for the rest of her life?

Chapter Nine

That night they dressed and went to dinner in the inn dining room, and afterward they wandered into the Grand Ballroom where a band played for dancing.

They sat at a small table, and Leigh felt completely and utterly relaxed. Maybe it was the champagne that Russ ordered, or maybe it was that she felt good about their day together.

"Wendy called while I was dressing for dinner," she told Russ. "She asked about you and me."

"What did you tell her?" Russ asked with more than a little interest.

"That we're spending a lot of time together," she said.

"And her reaction was—?"

"Interested, to say the least. She's always wanted to pair me off with someone since I've been alone."

Russ laughed. "I hope I'm the right someone," he said. "And how are the newlyweds?"

"Blissfully happy," Leigh said.

"Where are they honeymooning?" Russ wanted to know.

"She wouldn't say. All she said was that it was beautiful and cold and that she is very happy," Leigh replied.

"And may she live happily ever after," Russ said, raising his glass.

Leigh took a small sip of champagne and set her glass down. "Do you suppose it's possible?" she asked wistfully, wanting to believe.

"What?"

"Do you suppose anyone can live happily ever after?"

"Maybe 'contented ever after' is a better way to say it," Russ amended. "It'd be hard to be happy all the time. Besides, if you were, you'd probably be crazy. *Nobody* can have it that good."

"I worry about Wendy and Andrew," Leigh said slowly, tracing a damp ring on the tablecloth with one fingernail. "They think they know all the answers."

"So did we, remember? And we didn't even know all the questions. Speaking of questions, here's one that only you can answer. Would you like to dance?"

Leigh broke out of her contemplative mood and rested her hand in his. "Yes, I most certainly would," she said, smiling at him.

He led her out onto the floor, proud to see how all eyes turned their way. Leigh looked exquisite in a flame-colored chiffon dress that molded to her figure and broke into a cascade of ruffles at the hip. The back scooped low, revealing creamy skin; the sleeves were long and flowing.

He held Leigh in his arms, marveling at the lightness of her, at the grace with which she moved. They had always danced well together, but he was a bit rusty; nevertheless, he remembered all the moves and she followed him perfectly.

"I've always liked dancing with you," he told her, leaning away so that he could take in her face. She wore simple diamond studs in her earlobes; they glittered in the lights from the bandstand when she laughed. He loved the sound of her laughter.

"Remember the dances we used to do? The Frug? The Watusi?"

"Don't remind me," he said with a groan.

"They were kind of outdated by the time we were in college, but I distinctly remember one fraternity party where—"

"If you're going to talk about the time we had a toga party and invited two girls for every guy—"

"Was it only two? It seemed like three. What was the purpose of that, anyway?"

"My frat brothers and I wanted to meet girls," he said.

"Well, you certainly did. Not that *you* needed to. You knew far too many girls as it was."

"After I met you, I thought so, too. Remember that Betty Whatsername, the one who was slightly obtrusive of tooth?"

"Obtrusive of tooth!" Leigh said, stifling a laugh.

"She had *huge* teeth," he said.

Leigh snickered but managed to recover.

"She wouldn't stop calling me, even after I told her I was in love with you."

"I thought her name was Bonnie, and you *didn't* tell her you were in love with me. That was the problem," Leigh said.

"Oh, *Bonnie,* the one whose calves bulged like wine bottles. I was never into wine, I'm strictly a beer man," he said. He remembered that he hadn't liked Bonnie much. After he started going out with Leigh, he hadn't been interested in anyone else.

"Bonnie, Betty! I certainly had a lot of competition."

"No, Leigh," he said, suddenly serious. "You never had any."

Her smile faded into a nostalgic, faraway look. "Neither did you," she said.

He drew her closer so that her temple rested against his cheek, reflecting that he had never looked at another woman after he started dating Leigh.

When the song ended she smiled up at him, a bright spontaneous smile that melted his heart. They danced again and again, whirling around the floor, causing people to look up from their drinks and their conversations and remark about how well-matched they were.

And they were. She followed him instinctively, anticipating every movement, adjusting to him gracefully.

Like good sex, Russ thought. *Like last night.* It had been good until something had happened and she had run away. He pulled her close, feeling the way she adjusted to him, and he wondered what was going to happen tonight. Should they make love again? Should he wait for her to make the first move?

They drank another glass of champagne when they sat down, and her smile became softer and more reflective. She had so many faces, and all of them beguiled him with their countless expressions and the feelings that flitted so quickly across her features. His gaze followed the curve of her neck downward to where her breasts swelled beneath the bright fabric of her dress. She was womanly, desirable, and his throat tightened with the memory of how she had looked last night.

But Leigh coaxed him onto the dance floor again, and when she was in his arms, she tilted her head back and gazed up at him dreamily.

"I haven't danced like this in years," she said.

"Neither have I," he said.

"Why not?"

"I never had a partner as good as you," he told her truthfully, and was happy that the compliment pleased her.

"You taught me to dance," she said, surprising him.

"Not true," he said. "Definitely not true. You learned to dance in your cradle."

"Oh, I had the usual ballet and tap lessons at Mrs. Hand's School for Feet, but—"

"Mrs. Hand's School for Feet? You're pulling my leg!" His eyes glinted with humor.

"The neighborhood dancing teacher was named Mrs. Hand. I'm afraid her students added the part about feet. Anyway, I wasn't good at dancing until I met you. I remember how you taught me to waltz at the big fraternity dance that spring."

"I don't recall that at all. I remember what you wore, though. A dress with gold threads that shimmered when you walked."

"I loved that dress. But most of all I remember the corsage you bought me to wear that night. White orchids. My *first* orchids. They were beautiful."

"You were beautiful. And you still are."

"Oh, Russell. You always say the nicest things." She was gazing up at him mistily, and he would have kissed her then and there if he'd thought it wouldn't raise eyebrows among the others on the dance floor.

"You *are* beautiful," he said, his voice low. "I had thought you would have changed, but you haven't. You look the same to me, those same blue-green eyes, the same scent, the way you feel in my arms, the way you—" and he stopped, suddenly abashed. He had been on the verge of mentioning the way she murmured his name over and over during lovemaking, something she had done from the very beginning and which always had made him feel as though his name on her lips was some powerful kind of aphrodisiac that only he could supply.

"The way I whisper your name when we're in bed. I know what you were going to say," she finished softly, resting her cheek against his. He was stunned that she would speak the words out loud, but then he wondered why he was so surprised; she had never been shy about sex.

The song ended, and the band began to leave the bandstand. The other dancers drifted toward the door, and they realized abruptly that the dancing was over.

Reluctantly they broke apart, suddenly self-conscious with each other. She slid a slow glance toward him, wondering if he felt the same rising heat that she did. She wished it could be easy. If she could design lovemaking the way she wanted it, they would not have to worry about logistics—where it would happen, when it would happen, who would initiate it. It would occur spontaneously according to appetite, and people would have some sort of sixth sense that would tell them when and how and where. The thought made her giggle, and he said, "Too much champagne?" and she said, "You can't have too much champagne," and he laughed and pulled her close.

She felt so attuned to him that she knew he wanted to make love to her in spite of what happened last night. And she also understood that he was reluctant to be the one to suggest it in case she still had misgivings. She felt slightly tipsy; *had* she drunk too much champagne? No. She'd only taken a couple of glasses, and they were small ones at that. It seemed to her that the champagne had made things easier. Simpler.

She could think of no earthly reason why they should not make love. Her inhibitions had been carried away on champagne bubbles. Had floated away on the strains of music as they danced. Today they had grown closer; she was clearer in her own mind about what she wanted to happen. She had not resolved the problem of telling him about Wendy, and she knew it would have to be done sooner or later. But now she was operating under the heady influence of champagne and the physical attraction of a man who thought she was beautiful. She had never thought she would hear those words from a man again.

Silently she walked beside him to the elevator, and as it climbed past the second floor and came to a jarring stop on the third, she considered her options. She could ignore the enormous physical attraction between them and go to bed alone. She could wait for him to ask her to his room. Or she could invite him into hers.

He walked her to her door, and once there, he turned her around to kiss her good-night. Her desire for him flooded her senses; when she looked at him, he filled her mind and her heart. She lifted her arms around his neck and let her head drop until her forehead rested against his shoulder.

"Oh, Russ," she said on the breath of a sigh. "I had forgotten it could be like this."

"I hadn't," he said, his voice unsteady.

She felt warm and aroused and very, very lucky. If she had left this morning, this wouldn't be happening. She would be alone in the big, old house in Spartanburg, walking barefoot on cold floors because there was no one to remind her to put on her slippers when she went downstairs to check the doors. She would be drinking a solitary glass of milk and watching late-night television, worrying in her head about whether she should go to the store to buy another tube of naphthol crimson paint tomorrow, and the truth of it was that she didn't care one way or the other and neither did anyone else.

Instead here she was with a most attractive man, perhaps *the* most attractive man to her, and she knew that she did not want to sleep alone tonight, that if she did she would feel the utmost privation, and that waking up by herself tomorrow morning in the big queen-size bed would be depressing in the extreme.

She moved away slightly and rummaged in the small purse she carried, trying to find the key to her room, and he said, "Here, let me," and he reached into her purse, his big hand dwarfing it, and pulled out the key. She tried to take it from him, fumbling in her nervousness, and it slipped from her hand. He caught it in mid-fall, which elicited a gasp from her, and then he inserted it into the lock and swung the door open. When his eyes met hers, they spoke a question.

After one long, mute look she pulled him inside after her, and she stood before him, searching his face as the door clicked closed behind them.

She felt unsteady on her feet, but not from the champagne. She felt overwhelmed by the sheer import of this moment. Last night was nothing; it was a bridge they had to cross and that was all. The experience had served a purpose. Now whether they would make love was not an issue, and she was thankful for that. The issue here was something more; it was deciding if their lovemaking could represent anything more than good, quick sex, could transcend the physical.

She held out her hands and pressed them against the front of his suit, reaching for his heartbeat. She felt it, slow and steady, beneath her palms. Somehow it made her feel less tentative and more sure of herself. He reached up and circled her wrists with his thumb and forefinger, spanning them easily.

"So delicate," he said, rubbing his thumb against the bones.

She bent to him like a willow wand, and he slid his hands up her arms. He dipped his head and kissed her, a soft, swooping, brief kiss, and he inhaled the scent of her hair, sent feathery breaths along her jawbone, touched his lips to the warm shadowy hollow of her throat. Her hands fumbled with his tie, lost the knot, found it and untangled the silk until it fell away; the buttons on his shirt slid easily through the buttonholes. He shrugged out of his suit jacket, letting it fall, and it seemed to float away in slow motion. Everything seemed heavy, weighted with meaning, with time. Away fell his belt, his pants, his underwear, and somehow he found the tricky zipper of her dress and she was shivering out of it, so cold standing there in her underwear, and while she was pulling his head down for a long, searching kiss he dispensed with the gossamer wisps of lace and she was standing before him wearing nothing at all, champagne singing softly in her blood.

His hands began a slow exploration of her body. They were cool and smooth against her skin, and she knew she was shivering, but how could she feel so cold and so hot at the same time?

"Sweet, so sweet," he said, devouring her in a long kiss, and she clung to him, her limbs winding around him like tendrils. Once she had seen a slow-motion nature documentary depicting the way plants responded to light. Their stems and leaves had rotated to follow the sun in its course through the heavens; light was something they'd had to have in order to survive. She felt like that plant, a plant that had lived too long in the darkness and had discovered the warmth of the sun. If Russ turned, she would turn. If he moved, she would follow. He was the sun, and she needed his warmth.

His body, fit and lean, felt hard and smooth beneath her fingertips. She cupped her palms around his shoulders, slid them to the shoulder wings below, followed the curve of his waist and continued to the tight buttocks beneath. She pressed him against her, aware of his own hands curved around her breasts and amazed at how alive she felt. Compared to the way she felt now, she had been sleepwalking through life. Going through the motions. Doing what was expected of her. It all seemed flat and dull, from this perspective. Flat and dull and tiresome. But this—*this* was real.

He was lifting her up, and her legs twined around his waist, and their mouths were joined so that she could hardly tell where she left off and he began. He lowered her to the bed, his eyes dark behind tangled lashes, the pupils wide with pleasure. She felt him pressing against her, grinding down upon her, pushing her wide; she rose to meet him as if on wings, curving upward in flight, wild flight, opening to him as his lips bore down upon hers, and she couldn't breathe, only felt his breath hot upon her face, or was it hers? An exquisite tension built inside her, a singing electricity humming through her body, concentrated here and here and here, and mostly here, and mostly, mostly, mostly... ah! She gasped and pressed her wet mouth to his shoulder, tasting salt, tasting sweat and tears and whispering his name over and over, trembling beneath him, barely conscious of his own shuddering and release, and the tears were on her lips, her tears, and he tasted them on her kiss.

She sobbed in his arms, she couldn't help it. It had been so long, and it was still so good, so perfect with him. As though they had been doing it for years, with all the right moves committed irrevocably to memory, understanding things about each other that no one else could know.

"Leigh, Leigh, what's wrong?" he asked urgently.

She sobbed harder, wetting his chest and his neck, her fingernails digging sharp half-moons into his back.

"Nothing is wrong. It's *right,*" she said through her tears, and surprised herself by laughing.

"Crying, laughing, what is it with you?" he asked, rocking against her.

"Oh, I don't know. Whatever it is, I like it," she said.

"Since you like it, let's do it again," he said, sliding down until his lips found her breast.

"Mmm," she murmured, guiding his hands downward.

"There?"

"No, more—yes. *Yes,*" she said as his fingers found the right place.

"Ah," he said, and she lay back, letting his mouth and his fingers draw out delicious sensations more slowly this time.

"Enough?" he said later, when it wasn't nearly enough.

"Not yet," she said, sliding over him and teasing him with her tongue.

"It's like champagne—you can never have enough," he said, and in that moment she agreed.

Later, when their passion was spent, she lay in his arms in the quiet, darkened room and wondered why she had ever thought this would be complicated.

Because of Wendy, her conscience murmured, but she ignored it. Right now it was just her and Russ, and soon would be the beginning of the new year. It was a hopeful season, and she knew everything would be all right. It had to be. This was perfect. Wasn't it?

RUSS DREAMED THAT NIGHT, but it was not the kind of dream he usually had. Most of the time he dreamed action scenes where he was the principal player, reminding himself of Arnold Schwarzenegger. Afterward, when he remembered them, he was amazed at his feats of derring-do. This time, his dream resembled an impressionist painting—soft and blurry and emotional.

In the dream, he held Leigh's hand and they were strolling through a field of frothy wildflowers—Queen Anne's Lace, he thought they were called. The edge of the field was dotted with trees, and Leigh was wearing something filmy and yellow that billowed around her bare legs. As if he were looking through a zoom lens, Leigh's smiling face filled his vision. And then, surprisingly, the laughter of children, as liquid and warm as sunshine, swirled around them.

The children were his and Leigh's. There were four of them, the exact number they had decided they would have back in the old days when they planned to marry. Two boys and two girls, and one of the girls reached up trustingly and nestled her pudgy little hand in his. Her touch was so real that he could feel it.

He felt a sudden draft and opened his eyes. His legs were constricted, and as he began to understand where he was, he realized that his legs were tangled in the sheet. There was no field of flowers and his hand wasn't holding that of a small girl with blue-green eyes. Instead he was gripping Leigh's shoulder, and she murmured something and rolled over with her back to him.

Drowsily he pulled the sheet up and billowed it over both of them; he adjusted his position until he and Leigh lay as close as spoons. His hand rested in the hollow of her waist, his face was burrowed in her sweet-smelling hair, and he felt so content that he should have been able to go back to sleep but couldn't.

The children had seemed disturbingly real. He thought the boys had looked like him, and the girls had definitely resembled Leigh. Their faces had seemed so familiar that he thought he might have dreamed them before.

He couldn't remember such a dream. Perhaps he had pictured such children in his mind, however, during the years that he had been married to Dominique and she had kept refusing to start a family. They had argued about it frequently, and Dominique had stated obstinately that she wasn't about to give up her hard-earned gains in the business and that she had no intention of losing her figure. He had countered with a question about what good did it do to have all the proper female equipment if she wasn't going to use it, and she had commented heatedly that this was a particularly sexist remark and unworthy of him, and he had apologized, but he had still hoped that she'd see his side of it eventually. She never had.

Russ had thought often in those days about Leigh and the four children she'd probably had with David, and he'd envied her. He'd always known that Leigh would be a good mother, and now that he'd seen her with her daughter, he knew she was. Too bad that she hadn't had any more children; someone who is good at parenting should have a large family. *He* would have been a thoughtful, wise parent. He wished he'd had a chance to prove it.

Maybe he'd be a father someday, though he had come to doubt it as the years passed. He had a couple of buddies who had become parents after passing the age of forty, and fatherhood seemed to agree with them. They had married very young women, though, which wasn't an option for Russ. He liked women who could carry on a decent conversation about a variety of topics, women who had weathered a few storms in their lives, much as he had. Women like Leigh.

Leigh. If he married her—

But no. It wasn't time to be thinking of that. Maybe she didn't want to marry again. Maybe *he* didn't.

But children. If they married, would Leigh object to starting a new family? Probably their old dream of having four children was an impossibility, but perhaps she would like to have one more. A son, maybe. With his dark hair and her eyes. With curly eyelashes and a jaunty grin. He could picture such a boy if he let his mind drift...dreaming and drifting with Leigh's soft body pressed close to his.

Her daughter was grown. Why should he think that Leigh would want to start over again with diapers and sour milk and two o'clock feedings? She was forty-two years old and so was he.

He would help with a baby. He wouldn't mind. He was financially able to hire someone to run the stores; he'd be a better father than some of the younger guys who were never home because they were building a career. He had the energy to cope with kids. But what about Leigh?

She stirred and moved against him, and his mind focused on the present. She was warm and welcoming, and her skin was soft. Soon all thought of children fell away, and his whole awareness centered on the joining of their bodies, the joy and pleasure of it, again and again and again.

Chapter Ten

It was amazing, Leigh reflected as she waited for Russ to get out of the shower the next morning, how in certain circumstances making love obscured all the real issues in a relationship.

Not that she cared *why* they made love. At the moment, it seemed right. Oh, it was right to wake up in Russ's arms and to mold her body to his for warmth, and it was right to pick up the phone and call room service while one of his hands inscribed lazy circles around her breast. And it was right for him to head for the shower in her room, not his, and for him to sit with her at the small table by the window as they ate pancakes and sausage.

They could not stay inside; indoors seemed stifling and confining in light of this newfound freedom of their bodies. Instead Russ asked the restaurant staff to prepare a picnic lunch, and though the staff found it odd that two people would want to eat lunch outside in the snow, they obliged.

Leigh and Russ stopped to visit an antique toy train displayed in one of the rooms off the great hall, holding hands as they watched children approach with eyes that grew even rounder when the train chugged out of the tunnel and they saw that a small replica of Santa Claus sat in the locomotive. One little boy clapped his hands with delight when women dressed as Santa's helpers passed out lollipops all around, and Leigh and Russ took them, too, grinning at each other as they unwrapped them and popped them in their mouths.

Being around children and acting like children made them feel like children, and so they romped and chased each other around the small lake behind the inn until they reached the picnic area where they suddenly became grown-ups again and embraced and kissed and smiled at each other, scarcely believing their good fortune at being together again. Then, struggling to catch their breath in the thin mountain air, they cleared the snow off one of the stone picnic tables and a bench before sitting down to eat their lunch.

Leigh felt replete with happiness, so much so that she ate very little. Russ took up the slack, downing two chicken drumsticks, two ham sandwiches and a huge piece of chocolate cake. When he had finished, he swept the wrappings off the table and turned around so that he could use the table as a backrest, holding one of her hands in his.

Above them, snow blazed in the ridges of Briarcliff Mountain, and in front of them, the lake glittered with reflected sunlight. A bird landed in a spruce tree nearby, shaking clumps of snow to the ground. It took flight and wheeled in the air, a black speck silhouetted against the sky. Leigh sighed with pleasure and leaned back against Russ, surrendering herself to the moment.

The sun was warm, melting little rivulets that sparkled like jewels as they ran off the warm gray stones forming the bases of the picnic tables. The air was pure and fresh, and Leigh drew a deep breath into her lungs, energized by its crispness.

"Katrina and I used to come to this spot often during that summer when I first met you," she said dreamily. "It was where we met our boyfriends after dark."

"Boyfriends? And where was I?"

"In the kitchen. The boys we liked worked at the lake; they were lifeguards."

"They must have seemed glamorous compared to us kitchen rats," Russ said with a wry flicker of amusement.

"I'm not so sure of that. I can't even remember the name of the boy I liked."

"His name was Cal, and I was jealous," Russ told her.

She sat upright and turned to look at him. "Imagine your remembering that!" she said.

"Of course I remember," he said with an aggrieved air. "I spent the whole summer trying to get you to notice me, but I didn't have a chance with that guy walking around in a pair of skimpy swim trunks and flexing his biceps every chance he got."

"He did not. Besides, by this time he probably weighs three hundred pounds and has lost most of his hair."

"I'll bet that's what you thought about me before you saw me," he teased.

She laughed. "I didn't think you'd be fat. But I wondered if you were bald," she admitted.

He kissed the corner of her eye. "I was sure you'd be wrinkled," he said.

"I *am,*" she told him.

"Not very. And not where it matters," he said, kissing her mouth.

"What does *that* mean?"

"It means that I like the little crinkly places at the corners of your eyes. It means you've laughed a lot, and I'm glad. And I love the way your breasts have become more round, more full—"

She twisted away from him. "More fat?" she asked skeptically.

"Not fat. Round. I like it. I only wish I'd been around all these years to watch you develop and change." He seemed suddenly serious as he picked up her hand and traced her fingernails with one of his own.

She leaned back against him, uncertain about his change of mood. The sun flitted behind a cloud, then peeked out again.

"I dreamed last night about our children," he said at length.

She turned and regarded him with a puzzled frown. "I don't understand," she said.

"Have you forgotten? We were going to have four. Two boys and two girls."

"So we were," she said lightly, bending over to pick up a piece of plastic wrap from one of the sandwiches. She crumpled it in her hand, distracted by the sound of it, and dropped it in the basket that they were supposed to return to the inn.

"Anyway, there they were in my dream. One of the little girls held my hand so trustingly, looking up at me with enormous blue-green eyes. She had dark hair like Wendy's."

Something in his tone of voice made her catch her breath. Had he guessed?

"But," he continued, looking out over the valley, "the dream ended abruptly. Dreams often do."

He hadn't guessed. He didn't know Wendy was his daughter. If he knew, he wouldn't be so casual. In that moment, she realized that she wished he *did* know, because then all she would have to do was confirm his suspicions. If only she could tell him and be done with it!

I'm a coward, she thought with sickening clarity. It occurred to her that she could tell him right now, but in doing so, she knew full well that she would risk her happiness.

Leigh jumped down off the wall. "I think we should go back to the inn," she said abruptly. "It looks to me as if the sun is going to hide behind that bank of clouds, and it will be too cool up here if it does."

"The weather report distinctly predicted sunny weather today," Russ objected, but after studying her face for a few moments, he helped her pack up the basket.

She pretended to concentrate on the task, feeling that his eyes were on her whenever she turned her back. When they had finished, Russ hoisted the basket in one hand and followed her along the path beside the lake. She barged ahead, not waiting for him.

He caught up with her quickly. "Leigh, you're acting differently," he said.

She seemed to take stock of what he'd said. She shook her head. "I don't think so," she said, but he noticed that she avoided looking at him.

"It started when I was talking about the dream I had. You act as if I've struck a nerve."

"Nonsense," she said briskly.

"Do you have something against children?"

"Of course not."

"This isn't the first time you've shut me out," he pointed out. "Don't you think I get tired of this everlasting tango—forward and back, then forward and back again?"

"What I think is that this silly conversation is going nowhere," she said.

A boisterous group of cross-country skiers crossed the path where it forked toward the inn, and while he and Leigh waited for them to pass, Russ brushed the snow off a nearby bench.

From the set of Leigh's shoulders he knew that something was wrong. What it was, he couldn't say, but he was sure it had something to with his mentioning children. Why didn't she tell him what was on her mind? Why couldn't she be as open with him as he was with her?

The problem was that he didn't like unpleasantness any more than she did, which was why a lot of things never got said. He was struggling just as she was with trying to get their relationship back on track with too little time to do it; he was painfully aware that they had only a few days left. After that, he didn't know what would happen.

If she wouldn't discuss, however, then she wouldn't discuss. He would have to wait until she wanted to confide in him about whatever was bothering her, and there was no way he could force her to trust him with her innermost feelings. Either it would happen or it wouldn't. In the meantime, they might as well enjoy themselves; that was the way he looked at it.

"Have you ever tried that?" he asked, gesturing toward the skiers. "It's fun."

She sat down beside him and leaned forward, gripping the edge of the bench with her hands. "Cross-country skiing? David and I took it up one year in Utah," she said.

"I missed my morning run today. If you'd like, we could rent skis at the inn this afternoon. Are you game?"

"I was thinking of taking a nap. You could go while I sleep," she replied.

"I don't want to ski unless you do," he said, watching the skiers' retreating backs. His shoulder brushed against one of the laurel branches behind him, and it dumped a wad of snow down his neck.

"Ugh," he said, swatting at it, and Leigh said, "Let me." She whisked the snow away with one of her mittens. The wool felt harsh against his neck.

"Mountain laurel," he mused, looking over his shoulder at the big green, glossy leaves. "I've always liked it, especially when it blooms. Those huge pink clusters of flowers are one of the prettiest sights in the world. That reminds me—weren't we going to name one of our children Laurel?"

"The second girl," Leigh said faintly.

"The boys were Dirk and Matthew. The first girl was Elizabeth."

"Elizabeth is Wendy's middle name," Leigh said recklessly. *Let him make of it what he will,* she thought.

Russ focused a long, hard, incredulous look upon her.

Flustered, Leigh stood up. He was still staring at her when she turned her back and headed toward the inn.

He caught up with her near the gardeners' hut.

"I would have thought that the name was already taken," he said, his voice unnaturally quiet.

"Elizabeth is my sister's name. It's always been special to me," she said. The truth was that she had sentimentally bestowed the name upon Wendy in remembrance of the love affair in which she'd been conceived, but no one knew that, not even Katrina.

"If I'd been lucky enough to be a father, I would never have named my children any of those names. Never," he said, sounding slightly bewildered.

Leigh slowed her pace as they approached the inn entrance. She felt shaken; guilt stabbed through her. She wanted to say, *Wendy is our daughter. Can't you guess? Don't you see?* but the words stuck in her throat.

"I really think I'd like to take a nap," she said tonelessly once they were inside the inn. She looked pale, and Russ told himself that he could understand her fatigue. They hadn't fallen asleep until the early morning hours, and then they'd kept waking up, surprised and unaccustomed to finding themselves together. But they'd been happy. *She'd* been happy, but she wasn't now.

"All right," he said easily. "I'll go upstairs and jog around the track a few times." He made himself sound as natural as possible, but inside he was still reeling with the information that she had named her daughter Elizabeth; how could she have done that?

"Yes, do," she said, sounding immeasurably relieved, and when he walked her to the door of her room, she presented him with a cheek to kiss before slipping quietly inside. She didn't invite him to join her for her nap.

Russ went to his room, changed clothes, and ran around the track until he was so exhausted he almost dropped. Then he went to his lonely room and lay on the bed, trying to sleep. He never did, however; his mind kept trying to untangle some unknown puzzle and wondering what in the world it was.

THAT NIGHT THEY WERE lying in bed when Russ thought, in a burst of courage, that it was as good a time as any to broach the subject that he was sure she'd been thinking about as much as he had.

Leigh had never been one of those women who hurried away to wash after lovemaking; she was the kind who liked to kiss and cuddle and fall asleep wrapped in his arms. For that he was thankful. He was also glad that she liked the lights low so that she couldn't see his face when he first said the words.

"I've been thinking," he said slowly, "about what would happen if we got married."

He felt her shoulder muscles tense against his arm, and he stroked her cheek with his free hand. She remained completely motionless.

"Well?" he said, when there was no reply.

"Is this a proposal or what?" she asked finally.

"It's more like an 'or what,'" he said. "I'm merely throwing the idea of marriage up for discussion. You can do whatever you want with it—ridicule, argue, say you'll think about it tomorrow. I thought you should know that it's on my mind."

"On your mind," she repeated.

"You sound like a parrot," he told her, and he commenced sucking on her little finger, which happened to be handy.

She pulled her finger away. "It's a bit sudden," she said in a quavering voice.

"Hey, we've known each other for more than twenty-two years," he said, shifting his weight so that he could peer at her in the half darkness.

"Not all the time. It's not the same as *really* knowing each other," she objected.

"Nevertheless," he said. He paused. "You don't think we should be considering it?"

"I don't know," she said, sounding troubled.

"We wouldn't have to get married right away. We could be engaged."

"For how long?" she asked.

"A couple of days? Weeks? A few months? Whatever seems practical."

"Where would we live?"

He honestly hadn't considered this. He'd pictured them in his house in Charlotte, however; her self-portrait had decorated his hall for years; and it seemed only right that she should be there in person.

"My house," he said firmly. Then, seeing the dismayed expression on her face, he realized that it probably would not be so easy for her to leave the big, comfortable home where she had grown up, raised her child and lived so happily with her husband. "Maybe your house," he said in a spurt of generosity.

"What about your business?" she asked.

"I have employees who can take care of things with only an occasional visit from me," he said.

She rolled away from him and lay on her stomach with her chin propped on her folded arms. She stared broodily at the headboard of the bed.

He caressed her back, marveling at the silkiness of her skin. She seemed not to notice him, to be lost in some thought of her own. He wished she'd say something.

"Like I said, you don't have to make a decision right now," he reminded her.

Suddenly he was startled to see the silvery tracks of tears glistening on her cheeks. He reached out a forefinger and touched one; his finger came away wet.

"What in the world are you crying about?" he asked in mystification.

"About what we had. And about what I don't deserve," she said, turning her head sideways and away from him so he wouldn't have to look at her ravaged expression.

"Leigh, for God's sake," he said. He slid one arm beneath her and the other arm around her. Her tears fell on his clasped hands and he felt at a loss. What should he do? How could he comfort her? *What* was he comforting, anyway?

While he pondered this, she seemed to shrink within herself. Maybe he had been insensitive, although he couldn't figure out how. What was this rubbish about not deserving? *What* didn't she deserve? A marriage proposal? He thought he'd made it clear that he was only beginning a discussion; didn't she understand?

Twenty-two years ago he'd written her that fool letter, and she'd never received it; that was his first attempt at proposing marriage to anyone, and he had botched it. Now, as two adults without illusions about life or love, he thought that he and Leigh should be able to reason things out together; wasn't that what other people did? Or did Leigh expect surprise and hoopla and romance?

Not that he didn't feel romantic about her. He thought that this was a very romantic situation, lying in bed, engrossed in each other, the rest of the world busy someplace else. What could be more romantic than that? All the rest of it—the flowers and love letters and diamond engagement rings—weren't real. *This* was real, two people naked in each other's arms. But maybe Leigh didn't think so.

"I didn't mean to make you cry," he said.

"It's not your fault," she replied.

"If you're thinking about the past—"

"How can I help thinking about it?" she said.

"You could think about the future, instead. That's what I'm doing."

"Somehow I can't picture it."

"That's because you're not trying. You're clinging to old memories, and it's time to let go."

She sighed deeply and turned within the circle of his arms so that she was facing him. In the dim firelight, the shadows beneath her eyes looked deep and dark. She looked tormented and miserable, and his heart went out to her.

He stroked her hair as he would that of a child. She let her head drop against his shoulder, and he wondered what he could do or say to make her feel better. Since he didn't know the origin of her pain, he didn't know where to begin.

"I'd let go of the past if I could, but it's not that easy," she said finally, her voice barely audible.

"If I can, you can," he said firmly.

"I don't know what you mean."

He leaned back on the pillow and shoved one hand behind his head. In the fireplace, the logs glowed with an eerie light; one split and fell, shooting a shower of sparks up the chimney.

"I've had to live with the knowledge that you married David only weeks after I left for Canada," he said, deciding to lay it on the line. "It hurt. Oh, how it hurt."

She brushed away the dampness on her cheek with a sharp movement of her hand.

"Anyway," he continued, "it's past. Over. *Finis.* And what we have left is you and me. Now. Not then." The words were emphatic.

She brushed her hair back from her face with a weary hand. "It's not as finished as you think," she said.

He thought he understood. "I know you cared for David very deeply," he said gently. "I'm so sorry about what happened to him."

"It's not David," she said, her voice choking on the words. "It's Wendy." She looked so devastated that he drew her into his arms.

He was surprised to find that her skin was gooseflesh and that she was trembling.

"You're cold," he said. "I should put another log on the fire."

"No," she said. "No." She huddled against him, uncommunicative. He wrapped himself around her and eased her back under the blankets until their heads were side-by-side on the pillow.

"I would be good to Wendy," he said.

"It's not that," she said, her teeth chattering.

"She's gone, Leigh. Married. You have to let go of her."

He felt the infinitesimal shake of her head, a denial. He might have guessed that it would be hard for her to let her only child go so soon after her husband's death.

"Don't worry," he said soothingly. "It'll be all right. You have me now, you know."

Her eyes drifted closed, and he kissed her forehead, dismayed at the teardrops seeping out from under her lids. But he didn't speak of them and neither did she, and eventually they both slept.

Chapter Eleven

In the morning, neither one of them referred to the night before. Leigh marveled at how they could both get up, shower, dress and go on as though no unusual conversation had taken place. Russ was as even-tempered and smiling as always, and Leigh found herself thinking that this might be his greatest strength—his ability to remain on an even keel no matter what happened. It was one reason that she should feel comfortable telling him about Wendy, and yet she couldn't bring herself to do it. At least not yet.

But, she decided as she brushed her teeth, she wouldn't feel comfortable discussing marriage with Russ until he knew about Wendy. If she let him go on talking about getting married, she wouldn't be playing fair. *How* to tell him was the problem. All in all, she'd much rather he guessed.

Luckily the problem of how to tell Russ about their daughter did not overshadow the joy and pleasure of being with him. She was able to compartmentalize her feelings in such a way that their happiness in being together again was not overshadowed by her fear and uncertainty. She still looked forward to every minute they spent together, she enjoyed their companionability, and she soaked up his compliments and his admiration. Each magical day they had spent together was embellished with smiles full of memories, and the chemistry between them sparked the same old rapport.

"How would you like to get out of the inn today? We could go antique shopping on behalf of my staff," Russ suggested at brunch, leaning forward and smiling at her over the white tablecloth on their table in the dining room. Around them chimed the gentle clink of glassware and silver, and at the buffet table busy waiters were clearing away the last of the scrambled eggs and sausage, the French toast and cantaloupe.

"I'd like that. I think I can help you," she answered happily, and soon they were walking with light footsteps down the hill to the craft village, sucking on lemon drops and with Leigh's hand tucked inside Russ's big pocket for warmth.

She'd brought her camera; she hadn't taken any pictures at The Briarcliff yet, an omission that she intended to correct while everything was still covered with snow.

"The weatherman is predicting a thaw," Russ said. "It's supposed to rain tonight and become warmer by tomorrow morning."

"I thought I smelled a thaw in the air," Leigh said. "I'll hate to see the snow melt. This Christmas has been so beautiful. I've been so happy."

He squeezed her hand and smiled at her. "This has been the best Christmas ever, and it's because of you. By the way, I've bought our tickets to the New Year's Eve party."

She gave a little skip of delight. "I've always wanted to go to New Year's Eve at The Briarcliff. People come from all over to attend. They're having a jazz band, and a comedian in the lounge, and—and I don't have anything to wear!" she said at the sudden realization.

He laughed at her astonished expression; she looked as though the thought that she needed a dress to wear on New Year's Eve had never occurred to her.

"Wear what you wore to Wendy's wedding," he suggested.

"That suit is not the kind of thing I'd wear to a New Year's Eve celebration," she said.

"How about that bright dress with the ruffles? The one you wore dancing?"

"Oh, no, not that one. I'll buy something in the inn's boutique. Something special," and she smiled up at him, thinking that he would love the way she looked in the black sequined dress that she had spied in the boutique window on their way to breakfast this morning.

They turned into the antique shop, the little brass bells on the door tinkling merrily to announce their arrival.

Inside, Leigh steered Russ away from a rough-hewn cradle that she suspected was a copy, but cheered when he discovered an antique maple drop-leaf table that was suited to many uses. He also liked a small but authentic pie safe that had been painted Wedgwood blue and a lovely rocking chair with a handwoven rush seat, and he bought them all and asked that they be sent to the Charlotte store.

While Russ was standing at the counter arranging for the shipping, a man carrying a small child walked up and began to look at the cradle. The child was a boy, his chubby cheeks as round and red as apples as he peered out from under a bright green peaked cap, and Leigh thought that he looked like a little elf. He made a wild grab at her scarf as his father carried him past, and she was captivated by his wide grin.

"How old is he?" she asked as the man waited at the counter to be helped.

"Eighteen months," the man said. "And I have a newborn daughter, too."

"Bababa," said the boy.

"He can talk," the man said proudly. "Kenny, can you say 'doggie'?"

"Doggie," Kenny said obediently.

"That's very good," Leigh said. Russ turned and looked at them, and he smiled at the sight of Leigh and the baby together.

"Kenny, say 'cookie,'" the man said.

"Cookie? Cookie? COOKIE?" Kenny said, his voice rising on a shrill note of hope. He wriggled in his father's arms.

"Bad choice of words," the father said ruefully.

Leigh laughed. "Here, maybe this will help," she said, handing over a packet of melba toast that she had stashed in her coat pocket a few days earlier.

Russ folded the receipts for the furniture and stuffed them into his back pocket.

"It's all set," he said. He paused for a moment to chuck Kenny under the chin before they walked outside into the bright sunshine.

The snow had already begun to melt and was dripping steadily off the steep shingled roofs of the craft houses. Leigh felt a sudden pang, mourning the loss of the snow.

"I should take a picture of this," she said, snapping the lens caps off her camera. She set the shutter and the aperture in a businesslike way and experimented with several angles until she found one she liked. She clicked the shutter and advanced the film, and Russ thought how capable her hands were, how they belied the soft, gentle woman that she was. She saw him looking at her and sent him a questioning look, but he only smiled and slid his arm around her shoulders as they headed back toward the inn.

It felt right to be walking beside her, measuring his long footsteps to her shorter ones so that they stayed together. It was, he thought, a metaphor for marriage. If they were married, he would adjust his footsteps to hers; that's the way it should be both for husband and wife, but it hadn't been that way with Dominique.

He wondered about Leigh and David—how they had negotiated the inevitable compromises that go with being married. He gathered that they had adjusted very well, which should have made him jealous, but he only felt glad for them, both of them.

"I should take a picture of those bare tree branches—see how the branches make triangles out of the sky?" Leigh said suddenly as they began their walk up the hill. Ahead the forest loomed before them, the trees starkly beautiful against the snow-covered mountain.

Russ had never considered trees as geometric shapes, but now he did. The rays of the afternoon sun limned the branches in light; the effect was startling in its simplicity. Leigh fiddled with the camera, experimented with different angles, and snapped several pictures. He watched her, liking the way she concentrated so completely on what she was doing, entranced by the sparkle of her coppery hair in the sunshine.

"Why are you looking at me like that?" she said suddenly, as if she'd just noticed.

"I like the way you look," he answered. "You never gave me a Christmas present, you know."

"The two things," she said, "don't have anything to do with each other. And I apologize about the Christmas present, only I didn't know you'd be here."

"I'd like a picture of you," he said. "It would be the perfect present."

She laughed and looked embarrassed. "It wouldn't," she said.

"It would. Let me take one of you now. You could stand on that log over there," he said, pointing to a fallen tree trunk in front of a boulder shaded with interesting shadows.

"I don't want my picture taken," she said, but he pushed and prodded her until she was standing exactly as he wanted her, with her face slightly in profile and one leg on the log, and he snapped her picture just as she turned her head and taunted him with an appealing but saucy grin that made her look about ten years old.

"Now you," she insisted, making him sit on the fallen log and lean his elbows on his knees so that he was exceedingly uncomfortable, and then she ordered him to relax, which was impossible.

"You clicked the shutter before I smiled," he complained afterward, so over his good-natured protests she sat him down again and took another picture.

"Anyway, I wouldn't take a picture of you if you weren't smiling," she insisted as she put the lens cap back on the lens.

"Why's that?" he asked.

"I wouldn't want to miss capturing that off-center smile of yours for posterity," she said.

He had forgotten until now that she always referred to his smile as "off-center"; she was the only one who had called this particular peculiarity to his attention. He supposed his smile appealed to the artist in her, or at least the part of the artist that appreciated shapes.

"I'll ask the concierge at the inn about getting these photos developed," she promised as they hurried back to the inn. "You'll be pleased when you see how yours turns out."

"I can't wait," he said, and she laughed.

"If you don't like it, I can always take another one later," she told him.

This statement implied that they would have a future together, and this unexpected bonus made Russ's hopes turn optimistic. He was suddenly overwhelmingly glad that he'd taken a chance, that he'd tracked Leigh down at The Briarcliff. He'd had so many doubts about it at first. Back in Charlotte, when he was thinking it over, he hadn't been sure that it was the right thing to do. And then when he'd found her and she'd asked him to leave, his spirits had reached a new low. But now, things looked promising. He wasn't sorry; he'd never be sorry that he'd spent this special time with Leigh, no matter what happened in the end.

Leigh glanced at her watch when they reached the inn lobby. "Let's meet in the music room for tea in half an hour," she suggested.

"Good idea. I'd like to check on our dinner reservations for tonight," he said.

"And I'd like to change out of these wet boots," she told him, and when she left Russ watched her walking across the lobby, saw how other men turned to look at her, and felt wildly possessive in a way he had not felt about anyone in years.

In her room, Leigh changed into a pair of comfortable shoes and was preparing to go downstairs for tea when her phone rang.

"Mom, hi!" Wendy said, her voice brimming with happiness. "I'm so glad I caught you in. Where have you *been* all the times I've called, anyway?"

Leigh laughed. Wendy's curiosity about Russ was about to get the best of her, she could tell.

"Oh, I might have been at the craft village, or dancing in the Grand Ballroom, or walking to the overlook with Russ, or—"

"He really likes you, doesn't he?"

"Mmm-hmm, it's safe to say so," Leigh admitted. She was enjoying the suspense; Wendy seemed so surprised that she was actually keeping steady company with a man. *Keeping steady company,* she thought. My, those words would date her. What was the proper way to say it? Oh, *seeing.* She was *seeing* a man.

"Am I going to get to see him again? I mean, where does he live?"

"In Charlotte," Leigh said.

"Oh. So far away. Well, will the two of you get together after this week?"

Leigh thought about it. How much should she tell Wendy? That Russ had mentioned marriage? That the man was her real father? She felt slightly sickened at the idea.

"I suppose that Russ and I will see each other again," she said carefully.

"I'd like to get to know him better. He has kind eyes," Wendy said.

"Is that all you noticed?" Leigh asked, wondering if Wendy had picked up on any resemblance to her; probably not. Wendy was not one to beat around the bush. She would have come right out and mentioned it if she had.

"I noticed that Russ seems quite taken with you," Wendy said.

"I'm fond of him, too," Leigh said.

"Fond? Is that all? Merely fond? Or something more?"

"Wendy, ease up. We've only been together for a few days."

"I'm so glad you've found someone. I really am. Oh, here's Andrew. He wants to say hello," and Wendy put Andrew on the line.

They said a few obligatory words to each other, exchanging their usual friendly greetings, before Wendy returned.

"I'll call you again to wish you a Happy New Year," Wendy promised. "That is, *if* I can find you."

"I'll be in my room getting ready for the big party from about four o'clock until seven or so on New Year's Eve. You can call me then if you'd like."

"Will do. I envy your going to the New Year's Eve celebration," Wendy said.

"Will you and Andrew be going out to celebrate New Year's Eve?" Leigh asked.

Wendy laughed. "It's not likely. Andrew says I can tell you where we are—we're in a sweet little cottage on an island off the coast. The view of the ocean is wonderful and we're having a good time, but I'd love to go to a party." Andrew said something in the background, and Wendy laughed again. "Andrew says that the island's beautiful but cold. We think the heater is on the blink."

"Have you called a repairman?"

"There's only one man on the island who fixes things. He's at his sister's on the mainland. But don't worry, Mom. We're keeping warm."

"I know you can always go to Andrew's parents' house a day or so early if you'd like," Leigh said.

"They're not expecting us, but I'm sure it would be no problem. We're hoping the heater will be okay. Anyway, I'll call you on New Year's Eve, Mom, and in the meantime, say hello to Russ for me."

"Yes. Yes, dear, I will."

Leigh felt pensive as she hung up, and she remained so as she slowly descended the stairs to the music room. It seemed that there was no easy way to end the lie that she had been living for so long. She was painfully aware that when she divulged the information that Russ was Wendy's birth father, she would irrevocably change two lives.

You changed those lives before, you should be able to change them again, she told herself, but she was older now and much wiser. Things had turned out well enough for her and David and Wendy; in retrospect, she felt sad and increasingly guilty over her decision to keep the secret, because she knew now that it hadn't been good for Russ. He had never really found happiness, and perhaps it was her fault.

Also she cringed from letting Wendy know what she, Leigh, had done all those years ago. Once Wendy knew that Leigh had deliberately hidden her existence from her real father, her view of her mother would be forever changed. Leigh couldn't bear the thought that anything could disturb her happy relationship with her daughter; on the other hand, it was already changing because of Wendy's marriage. Perhaps Wendy was mature enough to take everything in stride. Katrina thought she was, but then Leigh was having a hard time accepting the fact that Wendy was an adult, a married adult who had shown every indication that she was capable of taking charge of her own life and in fact already had done so.

With these thoughts heavy on her mind, Leigh arrived in the music room before Russ. She sat down at a small card table in a corner and ordered tea for both of them, wishing there was some way to dispel her doubts and fears. She could think of no way out of the trap she had backed herself into; bleakly she acknowledged to herself that she was the one who was responsible for the current state of affairs, and ironically she had thought she was taking charge of *her* own life at the time she had made those far-reaching decisions.

Russ came in smiling, and in spite of her troubling thoughts, a tremor of recognition danced up her spine. *My love,* she thought involuntarily, and knew that it was true. She *did* love him, perhaps now more than ever before.

"Dinner is set for seven o'clock in the dining room," Russ said, sliding into his chair across from her. He smiled at her, and she relaxed. Nothing had to be done now, nothing but enjoying the present.

"I had a good time today," she said, picking up on his mood. "Going into the antique shop, taking the pictures—"

"Eating lemon drops, walking in the snow," he said, grinning at her. "And wasn't the kid in the antique shop cute?"

"He was adorable," she agreed without much enthusiasm; there were other things she'd rather have talked about.

What she lacked in enthusiasm was more than compensated for by Russ. "Eighteen months old—can all kids that age say a lot of words?" he asked.

"I suppose most of them can talk a little," she said, thinking back. Although her memories of Wendy at that age were vivid, she found more and more that she couldn't recall the specific ages at which Wendy learned the skills that all babies must learn. What was more, she didn't care. Every little accomplishment had seemed earth-shattering; now each one had diminished in importance. What was paramount in her memories now were her own feelings at the time—the sense of relief when Wendy first slept through the night, the delight when Wendy spoke her first word, the pride when Wendy took her first steps.

"That man—I think he said he had a newborn daughter, too," Russ said.

"Mmm-hmm," Leigh said, not really paying attention. A pianist walked through a door not far away and sat down at the grand piano in the middle of the room. He played a scale, a series of soft, tinkling notes, and the conversation in the room hushed and receded.

"His children would only be fifteen months apart. That seems a bit too close in age," Russ went on. He was oblivious to her lack of interest.

"Perhaps," she said.

"If we had children, we wouldn't have to have more than one," Russ said, and she turned astonished eyes upon him.

"We've talked about getting married," he said evenly, and she thought, *You've talked about it—I haven't,* but she held her silence.

"Oh, Leigh, don't look at me like that," he said seriously. "With marriage goes children. You're still young enough and so am I, and—" He stopped when he saw how pale she was.

She was speechless. She'd had no idea that he'd been thinking about this, no idea that he actually expected that if they got married, they would undertake raising a family together. It was so removed from the kind of things that she'd been thinking about that she was truly and utterly aghast.

"Leigh, don't look so—well, I'm not sure how you look. What's the matter?"

When she could make her mouth work again, she closed it, and for want of a better place to look, inspected the inside of her teacup, trying to gather her thoughts. She had the outlandish urge to giggle, but this wasn't funny. He was serious.

Russ leaned forward, his tea forgotten. He waved away the uniformed waitress who was approaching with a tray of dainty sandwiches.

"I know some people who have had children when they were in their forties," he said coaxingly. "It worked out well."

Piano notes filled the air, bridging the dead silence between them.

Leigh drew a deep, shaky breath. "I can't have any more children, Russ. I had a hysterectomy when I was thirty-five," she said. She was thinking that this was as good a time as any to tell him about Wendy. Or was it? He looked pained; no, it was more than that. He looked stabbed to the core.

"I see" was all he said.

"It wasn't elective surgery," she said, her words tumbling over each other. "I had a lot of physical problems and more than one indication that surgery was necessary. I'd always hoped to have more children and never became pregnant, but then I had the hysterectomy, and on top of the operation I had to realize that all hope for David and me to have any more kids was gone. It was tough, I'll admit that."

"That's why you never had the houseful of kids you planned on," he said. He felt sorry for her, but he felt sorrier for himself. He had woven a nest of dreams, and it was already unraveling.

"I've come to terms with it," she said.

He heaved a great sigh. "It makes no difference to me," he said heavily. "I want you more than I want kids. I hope you'll marry me. That way I'll gain not only a wife but a lovely daughter."

Leigh's knee jerked involuntarily and hit the side of the table, sending her tea sloshing into the saucer. When he saw the panicky look in her eyes he realized that he had upset her terribly, but he was confused. What had he said to set her off like this? What was going on in her head, anyway?

A waiter hurried forward with extra napkins and offered to bring a fresh cup of tea, but Leigh stood up abruptly. "That won't be necessary," she said to the waiter, and before Russ could speak, she ran blindly from the room.

He hurried after her, aware of the startled glances of the other people in the music room. When he came to the great hall, she had reached the row of elevators behind the bank of poinsettias, but when she punched the call buttons a few times, she must have realized that all the elevators were busy elsewhere and she headed up the large, sweeping staircase.

"Leigh! Wait!" Russ called, taking the stairs two at a time. A woman with a small child in tow stopped and stared after them openmouthed, but Russ didn't care. He only wanted to reach Leigh, to find out what the hell was going on.

She didn't stop until she reached the door of her room, where she fumbled in her pocket for the key.

He pinned her against the wall before she could unlock the door. His face was inches from hers and she closed her eyes to shut him out. Unfortunately he knew exactly what she was doing.

"Look at me, Leigh," he ordered, and slowly she opened her eyes. His expression was fierce and loving, and she tried to look away but he wouldn't let her.

"You have to face the fact that I love you and want to marry you. Why is it so hard to accept?"

"I'm not ready," she said miserably.

"I don't believe you," he said.

She swallowed, but the lump in her throat wouldn't go away. She heard the sound of children's laughter at the far end of the hall.

"We can't stay here," she said, twisting in his embrace. "People are coming."

Slowly he released her, and she shakily slid the key into the lock. "Come in," she said, when he hesitated.

He walked through the door and closed it firmly behind him. He looked around, not sure what to do with himself. Leigh was taking off her coat, and wordlessly he did the same. He felt exhausted after their exchange, almost too exhausted to go on.

It shouldn't be so hard, he thought wearily. When they were young, nothing had been easier than falling in love. All he'd had to do then was pick up on a certain look of Leigh's, act on an indefinable attraction to her, and after that everything—sex, intimacy, happiness—had happened naturally. Now love was so much more complicated—past issues to resolve, old hurts to be healed. And it was harder to love once you were experienced, because you knew that it could never be easy.

Leigh had wrapped her arms around herself as though she felt cold. He looped his coat over a doorknob and put his arms around her.

"I'm sorry," he said. "Sorry about Laurel, Elizabeth, Dirk and Matthew. And about everything that came between us. If it'll help you to know it, I'm sorry about the whole past twenty-two years. I wish things could have been different."

She looked up at him, her eyes haunted by ghosts of the past. "I had a happy marriage," she said.

"I'm glad," he said, meaning it. "You may not believe it, but I'm happy for you."

She drew away from him and sat down on the edge of the bed. When he didn't speak, she said, "David always liked and respected you, you know. He often said he admired you for the stand you took against the war."

He sat down beside her. She slid one of her hands into his, and he thought that she wouldn't have to tell him these things, that it wasn't necessary. She seemed to need to talk about it, though, and he'd always been curious about her life with her husband.

"David never was drafted?" he asked.

He could think of no explanation for the way her lips tightened into a grim smile. "He had a student deferment, and then we married and had a baby. Some men were drafted even though they were married, but fathers weren't subject to the draft. Wendy saved David from having to go to Vietnam," she said.

He sensed that she wanted something from him. She looked at him half-expectantly, but over and above her expectancy there was a tension and a fearfulness that he couldn't explain.

"Lucky David" was all he said, and he lay back on the bed and pulled her down beside him. She made no move toward him, only lay there with a look of despair and desperation on her face. He turned to her, slid his hand up the side of her neck, and turned her face toward his.

Slowly he lowered his lips to hers, seeking something in her response to him. Her passion and excitement and even her love for him had been amply expressed in their past lovemaking, but what he wanted and needed from her now was the certain knowledge that he brought her as much happiness as she brought him. He wanted to see his own pleasure reflected in her eyes; he wanted her to know the exhilaration that he felt when they were together.

But that was not what he found in her. Instead of joy, there was only melancholy.

She turned to him swiftly, pressing closer. "Oh, Russ," she said brokenly, burying her face in his collar. "I do love you, you know. I can't help loving you, even though—" Here she stopped, and he realized that she was trembling.

"Even though what, my darling?" he asked gently.

"Even though it may not be best," she answered in a tone so low that he could barely hear her.

"How can it not be best?" he asked. "Why shouldn't we love each other? I'll tell you this, Leigh—I never stopped loving you, and I never will. This time it's forever."

Her face was wet with tears when he kissed her, and before he knew it she had unbuttoned his shirt. He shrugged out of it and helped pull her turtleneck sweater over her head. Soon they lay together on top of the pile of clothes in the dim purple half-light of dusk, and when she reached for him tentatively, he yanked the phone cord out of the wall, gathered her into his arms and decided to forget about their dinner reservation. Outside a warm rain beat softly against the windowpanes.

He stroked her hair, and his mouth brushed her cheek, his breath gentle against her ear. *Just make love to me so I can forget everything else,* she said silently, feeling tired. Her emotions were tearing her apart, and she'd found no way to tell him why she was hesitant about marrying him. No way to tell him about Wendy. He hadn't picked up on her mention of Wendy's keeping David from being drafted, but then, why should he? All along she had tried so hard not to give Russ any clues, not to let any important details slip. Apparently it had never occurred to Russ to ask when Wendy had been born or to count up the months; he must have thought that his method of birth control in those days was foolproof. He had absolutely no idea that Wendy was his daughter.

His hand wandered lower, tracing her spine, and when she opened her eyes he was looking at her. He took in the long, slender curves of her legs, touched the indentation at her waist, slid his hand upward until it cupped her breast.

"You are so lovely," he said. "You always were."

He slid his leg over hers and pulled her so close that no space was left between their bodies. His mouth covered hers, and she felt herself opening to him, pleasure chasing care, eagerness overcoming doubt. This part was good; this had always been good.

She let her fingertips move of their own will, exploring the territory she knew so well; the wide shoulders, the firm pectoral muscles, the long, flat abdomen. His skin was hot against hers, and she melted beneath him the way the snow melts in the sun. Went all watery and weak because she loved him, and because she loved, she wanted to give him the most exquisite pleasure. And for an instant, only an instant, she could believe that this was twenty-two years ago and that they were in their secret glade in the park, loving each other as though they would never stop, no matter what.

"Russ, oh, Russ," she murmured, and he said, "Now I am you and you are me," and she answered, "Yes, yes," and felt him filling her at last.

When the world returned to normal, he said, "I love you so much, Leigh."

"I love you," she said, her voice a mere whisper.

He twined his fingers through hers and listened as her breathing became slow and regular. In this season of hope, she had brought him more hope than he could have imagined; he fell asleep beside her, his face nestled in her hair.

It was very late when a sharp knock on the door disturbed them.

Leigh sat up, her breasts shining white in the moonlight pouring through the window. She was disoriented until she felt Russ stirring beside her.

"Don't answer it," he said. "Whoever it is can go away."

She started to lie down when she heard a voice. "Mrs. Cathcart? Are you there? I'm afraid it's an emergency."

"I'll go," Russ said, pushing her back into the rumpled sheets with a cautionary hand, and he pulled on his pants and shirt and hurried to the door.

The word "emergency" woke her completely. Leigh sat in the dark with the bed covers pressed to her chest, trying to hear the subdued conversation, but she could make out none of the words. She struggled to stand up, wrapping the bed sheet around her.

Russ flipped the light switch as soon as he closed the door. Harsh incandescent light flooded the room, and she saw that his face was ashen and his look was pitying.

"What is it?" she asked sharply. "It's not Wendy, is it?"

"An accident," Russ said. "Andrew called and left a message at the desk when no one answered your phone. He and Wendy were driving back to the inn to surprise you and to spend New Year's Eve with us. Leigh, I'm sorry, but their car slid off the road. Wendy's hurt. Oh, Leigh, I am so sorry."

Chapter Twelve

The world began to spin and Leigh heard a roaring in her ears. She was only marginally aware that Russ was easing her onto the edge of the bed, was holding her head down between her knees, and she thought, *Am I fainting?* She had never fainted in her life.

When she lifted her head, Russ drew her into his arms. "It's all right, Leigh, it's going to be all right," he said. His voice sounded faraway.

"Where is she?" she managed to ask.

"The desk clerk wrote the telephone number of the hospital on this piece of paper," Russ said. "It's a hospital in Kettiston, North Carolina, not far from Fayetteville."

"*Kettiston!* What were they doing there? Andrew—is he all right?"

"Minor cuts and bruises, that's all."

"Thank God. Oh, Russ, I'd better call the hospital," she said. Her voice was shaking.

"Here, let me," Russ said, taking the phone receiver from her hand. Russ dialed the number and handed her the telephone.

The person Leigh talked to was an emergency-room nurse, who told her little more than what she already knew. Wendy had been brought in over an hour ago with a head injury. Period. For more information, Leigh would have to talk to Dr. Miller, the doctor in charge.

"May I speak with him, please?" Leigh asked.

"I'm sorry, he's with a patient," the nurse told her.

"With Wendy?"

"I don't know, Mrs. Cathcart."

Leigh's voice rose. "May I speak with my son-in-law? Andrew Craig. He was in the same accident, but I understand that he wasn't seriously injured."

A whispered consultation on the other end of the line, after which the nurse said, "He sustained a minor injury, a cut on his hand. He's being looked after by the doctor on duty now."

"I need to speak to him," Leigh said firmly, balancing on a thin edge between control and hysteria.

"I'm sorry, it's impossible."

"Page my daughter's doctor, then," she said, willing herself not to get angry.

Having the doctor paged yielded no results. The nurse, as impersonal as ever, noted the telephone number of The Briarcliff and promised to give it to Dr. Miller, Wendy's physician.

Leigh slowly lowered the receiver of the phone. She knew nothing. She could find nothing out.

"I have to go to Wendy. They won't even tell me how she is," she said. She lifted troubled eyes to Russ, who was standing beside her and looking concerned.

"Of course," he said immediately. "I'll take you."

"My car—it's probably low on gas," she said, beginning to function more normally. She let the sheet fall to the floor, gathered up her clothes and began to put them on.

"I'll check with flight service and see what the weather is like between her and Kettiston. I'll fly you, if it's okay. We could be there in an hour and a half."

With a sense of unreality that this was really happening, Leigh picked up a rubber band off the floor where it had fallen earlier and bundled her hair back into a ponytail. Her face looked so pinched and white, reminding Russ of another day when she had been upset, the day that he'd told her he was going to Canada. His heart went out to her; he could see her pain written all over her face.

"I'd better get ready," she said distractedly. "I'll have to pack something, anything..."

"Wait until I call flight service," he urged. He dialed the number and the phone rang on the other end, but no one answered. He glanced at his watch. It was after midnight; flight service was supposed to be available twenty-four hours a day to give weather reports to pilots. *Answer, damn it!* he thought, and at last someone picked up the phone.

He listened, then hung up and turned to Leigh.

"The airport's fogged in, but they expect the fog to lift in another hour or so. If we fly, it will take us a little over an hour to get to Kettiston; if we drive, it would take five."

"We'd better fly," she said tersely.

"It could take a while for the fog to clear," Russ warned.

"How long?"

"You never know what the weather will do," he admitted. "Still, flying would be faster, even if we have to wait a couple of hours."

"A couple of hours!" Leigh exclaimed. In her mind's eye she saw Wendy, bleeding and broken, lying in a hospital bed.

"It's possible," Russ said.

She wondered for one brief moment if he was trying to get out of this. "You don't have to go with me, you know," she reminded him.

"I want to," he told her firmly, allaying any doubts that she might have had. He gathered her hands in his. "You can't go alone, Leigh. You shouldn't drive when you're this upset."

At the look of concern on his face, concern for her, she broke. She began to sob quietly. For a minute or more he held her tight against his chest until she managed, with great effort, to pull herself together.

"I'll pack," she said, easing away from him.

"I'd better throw a few things in my duffel bag," Russ told her.

"You can still back out of this," she told him.

"Leigh," he said in a tone of reproof, and when she saw the reproachful look on his face she said nothing more.

When the door had closed behind him, Leigh moved like a robot to the closet. She threw the first things she saw into her smallest suitcase. Pants, sweaters, a skirt. Blouse, shoes, boots. In the bathroom, she yanked the curling-iron cord out of the wall plug. Shampoo. Brush. Mascara? No, she tossed it back onto the counter. She wouldn't need it.

In five minutes, she had finished. She zipped the suitcase closed and slipped on her parka, grabbed her warmest gloves off the closet shelf and opened her door as Russ was arriving, his muffler flying behind him.

"All set?" he asked in a low tone.

Mutely she nodded. She hadn't even brushed her teeth; she belatedly recalled that she wore no makeup. Neither seemed important.

He picked up her suitcase and set off at a trot. She had to run to keep up with his long legs.

Like Wendy's, she thought with a jolt, and then she thought, *She's Russ's daughter, too.* It seemed appropriate for him to be there, and strange. It was hard to reconcile herself to the idea that Russ was actually around when he was needed. It had always been David who had been there during other crises in Wendy's life.

People were still up and about in the great hall of the inn, walking in twos past the huge fireplaces where the fires were being banked for the night. Bright chatter wafted from the direction of the lounge. Russ turned to Leigh in the foyer.

"I'll get the car. It'll take just a minute."

She watched Russ as he loped down the curving driveway toward the parking lot. He was a good runner; after all, he ran every morning. She was immensely thankful for that. For *him.*

She saw a pair of headlights swinging toward her, recognized Russ behind the wheel of the car and picked up her suitcase. By the time she had reached the door, the car had screeched to a stop in front of her.

The trunk lid popped up, released from inside, and Russ erupted from the driver's seat to help her stow the suitcase in the trunk beside his duffel bag. He opened the door on the passenger side and made sure she was secure in her seat before he closed it after her. In a few moments they were on the highway to the airport.

Damp patches of fog swam past the car's headlights; wet tree trunks loomed on each side. Ragged remnants of snow remained here and there in places that the sun couldn't reach, and the pavement was slick from the thaw.

Leigh leaned forward in her seat, peering ahead. Russ masterfully guided the car around several curves where it was impossible to see what was coming from the other direction. They were descending the mountain; the airport was located at one end of the valley. The fog grew denser as they reached the lower altitude. Leigh's ears popped, adjusting to the change. All she really wanted was to get to Kettiston. The fog looked thick, too thick. They couldn't take off in this.

Russ sensed her agitation. "Don't worry," he told her. "I think the fog will lift before we reach the airport."

Leigh tried to relax, but it was impossible. The moment she let down her guard, her hands clenched and her fingernails bit into her palms. She prayed that Wendy would be all right and that the fog would lift so that Russ's plane could take off. She thought that she had never prayed so hard in her life.

When she stopped praying, she thought about Wendy and how she was beginning a new life with Andrew. She was so young, only twenty-one; surely Wendy deserved a chance to live the happiness that she had so recently found? And Andrew—he must be beside himself. He loved Wendy so much; together the two of them had planned their careers and had talked about having a family when the time was right. They had so much ambition and drive, so much love!

Great clouds of fog engulfed them within a mile of the airport, and Russ was forced to slow down. Visibility was so limited that it was impossible to see the curves in the road until they were upon them; the fog was a wall of white.

"We won't be able to get out if it's like this, will we?" Leigh asked nervously. She bit on a fingernail, a habit she'd thought she'd broken over a year ago.

"No," Russ said, clipping the word off short, and she sank back into the soft leather seat.

"Could we—could we still drive to Kettiston?"

"If you'd rather," Russ said.

"I don't know," she said fretfully, staring out at the mist. Russ had turned on the windshield wipers, and they seemed to taunt her. *Will you, won't you, will you, won't you,* they mocked, and she remembered that the refrain was a line from *Alice's Adventures in Wonderland,* one of Wendy's favorite books when she was a child.

She swallowed the lump in her throat and tried to think. She didn't doubt Russ's ability as a pilot; she only worried about the weather. She wanted to get to Wendy as soon as possible. What should they do?

Blindly she turned to Russ. "Tell me what you think," she said.

He braked the car to a stop outside a small white building—the airport. Somewhere out there in the fog were the hangar and planes, but they couldn't see the outlines of the building. Leigh had the crazy idea that maybe the hangars and planes weren't there after all, that this was some kind of nightmare from which she would soon awaken.

"I'll call flight service again," he said, going around to the trunk and getting their suitcases.

"I'll carry mine," she said, but he replied, "No, I've got it," his voice echoing eerily in the fog, and she followed him silently into the building where a stout man sat in an orange pool of light behind a messy counter and looked up in surprise as they entered.

Russ immediately picked up the phone and Leigh paced the small waiting area, barely conscious of the dog-eared magazines and the old leatherette furniture with its stuffing falling out.

"They say the weather should clear up soon," Russ told her, but when he saw her bleak expression, he hurried across the floor to where she stood. "We can drive if you want to," he told her gently. "My car has plenty of gas in the tank."

"It would take five hours," she said.

"Yes, I'm afraid so."

She whirled and looked out the window. If anything, there was more fog than before. Still, one hour was better than five.

"I'll hold out for the fog to lift," she decided.

"Okay," Russ said. "I'll get you some coffee, all right?"

She nodded, and the man behind the counter said, "Wouldn't you like to sit down, ma'am, and be comfortable?" but she shook her head, attempted a smile, and remained at the window, searching for a hole in the sky.

Russ brought her a paper cup filled with black coffee, and she tried to drink it. The first sip burned her tongue and she winced, but after that she didn't feel the pain of it. She was growing numb, both physically and mentally. She had slept earlier, but it was hardly enough rest. She knew she should probably sit down, perhaps lie down, on one of the couches, but she felt too jittery for that.

"Maybe it won't be too much longer," Russ said. "I'm going over to the hangar to do my preflight check on the plane. I'll be back in a little while."

Russ completed the preflight check; he came back and filled a cup of coffee from the pot. Once she glanced at him and he was staring out at the fog, a worried crease bisecting his eyebrows.

One hour passed and they were still waiting; flight service could offer no explanation for the continuing fog.

"I should have gone ahead and obtained my IFR rating last spring when I was thinking about it," Russ said.

"IFR?" Leigh repeated.

"Instrument rating. It means Instrument Flight Rules," Russ told her. "I could fly in this soup if I were instrument-rated."

"Oh," Leigh said, uninterested.

"Maybe we could find a pilot with an IFR rating who could be hired to fly us there," Russ suggested in a spurt of unexpected energy. He and the man behind the desk held a hurried consultation, and the man immediately began dialing numbers on the telephone. One after another, all the pilots he called said that they were unavailable.

"Another half hour gone by," Leigh murmured with one more despairing look at her watch.

"We could still—" Russ began, but the man behind the desk interrupted. "Look," he said. "I think the fog is lifting!"

The three of them went outside, slamming the door behind them. The hangar, which was about fifty feet away, was beginning to emerge; wispy tendrils of mist still curled around the roof.

"I'll get the plane out," Russ said, and he and the man took off at a run.

Slowly the plane rolled out of its shelter and headed toward the runway. Leigh went inside and tossed her coffee cup in a trash bin. The clock on the wall indicated that it was almost two-thirty; it had been hours since she'd learned of Wendy's accident, and she was still no closer to Kettiston than she had been at the beginning.

Russ slammed back inside and made a hurried telephone call. After he hung up, he grabbed Leigh's hand.

"Come on," he said. "The weather's clear all the way there. We'll be on our way in minutes!"

She ran beside him, her shoulder bag bumping against her hip, her heels barking against the asphalt runway.

When they reached the plane, Russ boosted her up on the wing. She angled into her seat, buckled her seat belt. The propellers began to whirl, slowly at first, then faster. The engine caught. And then they were lurching along the runway, the sky miraculously clear. Above them, Leigh could see a few faint glimmering stars.

Russ talked into the microphone, getting his guidance from the man back at the airport, who was now talking on the radio. The plane hurtled through the darkness, the familiar buildings receding into the night. Then the plane left the earth behind and below, leveling out above the trees. They were on their way.

Russ had to shout to make himself heard over the drone of the engine.

"Hang on to your seat, Leigh! We'll be there before you know it!" he said, and she ventured a halfhearted smile because he looked so jubilant.

Engine noise made it impossible to talk, so Leigh's thoughts turned inward. Her thoughts flew to Wendy. She had been such a beautiful bride. Such a happy bride. Had Andrew been driving when the accident happened? Or was it Wendy?

She glanced at Russ. He was concentrating on the remote and crackly sound of the radio, which Leigh found extremely hard to understand. Russ was much too busy flying the plane to talk to her, so she slid down in the seat and closed her eyes, but no sooner had she started to relax than they hit a pocket of turbulence. Her eyes flew open, and Russ touched her knee reassuringly.

Leigh settled back into her seat. Below a series of small towns skimmed by, their shapes discernible by the pattern of lights. She closed her eyes again, but she soon discovered that relaxation was impossible. She felt slightly sick to her stomach, which was probably a result of the turbulence. Russ did something to direct a small stream of cool air into the cabin, and after that she felt better. She did breathing exercises to relax, and she tried to remember the names of all the original Mickey Mouse Club Mousketeers, and she counted backward from five hundred. Anything, anything she could think of to dispel the image of Wendy in her hospital bed.

At last she felt the plane descending, and she bent forward, watching for the runway. Finally lights rushed up out of the blackness and the plane touched down, a rough landing that bounced her against Russ. She didn't mind being jostled, as long as they were here.

When Russ helped her out of the plane, she felt stiff and sore, but her muscles limbered up again as they took off at a trot for the Quonset hut where a single vapor light showed a cab waiting.

In answer to her questioning look, Russ told her, "I called ahead and asked them to have a taxi ready," and he hustled her into the back seat and climbed in after her.

They rushed past darkened houses and stores, and Leigh gripped the armrest as the taxi careened into a long driveway that puzzled her until she realized that it was the entrance to the hospital; it was such a small, forlorn-looking hospital with a too-bright light in front of a door labeled EMERGENCY ENTRANCE. She clambered out of the taxi with a feeling of dread in her stomach. Her palms were damp, but Russ held her hand anyway, and she had lost a glove somewhere but didn't care.

A glittery tinsel garland on an evergreen tree beside the door shivered in the chill wind. Russ held the door for her, and the overheated air inside felt like a blast from a furnace on her cold cheeks. To the right of the door a long counter shone under the fluorescent light, and on the counter a two-foot-tall Christmas tree's lights winked and blinked. A clerk greeted her with a smile, but the smile faded when she announced that she was Leigh Cathcart, Wendy Craig's mother.

"Follow me," an aide said in a hushed tone, and Leigh hurried after her, holding tightly to Russ's hand.

They were led to an empty office decked with smiling pictures of Santa Claus but smelling faintly of mildew. Leigh stood uncertainly as the aide turned and went back out the door.

"I'll find the doctor," the aide called over her shoulder, and Russ looked at Leigh's pasty face and said, "I think you should sit down while we wait."

"I don't like this place," Leigh said.

"It's a typical small-town hospital," Russ said with a shrug.

"It smells bad," she said.

"Look at the ceiling. There's been a leak, but it's fixed now," Russ told her, and she looked up, saw the stain on the acoustical tiles and shuddered.

"In Spartanburg—" she began, but she stopped when they heard footsteps in the hall. They both stood up when a tall white-coated man entered. He was accompanied by a nurse, and his expression was grave as he held out his hand. "I'm Dr. Miller," he said. "Please sit down."

He looked so serious. "Wendy?" Leigh whispered as a wave of dizziness swept over her. The nurse quickly handed her a glass of water, but she set it aside untouched as she sank back onto the chair.

The doctor went behind the desk, sat down and studied her for a moment as if to gauge how much she could comprehend.

"Your daughter has a severe concussion and a nasty cut above the hairline," he said. "That's the bad news. The good news is that there's no skull fracture or intracranial bleeding, as far as we can tell. We've put her in the intensive-care unit, and she's still unconscious. We have listed her condition as serious."

"Serious?" Leigh said.

His expression softened. "I have a good feeling about your daughter, Mrs. Cathcart. Maybe it's because I have a daughter of my own, also recently married. I want Wendy to be okay. I'll take good care of her, I promise," he said.

"I want to see Wendy," Leigh said.

"I can arrange that," he replied. He picked up a telephone and spoke a few words into it. "You may go to the second floor; they're waiting for you in the ICU. Wendy isn't a pretty sight right now, I'm afraid. But we have every reason to be optimistic." His smile was tired but compassionate, and she took heart from it.

"My son-in-law, Andrew Craig, came in with Wendy. May I see him?" Leigh asked.

"We can wake him if you like, but we've given him something to help him sleep, and he dozed off about an hour ago," the nurse said.

"I'll see him later," Leigh said. "After I see Wendy."

"Mrs. Billings will take you to ICU, and if you have any questions, please feel free to ask. If you'll excuse me, I want to stop by the radiology department," Dr. Miller said. He stood and shook Leigh's hand.

After the doctor left, the nurse, Mrs. Billings, told Leigh that she had to check with her supervisor before leaving the floor, and Leigh nodded mutely. She stood and stared out the window while they waited for the nurse to return. Outside, a gray dawn was breaking. Leigh struggled not to cry; crying would do no good.

Russ's hand touched her shoulder. "If you'd like something to eat or drink while we wait, I'll get it for you," he said.

"I couldn't," she answered. She felt chilled through to her bones; her face felt stiff.

For a moment she managed to transcend her own misery to consider Russ's. His eyes were rimmed by bluish circles, and the lines on each side of his mouth looked deeper than they had before. He was being so kind.

She reached out toward him and he folded her in his arms. She nestled her head against his shoulder, drawing strength from the beat of his heart. They were standing like that when Mrs. Billings appeared in the doorway.

"This way," she said, and they rushed along the corridor to an elevator which led to the ICU. They followed the nurse's stiff white back until she stopped in front of a windowed room, and Leigh pressed her face to the glass and strained to see the person lying in the bed. She couldn't see much; there were too many monitors and machines in the way. Mrs. Billings, a calm-looking woman with an air of competence, held a cautionary finger over her lips as she swung the door open.

When she saw Wendy, Leigh's hand rose to stifle a cry. She wouldn't have recognized her own daughter if she hadn't known who she was. Wendy seemed overwhelmed by the tubes and monitors; her head was swathed in bandages, and her face was white and still.

Leigh fought back tears as she approached the bed. Wendy's hand lay on the blanket, and she stroked it gently.

"Wendy?" she whispered softly.

"She can't hear you," the nurse murmured.

Leigh kept stroking her daughter's hand anyway. Wendy's chest rose and fell rhythmically.

"Come on, Leigh," Russ said. "There's nothing you can do. You should try to get some rest. The nurse is going to make up a bed for you in a room down the hall. You are welcome to stay there as long as Wendy is in intensive-care."

"But—"

"We'll call you if anything happens," Mrs. Billings said firmly, nudging her toward the door. With one last heartfelt look at Wendy, Leigh allowed herself to be steered down the hall and lay down on the bed that the nurse indicated.

When the nurse had gone, her tread whisper-soft on the faded asphalt-tile floor, Leigh sat up.

"I've got to make some phone calls," she said.

Russ had stretched out on the shabby recliner in a corner of the room. He brought the recliner to a sitting position.

"At this hour?" he said.

"I don't care what time it is. I'm moving Wendy out of this hospital."

"Moving? Leigh, I don't think it's such a good idea. Dr. Miller seems more than competent, and he said that they can provide the care that Wendy needs here." He regarded her with a puzzled frown.

Ever since she first saw Wendy lying in that bed, tubes and monitors surrounding her, she'd known what she wanted to do. Get Wendy out of here, that was it; move her to the clean, modern hospital in Spartanburg where she knew the doctors and nurses, and where her own mother had once worked as a volunteer.

"I want Wendy close to home," Leigh said stubbornly.

"Leigh, sweetheart, it's not up to you. It's up to Andrew. He's her husband now." She paled noticeably, and too late he realized that he had challenged her authority in the matter of her daughter, and that it hadn't set well with her.

"She's still my daughter. I'll talk to Andrew as soon as he wakes up," Leigh said.

He crossed the room and pressed lightly on her shoulder. "Please try to get some rest. Perhaps you'll see it differently after you've had a nap." Moving Wendy seemed like the utmost folly to him. In his view, there was no reason. Dr. Miller seemed more than competent, and what's more, he was sympathetic and interested in Wendy. The prognosis was good; it stood to reason that moving Wendy all the way to Spartanburg might result in a setback. And the hospital was clean enough; it was just old.

Leigh twisted away from him and stood up. She looked exhausted and probably was.

"Would you like something to eat before you rest? Or something to drink?" he offered, not knowing where he would find food or drink but willing nevertheless to try.

"I can't rest, Russ. Thoughts of Wendy keep ricocheting around inside my head," she said, and tears pooled in her lower eyelids.

"Tell me about them," he said, pulling her close.

"Oh, things like the time she found a butterfly with a broken wing in the woods and brought it home. She fed it sugar water and managed to keep it alive for quite a while. It never could fly, of course, and then it died, but..." Her voice broke because she realized now why she had thought of that incident; Wendy, lying helpless in her hospital bed reminded her of the butterfly. She sobbed softly against Russ's chest.

"Leigh, she's going to be all right. I know it," Russ said with conviction.

Impatiently she pulled away. "I think I'll go see if Andrew is awake," she said.

"Not yet, Leigh. It's too early. Let him get as much rest as he can," Russ said.

Leigh crossed the room in five steps and had her hand on the door. "I can't wait," she said, but he was beside her in an instant, barring her way.

Leigh had the determined look of a woman who was used to being on her own and doing things her way. He had to make her see that, where Wendy was concerned, she must relinquish control to Andrew. And besides, Leigh was being unreasonable.

"Russ?" she said. "Please get out of my way."

She was growing angrier by the minute; he had seen this resolute expression on her face many times before. He hadn't let her win last time, the time he left for Canada, and look what had happened to them. He suddenly felt uncertain; maybe he should let her have her way now.

But it was constitutionally impossible for him to give in, when he knew he was right. It always had been and still was. And he knew he was right about this. His experiences with both his sick parents in their later years had given him a kind of sixth sense about hospitals and doctors, and he knew instinctively that Wendy was in good hands here.

"Don't do this, Leigh," he said quietly. "It wouldn't be best for Wendy."

He couldn't have anticipated the effect this would have on Leigh. Her face flushed angrily, and when she spoke it was with a stone-cold fury.

"Best for Wendy?" she said, her eyes hard. "How would *you* know what's best for Wendy?"

"Sweetheart, it's just common sense," he said, suddenly more exhausted than he'd realized.

"Common sense? Let me tell you about common sense. It's what I had to have plenty of, Russ Thornton, to raise her."

"Of course you did," he said in an attempt to calm her.

"And now you're telling me how to take care of her," Leigh said. "Well, I won't have it."

Russ felt deflated. Maybe she was right—he was interfering. He tried to think about what they'd need to do if Leigh insisted on moving Wendy to the hospital in Spartanburg. They'd need an air ambulance, and as a pilot he was in a position find out where they could get one; and of course there was the matter of a hospital room in Spartanburg, which Leigh could attend to, and—well, perhaps the other details would fall into place. If only he weren't so tired. He felt as though he hadn't slept in a week.

"I don't—" he said, and he was only going to say that he didn't want to interfere, but Leigh seemed to think that he was going to say something else that she wouldn't like.

"Didn't you hear me? Get out of my way! You weren't around to take care of your daughter during the first part of her life, and you don't have any business butting in now!"

Horrified, Leigh clamped both hands over her mouth before Russ realized what she had said. He stared at her, his emotions deadened by fatigue.

"What?" he said, thinking that he hadn't heard her correctly.

Leigh's eyes looked panicked. "I—I—" she gasped.

"*My* daughter? Wendy is *mine?*" he said. He felt as though he was slipping into a state of total paralysis.

All the color drained from Leigh's face, and her eyes were deep pools of dread.

"Ours," she said. "Wendy is *ours.*"

Chapter Thirteen

Russ slumped in the chair, his head in his hands. There was no doubt in his mind that Leigh was telling the truth; her anguish was genuine.

He lifted his head and looked at her. She stood above him, tears streaming down her face. He stood and turned to the window; patches of blue sky showed above the trees. It was finally morning.

"She doesn't know?" he asked.

"No," Leigh whispered.

"David knew?"

"Of course. I told him before we were married."

"It's the reason you married him, isn't it?"

"Yes," she said. He felt her standing close behind him, but he didn't turn. All he could think of was that he had a daughter, and that Leigh had deliberately withheld that information for all this time. He wondered if he'd ever be able to forgive her.

"What else haven't you told me?" he asked bitterly.

"Only that. I couldn't," Leigh said.

He wheeled around. His eyes felt bloodshot, and his mouth was dry. "But you could blithely invite me to the wedding," he pointed out on a rising note of anger.

"I—I wanted you there," she said.

"You wanted me present on that day but not on any of the other days in her life? So when did you intend to tell me that I had watched another man walk my daughter down the aisle?"

"I don't know," Leigh said miserably. She lifted her shoulders and let them fall. "I really had no plan. I suppose I wanted to see how things went between the two of us."

"Oh, so it was something like, 'If Russ and I get along and we fall in love, I'll casually inform him some night when the lights are low that Wendy is his daughter.' Is that it?"

Leigh shook her head. "I thought that—that if we ended up together—"

"'Together?' What kind of together are we talking about? Married?"

She pressed her lips together to keep them from quivering and shook her head. She couldn't look at him, she couldn't.

An ache seized Russ's throat. All the long and lonely years through which he had observed happy families together and yearned for a child of his own; all the occasions that he and Dominique had argued about whether or not she would become pregnant; all the times he had been saddened by the thought that he was past the age when he could reasonably expect to become a father—and he already had a daughter! A beautiful daughter any man would be proud to call his own.

As if over a great yawning chasm he heard her voice, a placating voice.

"It wasn't possible for me to tell you, Russ, can't you see that? Certainly not while David was alive and when I didn't know where to find you. And after that, even if I had wanted to tell you, would it have been in Wendy's best interests? She was still a teenager when David died, and then she was working hard so that she'd make good grades at Duke. How could I have told her something that was bound to tear her life apart, even if I wanted her to know? And I didn't want her to know, I'll admit that."

Russ passed a hand over his eyes; his eyelids felt as though they were turned inside out.

"And now," Leigh said, "I wouldn't have chosen this time to reveal such a secret. It slipped out. Maybe it was the worst possible timing. But now you know. And I have nothing to hide anymore."

"You had everything I always wanted—a good marriage and family life, a child! You took that from me, dammit!"

"Russ—"

"Leave me alone. Go away. Please."

Leigh buried her face in her hands. She was going to lose Russ. Had already lost him, perhaps. And she could lose Wendy, too.

She heard a noise at the door, and, lowering her hands, turned around. It was Andrew.

"Leigh," he said, crossing the room in two steps and putting his arms around her. They clung to each other in their mutual sorrow until at last she held him at arm's length. His face had two really swollen bruises, one on the left cheek and the other on his chin, and there was a small cut over his left eyebrow. His left hand was bandaged.

"I'm okay," he assured her. "But Wendy—" and his eyes filled with tears.

"I know, I know," Leigh said, trying to comfort him. In the background Russ stared at them blankly.

Andrew pulled away and tried to get control of himself. Russ continued to look at her, a stranger now. Leigh knew she had to get out of there.

She picked up her coat from the bed, gathered her purse from the table beside it. She turned to face Russ, hoping he would keep his silence. She didn't want Andrew to get caught up in their own private hell; he had enough to worry about.

"Andrew and I will go to the coffee shop," she said to Russ. She couldn't stand the way he looked at her, his eyes so accusing. Russ nodded, his face as cold and as hard as granite. In that moment, she knew that he hated her.

What had she expected? Hadn't Katrina tried to warn her? All the deceit of the past twenty-two years pressed down upon her, crushing all hope for the relationship.

Blindly Leigh turned and took Andrew's arm, surprised that she was strong enough to walk out of the room and half expecting Russ to call her back. But he didn't. It was over.

In her state of mind at that moment, she grasped at anything that would help her go on. Wendy needed her. Andrew needed her. But Russ had never needed her, had never needed her at all.

Somehow she and Andrew found the hospital coffee shop and sat down at a booth. Somehow they ordered a breakfast of eggs and bacon that neither of them ate. As they sat watching the eggs cool and congeal on their plates, Andrew, who was almost too distraught to speak, told Leigh that the reason that he and Wendy had left the island was that the heater in the cottage where they were staying had stopped working altogether.

"At first we were going to go to my parents' house in Asheville, but when we called them to let them know, we found out that everyone had a cold, and they said that they didn't want us to get sick. That was when Wendy suggested that we drive back to The Briarcliff to surprise you and Russ. Wendy wanted to spend New Year's Eve with you in the worst way. So we set out, not realizing that it would be raining hard once we reached the middle of the state, and we skidded off the interstate when Wendy lost control of the car,'' Andrew explained, his voice breaking at the very last. He looked as though his entire world had fallen apart.

''She always drives too fast,'' Leigh said softly, remembering all the times she had cautioned Wendy to slow down.

''I didn't want Wendy to drive, but she insisted after we stopped for gas, and I wanted to let her have her way. I love her so much, you know,'' Andrew said, and he looked down at his full plate, fighting tears.

''I know you do,'' Leigh said consolingly.

''After the accident, before the emergency crew arrived, I found Wendy lying in the ditch and started to give her first aid. I sat beside her in the ambulance and held her hand, and when we arrived at the hospital I asked the receptionist who she thought was the best local doctor to deal with a head injury and made sure she called him. I tried to do everything I thought you would have done.'' His eyes seemed to plead for approval.

Leigh's eyes caught and held his. ''You did everything you could. She's going to be all right, Andrew,'' she said, though she was far from believing that herself. Her son-in-law looked so desolate that she didn't have the heart to bring up the subject of moving Wendy to the Spartanburg hospital; she would save that for later.

When she looked up, Leigh saw Dr. Miller's face in the window between the coffee shop and the hospital lobby. He swung the door open and came inside, sliding into the booth beside Andrew.

''I was going to ask you to come into my office to discuss Wendy's condition, but we can talk here just as well,'' he said. Leigh thought his smile was encouraging.

''Have you seen her? How is she?'' Andrew asked.

''I just came from her room, and I must report that she's doing very well indeed. Much better than I expected. In fact, she opened her eyes and was able to understand what I was saying to her. We've upgraded her condition to stable,'' he said. His round face radiated his own relief at his patient's turn for the better.

''May we see her?'' Leigh asked.

''Of course. Come with me,'' he said.

They followed him upstairs, Leigh wondering where Russ was. Perhaps he had left. Perhaps this whole scene was more than he could handle. She wouldn't blame him if he had gone to the airport and flown back to The Briarcliff or even to Charlotte; he probably never wanted to see her again. That thought should have made her sad, and at another time she would have been devastated, but with Wendy lying injured in the intensive-care unit, all she could feel about Russ was a curious kind of emptiness, as though her revelation about Wendy had purged all emotion from her psyche.

They were silent as they walked through the wide, empty halls of the hospital; in one wing, breakfast was beginning to be served, and people were starting to stir in the rooms up and down the corridor. In the intensive-care unit, a nurse named Bernadette showed them into Wendy's room. Dr. Miller walked purposefully toward the bed and enclosed Wendy's small hand in his larger one.

''Wendy,'' he said softly. ''Your husband and mother are here. Can you hear me?'' Nearby machines and monitors blipped and beeped; an IV unit hung over the bed.

Wendy's eyes twitched, then fluttered open. Leigh held tight to Andrew's hand and walked closer to the bed until she was in Wendy's field of vision. She bent over her daughter, trying to keep the horror she felt at Wendy's condition from showing on her face.

''Hi, Wendy,'' she said, forcing herself to smile.

There was an interminable silence while Wendy struggled to focus her eyes. Andrew leaned forward and took Wendy's other hand.

Finally Wendy managed to whisper one word, "Andrew?"

"I'm here," he said.

"Mom," Wendy said.

Leigh longed to hold her child in her arms and kiss away the pain as she had done so many times when Wendy was young, but this hurt was beyond healing with a kiss and a few kind words. Her eyes filled with tears, but she didn't want Wendy to see her cry, so she blinked them back and struggled to keep smiling.

"We're both here, and we're going to see that you're taken care of," she said firmly.

Wendy's eyelids drifted shut, and Leigh stepped back. The nurse, Bernadette, was standing in the corner, and Leigh approached her.

"Is she in pain?" she asked.

"No, I'm sure she isn't. We gave her something for the pain when Dr. Miller came in less than an hour ago."

Dr. Miller beckoned Leigh to the bed.

"She's sleeping now, but she's comfortable. You can see her again when she wakes up," he said. Gently he stroked Wendy's hand; it was a kind, caring gesture. Perhaps Russ was right. Maybe Wendy shouldn't be moved.

Leigh leaned over and kissed Wendy's cheek; Andrew did the same. Quietly they tiptoed out of the room, and Dr. Miller ushered them into a nearby alcove where they could speak privately.

"Wendy knows you're here, and she realizes that you're pulling for her. That means a lot," Dr. Miller said.

"Is there anything we can do?" Andrew asked.

"Nothing. Let us take care of her. It's what we do best," the doctor told them. "Now, how about you? If you need a place to stay, my office will arrange a room at the local motel. It's not The Briarcliff, I'm afraid, but it's only a block away and the people are friendly."

Leigh hadn't even considered where she would stay throughout this ordeal; she was grateful for Dr. Miller's help. She shot a questioning look at Andrew, but he looked confused, and she realized that he was still in shock and recovering from his injuries.

"We'd appreciate it," she said.

"How many rooms? Two?"

"Yes. Oh, but—" She had just thought of Russ. If he were still here, he would need a place to sleep tonight, and she was sure he wouldn't want to sleep with her. "You'd better make that three," she said hurriedly.

"Three rooms at the Hawthorne Motel," the doctor said, scribbling on a pad of paper. "My receptionist will call the motel for you. All you'll need to do is walk in and tell the desk clerk who you are. If you'd like, you may spend today in the ICU visitors' lounge, which is across the hall from Wendy's room. Help yourself to coffee and doughnuts. And, please—don't worry about Wendy too much. She's young and she's strong and she has a reason to live—she wants to get on with her new marriage. I have a feeling that this young lady is going to be all right."

Leigh gripped his hand gratefully. She had begun to have positive feelings about this man and about the hospital staff. When they passed Wendy's room, she looked through the window and saw the nurse, Bernadette, standing beside Wendy's bed, speaking softly to her and smoothing the covers. Wendy's eyes were closed, but that didn't mean she couldn't hear. Leigh had lost all her desire to move Wendy to Spartanburg.

Andrew looked at her bleakly. "We could go check into the motel if you'd like. You probably haven't slept much," he said.

"I'm not sleepy," Leigh told him.

"Did you bring a suitcase?" Andrew asked.

"I left it in the doctor's office last night—I mean, this morning," she said.

"I could take it to the motel, check us both in and leave it there. Then if you would like to rest later, all the formalities will be taken care of," Andrew said.

She had the feeling that Andrew wanted to be doing something useful; he must feel as powerless in this situation as she did.

"Okay," she said. "That would be really helpful, Andrew. Are there any phone calls you want me to make while you're gone?"

Andrew shook his head. "I called my parents last night after I called you. They were frantic to jump in the car and drive over here, but I talked them out of it because of their colds. Mother said they'll come as soon as possible."

Leigh patted his arm. "I'll wait for you in the visitors' lounge," she said.

When Andrew was gone, she walked back to the window overlooking Wendy's room and watched with her hand pressed to her mouth as Bernadette changed an IV. Wendy looked so small underneath those covers. She waited for some sign that Wendy was awake, but she never opened her eyes. *At least she's alive,* Leigh told herself. There had been moments when she was not at all sure that Wendy would still be breathing by the time she arrived at the hospital.

Slowly she went to the lounge, opened the door and walked in. To her surprise, Russ was sitting on the couch in front of the window. He was drinking a cup of steaming hot coffee.

She searched for some kind of sign that he had softened in his feelings toward her, but his lips were set in a grim line and there was a steely look in his eyes. His face, unshaven since yesterday morning, looked ravaged.

"How is she?" he asked.

Leigh stood as if riveted to the spot. "She's improved," she said. Her heart raced; she wished Russ had left. She felt too uncomfortable with him staring at her from underneath his lowered eyebrows with intense dislike.

"Her condition?"

"Upgraded to stable," she said, moving to the chair opposite the couch and sitting down, then standing up again. She walked to the coffeepot and poured herself a cup, aware all the while of Russ's eyes upon her.

"If you're still determined to move her, you should know that I object strenuously. *If* it makes any difference to you," he said.

Her hand shook as she brought the cup to her lips. She remained standing with her back to him.

"I don't think it's necessary to move her now," she said. "The doctor and the staff seem capable and concerned."

"You've come to your senses," he said. "I should be thankful for that."

She slammed the coffee cup down, and coffee jumped out and drenched a pile of napkins. She hung on to the edge of the table, telling herself not to break down in front of him. If only he would leave her alone to deal with this!

He stood up and turned toward the window as though he couldn't bear to look at her. When she raised her head, she saw that his shoulders were shaking, and she felt a wave of despair wash over her. She had never seen Russ break down completely before.

She mopped ineffectually at the coffee, finally giving up when she realized that she couldn't accomplish the task with the few napkins at her disposal. She wanted to go to

Russ and put her arms around him, but not if he would shake her off, not if he was as angry as he had a right to be.

"Russ," she said, and he took a deep breath and turned to face her.

"Is she going to be all right?" he asked, and his face was convulsed with grief.

"The doctor says he thinks so," she replied.

"My daughter," he said. "She's my daughter."

Leigh could only shake her head yes.

"She looks like me," he said.

"I know. I was afraid at first when I saw you at the inn that you'd guess. She has your nose, your chin, your shoulders."

"She has your eyes," he said, and she looked away.

"Didn't anyone else ever guess?" he asked in a low tone.

"Katrina was the only one who knew," she said.

"What about David?"

"Yes, he knew the baby was yours."

"How he must have hated me," Russ said bitterly.

She crossed the room, stood in front of him. She touched his arm. "You mustn't think that. David liked you, and he loved Wendy from the very first. He was grateful to you, he said, because you gave us Wendy."

"That's difficult to believe," he said.

"It's true. He and Wendy had a very special relationship. She never had any idea that he wasn't her real father."

"And now? Will you tell her?"

Leigh's face crumpled. "Yes" was all she said. Her face was full of the anguish she felt, and Russ couldn't stay angry. He had never been able to stay angry with Leigh.

Without a word he folded her in his arms, listened to her heartbeat, felt her tears drench the front of his shirt.

He was still trying to make sense of it all; he felt overwhelmed.

After a moment he led her to the couch and they sat huddled together, holding hands. After all the years, after all the words, they had nothing to say to each other. They could only comfort each other in silence.

Later they went together to Wendy's room to look through the window for any sign that she was improving; afterward they walked aimlessly up and down the hall outside the ICU. Whenever anyone went into or out of Wendy's room, they both hurried to see what was happening, and later, after Andrew returned, Bernadette allowed all three of them in to see her.

"Hi, Mom," Wendy said, her voice stronger now. Her eyes searched for Andrew. "I'm sorry I wrecked the car," she said. She spoke slowly, as if it were a great effort.

"Don't worry about the car," Andrew told her, reaching for her hand. "Right now it's in better shape than you are."

A flicker of a smile, and then she looked at Russ. "Russ came with you," she said in surprise.

"He flew me here in his plane," Leigh said.

"We were..." Wendy stopped and licked her dry lips. "We were coming to The Briarcliff to go to the New Year's Eve party with you."

"I know," Leigh said. "Don't talk too much, dear. You need to rest."

"But...but I'm afraid I've ruined your vacation," Wendy managed to say.

"Don't be silly. There's no place I'd rather spend my New Year's Eve than right here in beautiful downtown Kettiston with you," Leigh told her, knowing that Wendy would see the humor in this.

Another smile, and Wendy's eyes closed.

"You'd better go," Bernadette said, and with lingering backward glances, the three of them tiptoed out.

"Leigh, you look dead on your feet. You should try to get some sleep," Russ said to her when they stood in the corridor. "Is there a motel in Kettiston where we can stay?"

"Dr. Miller arranged for us to stay at the Hawthorne Motel. It's down the road about a block, and Andrew already took my things."

"Here are the keys to your rooms," Andrew said to Leigh, pulling them out of his jacket pocket. "Why don't you try to rest? I'll stay here and call you if there's any change in Wendy's condition."

"I don't think I should go," Leigh said with a backward glance toward Wendy's room.

"You won't be able to help Wendy if you're exhausted," Russ told her, and Leigh saw the sense in that.

"All right," she said. She held her hand out for her key.

"I'll go with you," he said, and so they walked out of the hospital through the lobby with its big Christmas tree decorated with red velvet bows and out onto the narrow tree-bordered Kettiston street.

It was a warm day, and the sun was shining. Overhead, a large, bedraggled white plastic snowflake was attached to each lamppost, trying in vain to dress up the small, dreary town for the holidays. Across the street, someone had painted a Christmas scene on the big plate-glass window of the gas company with tempera paint, which had already begun to flake. The whole scene was depressing, and Leigh looked away.

They turned right toward the motel and walked silently, heavy with fatigue. Leigh was so tired she could barely place one foot in front of the other; her hair blew in her eyes on a gritty wind, and she brushed it away impatiently. Her mind was concerned with Wendy; had she made a mistake in deciding to leave her in this hospital? Should she investigate the doctor's reputation? Was Andrew capable of making any decisions that needed to be made, or would she have to do it? She hated being in such a situation so far away from home.

"I didn't think you'd leave Andrew there with Wendy," Russ said suddenly.

"He's an adult, and he's her husband," she said with a shrug.

She noticed a brief flicker behind his eyes when he looked at her. "A few days ago, I wasn't so sure you were ready to let go," he said.

"A few days ago, I probably wasn't. Now—"

"Now what?"

She scuffed at some fallen leaves. "Now I see that Andrew, even though he is hurt and in shock, is capable of taking care of her. He handled the emergency very well, finding the doctor, calling his parents, calling The Briarcliff. I couldn't have done any better."

"I'm surprised," he said. "Surprised that you're letting go."

"I'm not letting go," Leigh said as she began to understand. "I'm merely moving over to make room for Andrew in Wendy's life."

They had reached the motel, but she thought that Russ was looking at her in a new way as they walked through the parking lot.

The doors of the motel rooms opened directly onto the parking space for each room; it was an old motel. "You're in Room 103, I'm in 104," Russ said, looking at their key tags.

"Andrew arranged our rooms that way," she said. She wanted Russ to know that she hadn't put him next door to her on purpose.

Russ said nothing, but he waited at the door to her room while she went in and flipped on the switch to the wall heater. When she looked up and saw him standing there, framed by the light in the doorway, she didn't know what to say. He seemed to be waiting for something, but she only looked at him blankly.

"I'll see you later," he said finally. "Shall I stop by for you in three hours or so? We could go back to the hospital after we grab a bite to eat."

"You don't have to—"

His head shot up. "She is my daughter," he said. "Of course I do."

"What I mean is—"

"Don't give me a rough time, Leigh," he said wearily. "I'll be back to get you like I said."

She nodded in reluctant agreement, and after he closed the door she made sure it was locked, stumbled to the bed, threw back the bedspread and fell asleep in her clothes.

RUSS DID NOT FALL asleep right away. Instead he lay on his bed and stared at the ceiling, thinking about Leigh and his daughter.

His daughter. He should have guessed when he saw her; Wendy was the image of his paternal grandmother when she was a girl. She had the Thornton jawline, too prominent for classical beauty, but beautiful nonetheless. When he had looked at her, all he had seen was the eyes, Leigh's eyes.

If Leigh had only told him that she was pregnant back in 1969, he could have come home from Canada and married her. But she couldn't have told him. She didn't know where he was.

Why didn't Leigh contact his parents when she realized that she was going to have a baby? They could have found him for her. They always knew his address. Yet Leigh would have been too proud to do that. She wouldn't have wanted his parents to think she was chasing after Russ; she couldn't have told them she was pregnant because in those days nice girls didn't get pregnant before marriage. And anyway, Leigh had thought he didn't love her.

What a mess! So many problems, so many sorrows, and all because he and Leigh had been young and in love and too innocent to realize that the very private act of making love could have public repercussions. They'd never thought how an illicit pregnancy could affect other people's lives, and if they had they wouldn't have cared. The only thing that had seemed important to either of them in those days was to make love as often as possible, never mind the consequences. Leigh had relied on him for birth control, and something had gone wrong, and for that he felt immeasurably guilty and always would.

And Leigh—what about her? How had she managed to come through the experience as well as she had? A lot of the credit had to go to David, who had jumped in and solved the problem that he, Russ, had caused. From what Leigh had told him about Dave, the guy had been a prince.

He heaved a giant sigh and turned over on his stomach. He punched the pillow, trying to get comfortable, and he wished that Leigh was lying beside him. He'd been so hard on her, had said some things that he shouldn't have said. She'd suffered, they'd all suffered enough. Whatever was the outcome of all this, he didn't want any more suffering.

Before he did anything else, he'd better go to sleep. Things would look better when he woke up. Things had to look better, because it was hard to imagine their being any worse.

LEIGH'S WAKING UP was gradual, and before she was fully awake she wondered why Russ wasn't sleeping beside her. Then she remembered about Russ and about Wendy, and all she wanted to do was pull the covers up over her head and never come out. But that would never do.

Slowly she eased herself to a sitting position and rubbed the back of her neck. She was stiff and sore; her mouth felt dry. She went to the bathroom and filled a glass with water. Her face stared back at her from the mirror as she drank, her eyes red-rimmed and her cheeks gaunt. At her throat, Russ's locket, engraved with their initials, mocked her. Slowly she unhooked the clasp and, after staring at it for a moment, dropped it into the depths of her makeup case.

She showered quickly and put on lipstick, and she wondered if Russ had been serious about returning for her; his knock on the door convinced her that he had. When she opened the door, she found him looking rested. He had shaved and looked more like his old self.

"Shall we get something to eat?" he asked stiffly.

Leigh didn't think she should go with him. They clearly had nothing of importance to say to each other. But what else was she to do? She didn't want to walk around in a strange town by herself, when it would soon be dark. She silently put on her parka and joined Russ outside the room, pulling the door tightly shut behind her.

Neither of them talked as they walked to the restaurant two blocks away. The large plastic snowflakes on the lampposts had been lit, looking slightly better than they had in the daytime, and they lent a soft white glow to the night. Leigh had no idea where she and Russ were going from here. Nowhere, probably.

They found a table in a corner of the small restaurant that had been recommended to Russ by the desk clerk at the motel, and without enthusiasm they ordered the daily special, which was meat loaf and fried potatoes. Leigh was staring out the window at a plastic snowflake when Russ spoke.

"I thought at first that I could never forgive you," he said. She turned startled eyes upon him. She hadn't expected him to talk about what was weighing so heavily on their minds.

"I don't expect forgiveness," she said in a strangled tone.

"But I have forgiven you," he said, and she stared at him in shock.

"I've had time to think about it since you told me, and I understand why you did what you did," he went on as she focused disbelieving eyes on his face. "In those times, under those circumstances, there was nothing else you could have done. Nothing else that would have made any sense, that is. I want you to know that I understand."

Her eyes filled with tears, and she looked down at her lap, unable to risk looking at him. If she did, she was sure that she would fall apart before his very eyes.

He reached across the table and put his finger to her cheek with a touch as delicate as a feather.

"Please look at me when I talk to you," he said gently.

She lifted her brimming eyes to his and saw through the blur of tears that he was smiling. She couldn't believe it. She felt as though under the circumstances, his goodwill toward her was completely unwarranted.

His expression was one of infinite compassion. "I cared about you when we were twenty, and in those days the world seemed as young as we were. It was all an illusion, wasn't it? The world was old and careworn, only we didn't know it. The irony is that we become that way, too, as we grow older. We take all the burdens of the world upon our own shoulders, and sometimes we become weary and blasé about everything," he said, watching her intently.

"I—" she began, but he said, "No, let me finish," and she subsided.

"The point is that I've felt like a new person since I've been with you. Christmas seemed like Christmas again, and everything was fresh and new and yet it felt comfortable and right. We belong together, Leigh, now as never before. I've discovered that I love you more than ever, and I love our daughter. I need you, and I need her. I hope you need me, too," he said. His eyes were bright, too bright, and she saw that they were swimming with tears.

As the realization dawned that he was serious, that he was not only serious but was pouring out his heart to her, she was rocked by a rush of gratitude so strong that she felt as though she were drowning in it. Her heart expanded to take it all in, and she knew that this was more than gratitude, it was a love so perfect and so right that it could never die, that it had never gone away completely but had slept dormant in her soul until she had found Russ again.

"I do need you," she whispered. "So much. So *much.*" Her hand rose and met his over the table, and he slowly lowered their clasped hands to the tabletop.

"Where do we go from here?" she whispered, still only half believing, and he said, dispelling all doubt, "Wherever it takes us, Leigh. Wherever you want to go."

Chapter Fourteen

Later that night, a jubilant Dr. Miller told them that Wendy would be moved out of the ICU the next morning.

"And then?" Leigh asked.

"We'll watch her closely. She's making wonderful progress, but we don't want her to overdo it," he said.

After the doctor left, Leigh and Russ simply stood and held each other in the hall, sick with relief and weak with the knowledge that it could have been much, much worse.

Andrew, his spirits bolstered by the positive report, volunteered to sleep that night in the room that had been made up for Leigh down the hall.

"You'll sleep much better at the motel, and there's no need for all three of us to be here," he told her. "I'll relay any information you need to know."

Leigh hugged him, this man who was so capable, and turned toward Russ, her spirits lifting.

"Will you stay or go?" she asked.

"I'll go with you," he said promptly, and when Andrew had started to walk away, he said, "Always."

They slept in each other's arms that night as they had at The Briarcliff. In the night Leigh woke often and when she did, she always opened her eyes, half fearful that Russ wouldn't be there. Each time she was immensely relieved to find him there, his face serene in the light penetrating the thin motel curtains. Once he stirred briefly and muttered, "What's wrong?" and she said, "I can't believe how lucky I am," and he pulled her closer and nestled her head in the hollow of his shoulder.

The next morning when they were walking back to the hospital, Russ said suddenly, "We're going to miss the New Year's Eve celebration at The Briarcliff," and he said it as though the thought hadn't occurred to him before.

"Do you think I care?" she said, swinging their hands between them. She thought guiltily of the black sequined dress that she had ordered but had never tried on. She would pay for it, of course, and wear it sometime, but not this New Year's Eve, which was tonight.

At the hospital they went directly to Wendy's new room and found Andrew sitting beside her bed holding her hand. Wendy's smile was weak and she looked groggy, but she had eaten oatmeal for breakfast and was feeling stronger. Her huge head bandage had been replaced by a smaller gauze pad.

"Dr. Miller says I might even be able to start the semester on time if I keep improving at this rate," she said.

"Oh, I don't know," Leigh began, but she checked herself in time, when she realized that this decision wasn't hers to make.

During the intermittent times that Wendy was sleeping, Leigh and Russ walked the hospital corridors until Leigh thought she would gag on the hospital smell, and then they walked outside until they couldn't stand to look at downtown Kettiston anymore. For dinner, Russ went to a nearby fast-food restaurant and brought back a pizza for Leigh and Andrew and fried chicken for himself, and they all ate in Wendy's room.

"A lovely New Year's Eve dinner," Wendy said apologetically.

"Any dinner is a celebration when you're with people you love," Russ said, and he meant it.

Later, when Wendy had closed her eyes for a nap, Leigh told Russ, "I should call Katrina. And Bett. And a lot of other people who will want to know about Wendy and Andrew's accident."

"I called Bett this morning," Andrew supplied. "I phoned some of Wendy's and my friends from the university, too. A couple of them will probably drive over to see Wendy tomorrow, if she's feeling up to it."

Leigh went to phone Katrina, thinking again that Andrew seemed to have things well in hand. It was good to be able to give him some of the responsibility; he was someone to lean on, and for that she was grateful. She thought, not for the first time, that Wendy had chosen a good husband.

She left Russ talking with Andrew and Wendy and went to the hospital lobby where she found a pay phone. She punched in Katrina's Spartanburg number from memory.

Katrina was stunned when Leigh told her about Wendy's accident and quickly volunteered to do anything she could do to help.

"You have your hands full with your mother and her broken foot," Leigh said.

"True, but my cousin Ginger is visiting us for a couple of days, and she could stay with my mother. Would it help if I came to Kettiston?"

"Andrew is taking care of things quite well, and I have Russ. Thanks, Katrina, but I don't think it's necessary."

"How is Russ, Leigh?"

Leigh jiggled the change-return pocket in the pay telephone; there was nothing in it. "He knows," she said.

"He knows about Wendy?" Katrina asked sharply.

"It slipped out. It was awful, Katrina, just like you, in all your wisdom, warned me it would be. After we came to the hospital and saw Wendy linked up to all those machines, I was upset and kind of crazy, thinking I wanted to move Wendy out of this hospital, and Russ was doing his best to talk me out of it, but I wouldn't listen. And I just started screaming at him, and suddenly I said it," she said.

"And then what?" Katrina sounded awestruck.

"I thought he hated me. Then later we went out to dinner and he told me everything was okay. He loves me, and he loves Wendy. Only she doesn't know yet that he's her father."

"You'll tell her, I suppose," Katrina said.

"Not now. Not yet. She's not ready to hear it. She's curious about Russ and our relationship, though, so I think there will soon be a time when we can tell her naturally and easily. She likes him, which will make it easier."

"What about everyone else? Bett and Carson, my mother, Andrew's family? Will you tell them, too?"

"You know, Katrina, I think I've carried this burden too long. I'm going to leave it up to Russ and Wendy to help me decide things like that."

Katrina expelled a sigh. "Maybe that's good. Yes, I'd say you're making progress."

Leigh managed a rueful laugh. "Finally," she said.

"Tell Wendy I love her, and I'll call her when she feels more like talking. And tell Russ—" Katrina stopped in midsentence.

"Tell him what?"

"Tell Russ that this year, he'd better drink a cup of kindness for auld lang syne," Katrina said.

Leigh had talked to Katrina much longer than she had intended, but she called Bett, too, mostly to assure her

that Wendy was recovering. By the time Leigh went bac
to Wendy's room, it had been dark outside for a lon
time. Andrew was sitting beside Wendy's bed, and he an
Wendy were holding hands, clearly enjoying a quiet mc
ment. Leigh stayed for only a short time; she felt a
though she was intruding on their privacy. They were, sh
reminded herself, technically on their honeymoon.

"Do you know where Russ went?" she asked Andrev
as she was preparing to leave.

"He said to tell you not to worry, that he'd be back a
soon as he could," Andrew said.

Leigh hesitated in the corridor looking for Russ, but h
was nowhere to be seen. People were beginning to arriv
on the floor with paper-wrapped packages shaped suspi
ciously like bottles of champagne, probably to cheer thei
friends and relatives who were confined to the hospital o
this festive night. At the nurses' station down the hall
someone had set out several plates of hors d'oeuvres.

"Have one," offered the smiling aide who was sittin
at the desk, and Leigh did.

"We try to make it as much like a party as possible fo
patients who are here during the holidays," said a nurs
who arrived and sat down with a pile of charts. Behind he
a tiny Christmas tree with bulbs too big for its branche
glittered in the glare of the fluorescent light overhead an
a red-and-green banner proclaimed HAPPY NEV
YEAR. Voices rose in the patient's room nearest th
nurses' station, and Leigh realized that the people in ther
were having a party. Several people were singing,

Should auld acquaintance be forgot,
And never brought to mind...

but someone had trouble singing on key, and the song fe
apart as everyone laughed.

Leigh felt very much alone and out of it; she wouldn't feel comfortable going back to Wendy's room, and she was tired of waiting for Russ in the drafty hall. The hospital chapel was located around the corner from this station, and she supposed she could duck in there for a few minutes.

"If Russ Thornton comes back, will you please tell him I'm in the chapel?" she asked the aide, who would recognize Russ because he had given her the leftover fried chicken and pizza that they couldn't eat, and the aide looked up from her paperwork and said that she would.

The chapel was blessedly quiet and warm, and stained-glass windows glowed in the light of several candles that someone had lit on the altar. Leigh slipped inside, tiptoed down the aisle and sat down in the first pew, relaxing, thinking. She was glad she had found this peaceful spot. Tonight, New Year's Eve, it was deserted.

She bowed her head and said a short prayer for Wendy and Andrew, thankful that the accident had not been any worse. She lifted her head sharply when she heard the door behind her open.

It was Russ. He walked down the aisle and sat beside her, taking her warm hand in his cold one. He was wearing his coat, and she realized that he must have recently come in from outside.

"Where have you been? I was beginning to wonder if something had happened to you," she said.

"I had an errand to do," he said, and she thought she detected a shred of mystery about the way he said it. "You weren't worried, were you?"

"A little. I keep thinking you're going to disappear."

"Never again," he said comfortably, squeezing her hand. "Where you go, I go. And I can promise you I'll never go as far away as Canada again."

"I wish you hadn't gone that far before," she said.

"So do I. Have I ever mentioned how much I missed you after I left?" he said fondly, looking down at her with serious eyes.

"Missed me? No, I don't think you ever told me that," she said.

"Oh, I thought about you twenty-four hours a day. I even telephoned your parents' house in Spartanburg shortly after you went back to Duke for the fall semester to ask the telephone number of your new dorm at school, and I was plunged into a state of despair when your father wouldn't give it to me."

"He wouldn't *what?*" Leigh said, staring at him in disbelief.

"Your father said you didn't want to talk to me, and that you didn't want to have anything to do with antiwar protesters. Afterward I felt like crawling under a rock someplace and eating worms."

"He never told me you called," Leigh said slowly. "I had no idea. And it wasn't true that I wouldn't talk to you. My father probably just didn't want me to see you." She remembered that she and Katrina had moved to a different dorm that year, and the number of the lobby phone had been a new one and was not listed in the telephone directory. It had caused them no end of inconvenience, but she'd never known that it had also cost her the chance to talk to Russ.

"I'd called the old dorm, but no one seemed to know or care about the number of your new dorm, and after someone walked away and left the phone hanging, I gave up. I thought your parents could give me the new number, so I called them. After your father told me that you didn't want to talk to me, I figured there was no point in trying to reach you again. Later I heard that you were married. Anyway," he continued, "that was a long time ago."

"A long time," she agreed, but she was incensed that her father had told Russ she hadn't wanted to talk to him. She'd had no idea that her father would take it upon himself to censor her relationships. Of course she had wanted to talk to Russ! Those were the days when she'd been scared and worried about her pregnancy; she would have given anything to have spoken with Russ for only a few minutes. If she had, maybe things wouldn't have turned out the way they did. Everything would have been different. Or would it? And hadn't she been happy? Hadn't she loved David? Had things worked out for the best, after all?

The chapel door hadn't closed properly when Russ had entered, and through the open door came the soft strains of the group down the hall singing "Auld Lang Syne." They'd added a few good singers; someone was attempting the harmony.

"That song always makes me feel nostalgic," Russ said, pulling her into the shelter of his arms.

"They were trying to sing it before, and they had to stop. This time I think they're getting it right," she said.

"There's something *I'd* like to get right," he said. He moved away slightly, and his eyes sparkled at her in the candlelight.

She watched him pull a velvet box from his coat pocket; her eyes grew round as he opened it. Inside was a ring; a huge brilliant-cut diamond winked up at her.

"For me?" she whispered.

"If you'll say yes," he said.

"Yes," she said without hesitation. "Yes, yes, yes!"

"I've been waiting most of my life to hear you say it," he said, and he slipped the ring on the third finger of her left hand.

"I would have said yes the first time you proposed, you know. I'd have married you in an instant," she said.

"It's funny about that," Russ said. "I wonder where the letter was for all those years."

Leigh smiled. "All I can tell you is that the mail carrier was one of those temporary postal workers that they hire for the holidays. He was short and fat and had a long white beard and—"

"If you're going to tell me he wore a red suit with white fur trim, I'm not going to believe you," Russ said.

"No, I'm not going to tell you that, but it does make you wonder, doesn't it?"

They laughed together, and he pulled her close again.

"I love you, Leigh," he said. "And now I have a daughter to love, too. It's a wonderful present, you know."

She smiled up at him, at his curly eyelashes, at his square jaw, at his sharp nose; Wendy's features in Russ's face. She slid her arms around his neck.

"Where did you get the ring?" she asked.

"I made the town's only jeweler desert the New Year's Eve preparations at his house and open the jewelry store. He grumbled a bit, but not after I told him our story. I hope you like the ring," he said.

"It's beautiful," she said. The ring Russ had chosen for her was gold, and the diamond was flanked by four channel-set baguettes, two on each side. The diamonds flashed and gleamed in the light from the candles on the altar.

"I bought a wedding ring, too," he told her. "When will you marry me?"

"As soon as I can. As soon as we've told Wendy," Leigh said.

"Told Wendy—?"

"That you are her father. We'll find a way," she said, strong in her conviction.

"The two of us will always find a way," he assured her, and then he kissed her, and in that moment she knew that nothing, nothing and no one, could ever keep them apart again.